EVE . . .

She's a captivatingly beautiful
photographer's model . . .
She's a bright, new television
anchorwoman . . .
And she's the object of every
man's desires . . .

From the breathtaking
northern California coastline
to the fierce, competitive media worlds
of Los Angeles and New York City—
Eve is caught in a whirlwind
of the beautiful and the rich,
and the uncontrollable desires of
Brant, a cruel sensualist, to
whom nothing is forbidden—nothing.

THE
INSIDERS

ROSEMARY
ROGERS

 AVON
PUBLISHERS OF BARD, CAMELOT AND DISCUS BOOKS

THE INSIDERS is an original publication of Avon Books. This work has never before appeared in book form.

AVON BOOKS
A division of
The Hearst Corporation
959 Eighth Avenue
New York, New York 10019

First Avon Printing, January, 1979

AVON TRADEMARK REG. U.S. PAT. OFF. AND IN
OTHER COUNTRIES, MARCA REGISTRADA, HECHO EN
U.S.A.

Printed in the U.S.A.

THE INSIDERS

CHAPTER ONE

EVE MASON SAT cross-legged in the center of her bed, Yoga-fashion, with eyes closed while she concentrated on trying to relax. She was also trying to ignore the bright sunshine outside the blinds that masked her windows, and to forget the fact that the telephone hadn't rung, even once. But what did she expect? She'd changed her telephone number because the constant ringing used to make David uptight when they were together. And the other men, those casual dates she had begun to accept when she'd felt she'd needed something to fill the emptiness in her life after Mark had died—after a while they'd stopped calling.

She squeezed her eyes shut tightly, fighting the feeling of tension in her body. She'd been getting quite good at relaxation before David. Damn him! But this time she wouldn't try to push the thought of David out of her mind. Peter, handing out free advice last night, had told her to try stream of consciousness. Think about it, remember. Maybe after a while you'll get tired of thinking about the bastard, he'd said.

Lately, Eve had started sleeping with Peter, but only on weekends (to fill up the empty space that had once belonged to David). Doctor Peter Petrie, San Francisco's most fashionable analyst. So damned busy, his time all booked up, that he couldn't fit her in as a regular patient.

However, when he was feeling magnanimous, he'd occasionally give her some free counseling. Maybe to keep
her sane until the next weekend, when, no doubt, he'd
want to screw her again.

Peter had been David's friend—and David was her
sickness, her obsession, her madness. She wouldn't call
him her love, because she was trying to kick the habit
of being in love with David. That was another thing
Peter had told her. Stop trying to fight it. Analyze it instead. But how could you put feelings and emotions
under a microscope, especially if they were your own?

Eve, you idiot! How could you have fallen so deeply
and irretrievably in love with a guy that you lost all
shame, all pride?

Thinking about it, she felt herself shudder. *Now* she
could feel revulsion at herself for her spineless, prideless
crawling to David; clinging to him even in the face of
his rejections. Peter, of course, was a rebound lover; but
then, Peter had admitted that that was his specialty.

"I take other men's rejected lovers and make them
over, doll," Peter had told her once. "I *make* them; I fuck
them into forgetfulness. Pretty soon, they've forgotten
whoever it was threw them over—they're new women,
rehabilitated, you might say. It's my small contribution
to the cause of womankind."

"It's nice to know I'm a good cause," she had responded waspishly.

But she wasn't depending on Peter to make her over.
Since David, she'd had a lot of casual affairs—one-night
stands with men she wouldn't go out with again and
wouldn't give her unlisted telephone number to. Funny,
that. Once she had despised women who screwed around
for the hell of it, or just to prove they were the equals
of men, as if that were the only way they could think of
to prove it. But God, then she'd been so independent
and so sure of herself and where she was going!

Eve had told Marti, who shared the apartment with her, that she felt as if her life could be divided into two segments—before David and after David. Marti, who had been indirectly responsible for her meeting David in the first place, had merely looked sourly at her. Marti didn't like David—never had, from that first evening, when he'd walked in with Stella. . . .

Stella—Stella-by-starlight, with the platinum hair curling damply around her face; at the nape of her neck. Stella with the soft, demure manners, the voice of a lady —and the body of a wanton.

At first, Eve had thought that Stella belonged to David. Or the other way around. But Marti soon clued her in. Marti was a lesbian, and Stella was her lover of the moment. But Stella, who was also David's secretary, could never admit in public what she was. So Stella always carried a "front" with her.

On this particular occasion the front had been her young, open-minded boss, David Zimmer. Good-looking, sharp dresser. Up-and-coming fast—he was the type. Eve, walking in late, had noticed him right away. And latched onto him.

Maybe it had been only because she felt sorry for him —he was obviously straight, and none of Marti's other friends were. Maybe because he was so tall, and had the nicest brown eyes and a sexy, full-lipped mouth—she always looked at eyes and mouths first. But there he was, with a glass in his hand, standing slightly apart from the rest of the crowd, ten gay friends of Marti's.

Eve had had a particularly hard day, filming "The Regeneration of the Haight-Ashbury." Since she'd moved up to being anchorperson on the KNXT morning news, she hadn't had too many chances to go on location, interviewing people on the streets, and she had enjoyed this particular assignment. But it had been a tiring day, and she'd intended to go straight to her room and to sleep.

Instead, after she'd kicked off her shoes, she'd asked him teasingly to fix her a drink.

It amused her to watch him studying her, obviously sizing her up, wondering. . . .

"Hello." He had a nice voice, too. Deep, definitely masculine. "I'd love to fix you a drink, but I'm afraid I don't really know where everything is—I'm just an observer here."

"So I noticed!" In those days, not really knowing David, she could tease him—play it cool. "Everything's hidden in that cabinet behind you. I'm Marti's roommate, by the way."

He'd fixed her the drink she asked for—and two more after that. She remembered the relief in his voice when he'd become bold enough to say, "You're straight? You mean that?"

Later, he had escaped with her into her bedroom. That was after the others had left to go dancing, after Marti had announced that she'd drop Stella off and it was okay if Eve and David wanted to party it up by themselves. . . .

Throwing her head back, trying to concentrate on her breathing, Eve caught her bottom lip in her teeth. Go back, Peter had said. If only she could!

That first night—why had she forgotten to be wary with David as she was with the other men she'd started to date after Mark? He'd asked her questions about herself, her job. He'd caught a couple of the news programs she'd been on, had thought he recognized her when she walked in. But she came on too early or too late—he was usually on his way to the office by eight o'clock. He was an attorney. . . .

They'd both known at that stage that he would end up spending what was left of the night with her. But he'd taken his time, he had seemed really interested in getting to know the real person under the getting-to-be-well-known face and figure of Eve Mason, KNXT newswoman.

And maybe that was when he'd gotten to her, that very first time he'd penetrated the shell of reserve she'd learned to erect around herself. Or had it been later, when they'd gone to bed? There his concentration had shifted from her mind to her body, and the contrast between his detached, friendly manner of moments before and the uninhibited lover he showed himself to be excited her beyond measure. Eve found herself giving, doing freely and naturally with him things she hadn't done before with any man, not even Mark.

"Eve—Eve! You're like your name. Woman. I like the way you don't hold back."

"Do you always talk while you're making love?"

"I don't make love often. Mostly I just screw around. You're different."

Nothing unique about that, but it was the way he said it, the sincerity in his voice that made the meaning different. And right then he'd told her he wanted to go on seeing her. They made plans to have dinner the next evening; to go down to Albany during the weekend when she was free, to meet his family.

Who could resist a man like David—beautiful, tender, fierce, and knowing.

His parents had died together in an automobile accident four years earlier, leaving David responsible for his three younger brothers and sisters. Francie, who was seventeen, pretty, and knew more about life than she let on; Rick—thirteen and an average baseball-crazy boy. And Lisa, who was only seven, and silent. Silent since the death of their parents. It wasn't that Lisa was retarded, David had been quick to point out. Just that their parents' death had come as such a shock—he was sending her to a speech therapist, who said she was making progress. . . .

What Lisa needed most was loving and cuddling—someone to tuck her in at night and read her bedtime stories. Once, Eve had tried to tell David so, and he'd laughed at her.

"Is that why you give her all the attention? You're just a born mother, Eve, in spite of your career-girl surface!" He hadn't said anything about making her his wife. But then she'd thought that the time would come. When they were both ready. Stupid of her! That time would never come now.

The hell with David—so quick to jump to conclusions. Right now, Eve thought she almost missed Lisa, who had just begun to open up to her, more than she missed David. Lisa had been like her sister Pattie, crying when Eve left home after that flaming row with Pop. Like Eve herself at seven years old, all skinny legs and hair.

"All that hair!" her mother used to complain. "Darling, can't we do something with it? Braid it or tie it back or something if you must have it long. You can't have it hanging in your eyes and hiding your pretty little face."

Her hair hid her from the world—she deliberately let her bangs grow until they almost obscured her eyes from all the ogres of her childhood. Especially her father, with his heavy hand and loud, shouting voice.

He'd raised Cain when Eve had announced, after the years of parochial school that she was going to college. Even her mother hadn't understood.

"But darling, you don't need college! Allen Harvey has such a good job, and he's going to take over his father's store—"

"Mother, I'm not going to marry Allen! For heaven's sake, just because I dated him—"

"We'll leave heaven out of this, if you please!" A big vein throbbed in her father's forehead—she could tell from the way he rubbed his palm against the side of his pants that he itched to smack her, as he would have without hesitation a few years ago. "Now you listen here. College is bad enough, but this place you've picked, Berkeley—isn't that the place all the damned radicals go? Always in trouble, always making protests and demonstrations—I tell you, no daughter of mine—"

"Pop, I want to major in political science. And maybe take journalism as well. Berkeley's one of the best universities, and I won a scholarship, so you won't have to support me! I'm only going to *college*, Pop, not taking to a life of sin!"

"I wouldn't be too sure of that, after the things I've heard about that place!"

The arguments and the rows had gone on, up until the day Eve had finally walked out, with her father's shouted threat that she'd better not get in trouble and she needn't bother to come back home if this was how little her family meant to her ringing in her ears.

But she'd won out! The first time she'd ever fought a battle for herself and won it. The first time she'd really been free; completely on her own.

By this time, the skinniness had turned to slenderness, offset by curves in the right places. Her hair, still long, was tamed—shining copper-brown, thick. "Skinny little Eve" had blossomed into a natural beauty, but on the inside she was still shy—a little scared by her new environment and suddenly full of doubts about herself.

Eve had picked the Berkeley campus of the University of California mostly because it symbolized, in those days, the kind of freedom she thought she craved. The freedom to think and speak out as she pleased— not to have to go to church—the freedom to fuck if she wanted to, although at that time in her life she would never have used that word.

She found, in the end, that between classes and her part-time job and studying hard to keep her grades up so she wouldn't lose her scholarship, there was really no time for anything else, not even serious dating. The few times she did go out with guys, she discovered they expected to make it with her. She hadn't become liberated enough to accept casual sex, and she didn't have

the nerve to let any of them know she was still a virgin
at eighteen.

Nothing exciting happened to her, and she had begun
to despair that anything ever would. She was getting
good grades, and she had switched to journalism as her
major, discovering she had an aptitude for writing. And
then, toward the end of her second year, everything
seemed to happen at once.

Her father died—he had refused to speak to her since
she had left home—and her mother needed help to support the family. Eve was thinking of dropping out,
taking a job—but what could she do?

That was the year that *Good Taste* magazine decided
to run a feature titled "Undiscovered Beauties on American College Campuses," and their photographer, shooting pictures in the library one rainy day, discovered
Eve.

The *Good Taste* fashion editor made her over, gave
her pointers on makeup and how to dress, but it was the
photographer, Phil Metzger, who made Eve look beautiful.

"You'd be perfect for modeling, baby—you're one of
the lucky few who's got curves and still photographs
slim. And that *face*. You're really beautiful, you know
that? Got bones in all the right places."

Phil tried to make her all the time they were shooting,
and, in the end, she gave herself to him on his last night
in town.

Phil had been at first disbelieving and then honestly
astounded when he found Eve was a virgin.

"Oh, my God!" he kept saying, "I didn't think there
were any left! I mean—hell, don't the guys around here
have *eyes*? Christ, baby, you're my first cherry, you
know that?"

Halfheartedly, he tried to persuade her to go with
him to New York, but they both knew that it was only

because of her now-lost virginity and not because there was anything really going between them.

Eve turned him down politely and sensed his relief. And, maybe because he was relieved that she had let him off so lightly, he gave her prints of all his best pictures of her, told her how to put them together, and added a letter of introduction to the head of the Ray Burnside Modeling Agency in San Francisco.

CHAPTER
TWO

IT DIDN'T TAKE Eve long to discover that she didn't really want to become a model. There wasn't anything exciting or challenging about what was supposed to be a glamour job, standing around posing—either baking under hot lights or freezing outdoors and there just weren't enough openings and opportunities in and around San Francisco to make it worthwhile—New York was where the big money was. But after the training, Eve did take a few assignments, mostly out of a sense of gratitude, partly to find out for herself how it really felt. And that was how she met Marti—and Mark Blair.

Marti came first. Marti Meredith was an established model who had made the six-hundred-dollar-an-hour bracket before she left the East Coast. An inch taller than Eve, who was five foot seven, Marti had a truly patrician face, with a polished-ivory complexion and large dark eyes fringed with spiky black lashes. Where Eve had curves, Marti was all angles.

They were introduced by one of the secretaries at the agency when it turned out that Eve was looking for a place to stay in the city and Marti, who had just taken on a too-large apartment, needed a roommate.

When they were first introduced and went out to look

at the apartment together, Marti didn't waste time beating around the bush, either.

"There's something you'd better know before you decide to share an apartment with me, Eve. I don't dig men, except as buddies. I dig women. I'm a lesbian. Most people in our crowd know it."

There was more—and Marti said it all, flat out, while Eve just stood there looking at her. Later, she thought it was mostly the challenge that Marti had indirectly thrown at her that had led her to accept both the apartment and Marti. Now, three years later, Eve and Marti not only accepted and understood each other, they really liked each other. As Marti had pointed out early in their acquaintance, there were several advantages to roommates who dug playmates of different sexes—the main advantage being that you didn't have to worry about poaching on each other's preserves.

Now . . . Eve opened her eyes, seeing her own reflection in the full-length mirror that was angled on the wall across from her bed. The mirror had been David's idea—he had hung it for her about four months ago. And damn David again for coming back into her mind! She felt like a child again, crying for the moon or the stars when she had everything; didn't other people always say so enviously? Why did she still want David when she had done quite well without him before?

David, David, David. Just saying his name, over and over like a litany, a cry of pain and passion. David, who had been *her* David just two months ago. Who had him now?

Eve's reflection stared back at her—smudges under her eyes. Concentrate, Eve. Assess yourself; this won't do. All your good points. Face. That's okay. Cheeks slightly hollow now (good for camera angles) from too much thought and too little nourishment. Green-tinged hazel eyes (they were really more green than hazel),

copper-brown hair, cut to shoulder length. Nice breasts.
Not too big, thank God, but definitely *there*. And long,
slim legs, too long to cross comfortably behind the desk
in the newsroom. She had begun, again, to play tennis
and the exercise was good for her. Mental and physical
discipline, that's what she needed!

Why can't I turn David out of my mind? I made myself stop thinking about Mark. . . . Dear Mark, why did
you have to die?

Eve thought about Mark deliberately now, about her
first meeting with him. It was one way to keep David
out of her mind, wasn't it? Dear, helpful Peter and his
helpful tips. Self-analysis for the masses. Do-it-yourself
head-shrinking. Stop it, Eve! It's Saturday, and you have
nothing to do until four-thirty Monday morning when
the clock goes off again. Remember Mark. He, at least,
was kind.

She always noticed men who were taller than she was.
And she had known he was someone important from the
way everyone seemed to fawn over him the minute he
walked in. Mark had *presence;* he was the kind of man
one couldn't help noticing.

Eve had been modeling gowns at a charity ball, given
just two weeks before the San Francisco Opera season
opened. She had been feeling desperate that evening because she knew she had to get a job—a real job. She'd
switched over from Berkeley to San Francisco State University, but the question remained. Scholarship or not,
she had to have a part-time job so she could send money
home and still have enough to live on.

"Mart, I've *got* to find something! Mr. Higgins gave
me this really great letter recommending me to the editor of the *Record,* but it's been two weeks and I haven't
heard—"

"Well, you will. And wipe that sick look off your face,
for Christ's sake. You're not playing Violetta, remember,

just modeling the gown Beverly Sills is going to wear. Go on out there, baby. You're on."

The gown, really a costume, was gorgeous. Yards and yards of skirt and a tightly fitting bodice that exposed her arms and quite a bit of cleavage. Eve walked out to the lilting waltz theme from *La Traviata*, and the first person she noticed was Mark.

Tall, with silver-gray hair. Piercing blue eyes in a tanned, ruggedly handsome face. His gray suit almost matched the hair. And she knew, without having to look after that first glance, that he was watching her.

She hadn't known until later that he had arranged to sit next to her at dinner. Or that he had been the reason the five models had been asked to stay on for dinner. Another of the things she was to learn later was that Mark Blair always got what he wanted. He wanted Eve, and she didn't even realize who Mark Blair was and what he represented until Marti clued her in, much later on that evening, when Eve had floated back to the apartment on a champagne cloud.

"Darlin' child, your future is assured. Mark *Blair!* The elusive, aloof Mr. Blair, who just happens to own— almost everything around here! Do you feel like Cinderella?" Marti was half-drunk herself, but honestly happy for Eve, who hadn't really recognized her luck yet.

Eve wasn't thinking "luck"—she'd never met anyone like Mark Blair before, and she'd been more impressed by the man himself than the aura of power that clung to him. He hadn't been distant with her, and he was both a fascinating companion and a tender and undemanding lover.

It was not until afterward that Eve realized just how much Mark had done for her. He'd taken over. She'd got the job working as a feature writer for the *Record*, one of the newspapers Mark owned, and had finished college. And it had been Mark who'd found her the job at KNXT, insisted she must take it. It was almost as if he had been preparing her for what would happen—for learning to live without him. All she had left of the two years with Mark was memories. Sudden, surprise "vacations" all over the world, an education she could never have had in college. A closet full of expensive clothes and a few pieces of expensive jewelry.

All that was left of Mark Blair was cremated one incongruously sunny morning. Eve hadn't gone to the funeral, which was attended by his grown-up children. His bedridden wife, who had been "dying" for the past ten years of some mysterious illness, hadn't attended, either. Mark had died of a heart attack, playing tennis.

Two years. Eve hadn't cried over Mark since he'd died, but now the tears came slipping far too easily down her face. Was she crying for Mark and the love and safety and security he'd given her, or for David? Or were they tears of self-pity, for Eve Mason who was young and beautiful and bright, and had everything— and nothing?

CHAPTER
THREE

"PETER PET, I tried everything—Yoga, stream of consciousness, reminiscing over past mistakes—I can't exorcise him."

Why, Eve wondered, did she tend to talk like Peter whenever she was with him?

She looked at him expectantly. Waiting for the rabbit to be pulled out of the hat; waiting for him to snap his fingers and tell her it was okay to wake up now—the breakup with David had been nothing but a nightmare.

They lingered over Saturday night dinner at Peter's favorite restaurant, one of those "in" places where everything was lousy but the food.

Peter sighed theatrically, shaking his head at her, but underneath the table Eve could feel his hand searching for her knee, moving upward to rest on her thigh. Peter liked touching, especially in public—and most of the time she let him because it gave her a strange, exciting feeling.

"I told you, Eve darling—I charge for analyzing you, but I screw you for free. Now, which is it going to be?"

"Stop giving me ideas, Peter—maybe I should start charging you. Wouldn't you like to use me as a case history? I'll talk into your little tape recorder in my best little-girl voice and use all the dirtiest words I know—it should make a best-seller."

He leaned over the table, pretending to look into her eyes, but she had felt his hand tighten on her thigh, and now his fingers probed delicately, carefully, until she rewarded his persistence with a tiny sigh—a relaxing of her muscles.

"Clever Eve. You always say exactly the right thing, don't you? Let's skip the café royale and go to my place so we can fuck."

"Mm-hmm. And I get to talk afterward?"

"Fuck first, darling. Talk later."

That night, Eve made the first of what she was to call the "Peter Tapes." She rationalized that she was doing it for herself because she needed help and Peter was a psychiatrist—normally she would never have been able to afford Peter. Whatever her subconscious reasons were, she had to admit to herself that having their lovemaking taped gave her the same sexy-dirty feeling that Peter's hands groping up her skirts under restaurant tables did.

Peter didn't like her to call it screwing.

"Screw is such a mechanical word, my sweet. You're not a machine; I'm not a machine. Fucking is so much more human, more personal, don't you think?"

Peter was good in bed, very efficient, even considerate —making sure she got hers. But he wanted her to talk dirty. All the other times she had refused, why should she put herself, her voice, her moans on one of his tapes?

At least he had been honest enough to tell her about his collection of porno tapes and to ask her if she'd mind having the tape recorder running while they fucked.

"But what do you do with them, Peter? Do you play them back when you're alone? Do you play with yourself while you listen?"

"I'm the analyst, Eve," he had said reprovingly. He had explained that one day he was going to make up a kind of tape collage that included the voices of all the women he had ever fucked. "Everybody has some secret ambition, luv—that's mine." She had not been able to help laughing. In a way, she really liked Peter. He was honest, he didn't bother to play games; and because she was not one of his society patients, he didn't bother to be tactful with her.

Tonight, Eve was going to play Peter's game. Why not? Maybe he'd play the tape for David sometime; it might even make David jealous. Somehow, she knew David was still jealous, still cared what she did.

And after she had put herself on tape to Peter, he'd let her keep talking, putting herself on tape for herself. It was supposed to help her understand her own hang-ups better when he played it back for her the next time. Therapy, Petrie-style.

THE FIRST TAPE:

The damn thing is running. Peter, how do I start? What do I say? (Sigh.)

Eve, you were very good tonight, and I'm very sleepy. You just talk—just say anything you can think of. That tape's good for a whole hour more, and it's all yours.

Oh—shit!

No more dirty words, angel, or you'll get me aroused again. And do try to make any questions you might have rhetorical, would you, please? I'm going to take a nap.

Peter, you really are a cold fish. No—I take that back. You're not too bad, really. For a man. I can see you shrugging in the dark. Don't you like it when I say something nice about you for a change? Oops, sorry, purely a rhetorical question.

You know, this is really a strange feeling. Sitting up in bed talking to myself. At least, it seems like that. I know you're there somewhere, tape recorder, but I can't see you. I should talk to myself more often; it really is kind of fun.

What am I going to talk about? David, natur-

*ally. That's why I'm here. You're going to have to
answer some questions later, Peter, dear. Maybe
when you play this back. After all, I'm here
courtesy of David, aren't I? Does he do this often?
Do you tell him what happens between us? Oh,
damn, I wish I could have the answers right now,
but there you are, pretending to be asleep.*

*All right. Back to David. I don't understand him.
Do you, Peter? I suppose I never did understand
David, even while I was falling in love with him.
I thought I did, of course. I thought I knew everything about him—the way he thought, the way he
could turn me on without even touching me. God!
Here I was, thinking he'd turn out to be just another guy, looking for some fault, something about
him I'd begin to hate. And suddenly it hit me, out
of the blue.*

*I love David. My God, I'm really in love. That's
a big moment for any woman—sort of like losing
your virginity, only better—more scary, too. Isn't
there a song that goes "I've never been in love
before"? Well, I haven't. I was beginning to wonder if I'd ever feel that way about a man after
Mark, whether I'd ever find another man, one I
could really trust. And then, without even realizing
it, I was in love with David.*

*He didn't call. That's when I knew. He used to
call me every day, from the first time we met. It
was like—like something to look forward to each
day. At first I thought it was kind of amusing—
David didn't seem the romantic type at all; he
seemed very prosaic, very straight. But as I got to
know him, I felt as if he was opening up his real
self, letting me in, and it was a very private thing—
I was the first, the only woman. He made me feel
that way.*

Anyhow, David would call me. At least once a

day. Every day. I started to look forward to his call,
you know? I used to unwind while I talked to him,
he's—he was, I mean—he seemed to understand.
He even let me talk shop, tell him about my aching
feet—oh, I begin to see something already. This is
an aside to you, Peter; you really are clever. I guess
David was my very own tape recorder, only not
quite; a tape recorder can't fuck and make you feel
like you're the only woman in the world—that's
another little knack David had. He would concentrate on me; he made me feel—unique.

And then one day he didn't call! I couldn't get to
sleep; I was frantic! I found myself pacing around
the apartment like a caged animal, getting on
Marti's nerves, and then it hit me, and how it hit me
—I loved David. I mean, I'd fallen in love. And he
hadn't called. So I made mistake number one—the
first in a long line of them. I called him. In the middle of the night yet.

"David," I said, "I love you." And he laughed.
"Eve, you're an idiot." That's what he said. Then
he said he was sorry he hadn't called—there had
been an emergency and he'd had to stay late at the
office, working on some brief. And afterward, he'd
just fallen asleep. I felt stupid. But good, too. Now
he knew. Don't ask me why I wanted to tell him.
Maybe I wanted to hear him say the words back.
But he never did. Smart David.

Peter, did you analyze David, too? How did you
become friends? What did David tell you about
me? Ah, come on, Peter, I know you're not asleep
—I can tell by the twitch of your shoulder. You
want to fuck again, I can tell that, too. Peter? Did
he tell you about the quarrel?

Time's up, Eve. You can save the quarrel for the
next tape. Roll over now, like a good girl, and tell
me you want to get fucked. Come on, there's a few

minutes left on that tape, enough for lots of sexy words and noises.

You're a bastard, too, Peter . . . no, stop it, I don't want . . . damn you anyhow!

Tell me, Eve.

Fuck me, Peter. Fuck me, fuck me!

END OF TAPE.

CHAPTER
FOUR

When Eve got back to the apartment, very late, Marti was still awake, listening to Rod Stewart records. As usual, she had been drinking; a half-filled glass sat on the coffee table within reach.

Eve was worried for her. So far, Marti's drinking had not started to show in her face or her figure, but if she kept it up, it inevitably would.

Marti and Stella must have quarreled again. Eve wondered with a trace of bitterness whether Stella was still confiding in David. Two-faced Stella who stood between two camps and wavered.

"Eve, baby, Want a drink?"

"Uh-huh. I'm beat. That Peter, sometimes he gets in a mood and he seems insatiable. Even my legs ache."

"You must've turned him on, baby."

Eve laughed shortly, easing off her shoes.

"Not me, really—it was the tape I made for him. Peter taped everything—words, sounds. Would you believe that he's even fixed his bed so it creaks every time someone moves?"

"I believe. Peter sounds like a riot. Sure is a shame I'm not a switch-hitter like Stella, or I'd get him to give me some of his bedroom therapy."

"Marti—"

Marti picked up the glass and waved it vaguely in Eve's direction.

"Go on to bed, baby, and don't worry about me. In a mood like this, no one can help me. We had a big fight, Stel and I, but we'll make up. Don't we always?"

Marti didn't sound convinced, but it wasn't any of Eve's business.

"Well, I guess neither of us will be getting any telephone calls tomorrow, so we can both sleep late! 'Night Marti."

After Eve had gone into her bedroom, Marti fixed herself another drink. She thought about what Eve had said, about the tape recorder. Maybe she should get herself one and talk into it on nights like this. It might be better therapy than alcohol, at that. The drink was much stronger than the last one she'd had, and she grimaced at the taste. Mustn't turn into an alcoholic; it ran in the family. When she lived at home, very long ago, someone was always warning her about her drinking. And then she'd quit. But Stella—Stella was enough to drive anyone to drink.

Oh, God, what a bitch Stella was. But how beautiful, how very clever with her hands and her tongue and her soft, ladylike voice that could make even the dirtiest words sound like a love poem.

Marti supposed it was funny, in a sick sort of way, that she and Eve should both be in the same boat. Eve had lost David, and she had lost Stella. Wasn't it odd how all their lives were mixed up together in some way? Here were Marti and Eve sharing an apartment; Stella and David sharing office space. At least, she hoped that was all they shared, but with Stel, who could tell? "Mr. Zimmer," she called David in the office. When she brought him to the party, it had been "David." And how could anybody really blame David or any man for looking twice at Stella, for wanting her? Stella was lovely;

if she hadn't been so petite, she could have been a
model, too. So innocent, Stella could look, and when she
cried, so pathetic, so sad!

Tonight, Stella had cried.

Marti had known, from the time Stella walked in, that
something was going to happen. Stella was tense, edgy.
When Marti kissed her, she had ended the kiss quickly,
drawing away.

"Okay, baby, give. Something's bugging you, and
you might as well tell me now as later."

Marti had been pouring drinks, her face turned away
from Stella's. Why let Stella see how much she was af-
fected? Stella was already too sure of her power over
Marti.

"Mart," Stella said nervously, chewing on her lower
lip. She paused, and Marti could almost feel her gathering up her courage. The words tumbled out in a rush.
"George asked me out. George Cox—you remember I
told you about him? And—I said I would. Marti, I've *got*
to try it, don't you see? I—I want to."

Marti had heard her own voice bridge the distance
between them, sounding calm, so damn calm!

"Well, darling, if you want to, there's nothing I can
say, is there?" She came back with their drinks and
handed one to Stella. "I don't exactly own you, baby."

Stella reached out and touched her lightly on the arm,
and she had to force herself to remain calm, casual.

"Marti?" Stella's voice pleaded with her. "Baby, it's
just a *date*, that's all. And he's so old. All he wants is
companionship—he said so. And to be seen with a girl,
someone young, you know? It's just an ego thing."

"And what is it for you? Do you have to be the one
to feed his damned male ego?"

Stella pouted, bending her head to study the liquid
in her glass.

"There's nothing wrong with being nice to someone,
is there? And he's a friend of Mr. Bernstein's—he can

help me get ahead, don't you see that? He won't make any demands of me; we'll still have each other, see each other. Oh, Marti, darling, please understand! I'm so damned weak; I'm not strong like you are. I have to put on an act like I'm—I don't want people to know. My never going out on dates—people are bound to think it's not normal, not natural. I feel as if they've started to wonder already, to talk about me. And I can't stand that thought, Marti."

Marti ground her teeth, her hands clenching, but she managed to make her voice come out even.

"Stella, I *do* understand. You've made up your mind already; you've been thinking about this, and you think you're doing what you have to do. But think about this, baby—I *love* you. Marti loves Stella—does George? Or does he just want a pretty face to take out to dinner? I want more than that, Stel. God, sometimes I wish *I* were a man, so I could take you out in public and show you proudly to the world as mine. But I'm a goddam coward, too. I'm not going to fight for you. Know what, baby? You go ahead, go out with George. Me, I think I'll get good and drunk!"

Stella began to cry, leaning her head against Marti's shoulder.

"Marti, don't! Please don't make me unhappy, because I do love you, you know I do! I'm just afraid, that's all. What's there for us, Marti? In the end, I mean? I don't want to end up old and living with another old maid. Old maids—old dykes, they'd call us. And laugh, and snigger at us. And—I've seen it, Marti! We'd get to looking so *ugly;* all square-bodied and thick, like men. Oh, I couldn't stand that. I'd kill myself first!"

"Stop it, baby, stop it! You're young and you're beautiful and you'll never get old—all it takes is money and face-lifts. So cut out the tears. Go out with George; take him for whatever you can get; go out and fool the god-

dam world, then. But baby, come back to me afterward
—never stop coming back to me!"

Marti's hands touched Stella, stroked her trembling
body, caressed it until the trembling had become a need
that made her gasp and squirm.

"Oh, God—yes, baby—yes, yes! Do it to me—let me,
too—Marti—Marti, darling—darling!"

They fell together onto the thick shag rug, tugging at
their clothes, touching, kissing greedily. Marti kept
thinking that at least she'd leave nothing of the life, the
passion, the loving that brimmed up in Stella for old
man George with his distinguished gray head and mani-
cured hands.

Marti made Stella climax, screaming and whimpering
with desire and lust—that soft, babyish mouth was open
—little tongue licking greedily out at Marti's nipples. Of
course Stella loved her back! Stella would use George,
but it was Marti that Stella loved. Stella was hers, hers!

Marti gave herself up at last to pure feeling, ceasing
to think and to calculate. Midnight-black hair and blond
were all mixed up; their bodies met and tangled and entwined in the age-old Sapphic patterns.

Marti had never been so forceful, so demanding, so
generous, and so tender. Under her avid, seeking mouth
she felt with joy how Stella seemed to quiver and burn
and then melt. Stella's beautiful body lay opened to her
hands and lips—possessed completely by her. And as for
her own needs—had Stella ever loved her so well? Stella
was usually shy and inhibited about the things she
would or would not do. But tonight, as if she had to
prove something, Stella seemed to go wild. Her hands
and tongue were merciless, taking Marti to peak after
peak of joy.

After it was all over, they lay panting against each
other like animals. Stella's skin still quivered and shrank
with sensation—she lay on her back with eyes closed

and her pink lips parted, still moaning softly. Marti, lying on her stomach with an arm and a leg thrown possessively over her love, was, at that moment, content.

Now let her go out with George—let her try finding out if that was what she wanted, whether George could give her pleasure.

It was only after Stella had left, still half-dazed with the passion that had exploded between them, that Marti let the depression catch up with her again. The last thing Stella had said as they kissed good-bye at the door had been, "Marti, I love you. Please understand!"

So Stella would go out with George after all. How could George resist her? Marti was well aware of Stella's loveliness—and Stella's selfishness. Always, Stel would come first—to Stel. If it hadn't been George, then eventually there would have been someone else. Marti knew that, had always known it. But how could you stop yourself from loving, from needing one particular person?

The last record had ended, and the silence hurt her ears. Why couldn't Eve have stayed up? They might have gotten smashed together, consoled each other. Poor Eve, as unhappy over her stupid, undeserving David as she was over Stella.

Her drink was finished. Should she have another, maybe? Standing up, Marti felt herself sway. A sudden wave of nausea hit her, and she felt beads of sweat pop out on her brow as she clutched onto the arm of the chair. No more drinks—she hated to get sick, hated the agony of vomiting. Carefully, she began to walk toward her bedroom.

On the way, she leaned against Eve's door for a moment. Eve, wake up—I need someone. Hold my hand; talk to me; tell me she'll be back. But there was only silence. Well, she could cry herself to sleep!

CHAPTER FIVE

IN THE WOMEN'S WASHROOM at Hansen, Howell & Bernstein, Stella Gervin studied her reflection in the mirror. Thank goodness last night didn't show, except as a very faint shadow under her eyes, hardly noticeable under her makeup. Stella's lips curved in a smile. Smiling, she gazed back at her mirrored self with a kind of complacence. No wrinkles. And her hair looked pretty this morning; she was glad she was letting it grow again.

Stella's new blue dress brought out the color of her eyes; its demure ruffled collar made her neck look slender, and the skirt was midlength enough to show that she had extremely pretty legs. She wondered suddenly if David would notice. She had had the feeling that just recently he had been noticing her a lot and trying to hide it. Well, men who knew she was Marti's special friend were usually intrigued. Every man wanted to be the one who could make a lesbian come.

Under her pale skin, Stella flushed. More of Marti's philosophy—she herself hated the word. I am not a lesbian. Bisexual, maybe. It sounded properly clinical, better than lesbian, les. Never. I can always get it from somewhere; it doesn't have to be a woman. A man with soft hands who understands women and likes to go down on them could have the same effect. Against her will, she thought of Marti as she had been last night.

29

Beautiful, slender Marti with her hard-muscled dancer's body, giving her pleasure—and such pleasure! Could a man ever do the same for her?

One of the other secretaries came in, and Stella turned away hurriedly, the flush still on her face. She picked up her purse and started to hurry out, smiling at the other girl. Thank goodness it hadn't been Gloria. Gloria always managed to make her feel plain and insecure. Privately, Stella knew it was because Gloria had her eye on David Zimmer, who was Stella's boss. To Gloria, any female who worked around David had to be competition, especially since Eve was out of the picture now. So Gloria invariably made it a point to remind Stella of her position, which was *outside* David's office, and safely behind her desk.

Back at her desk, Stella put her purse away and sat down, crossing her legs. David wasn't in yet. Mr. Zimmer. She always called him that in the office; it made for better business relations, and it kept Gloria off her back. It was Gloria, in fact, who had made a point of bringing George Cox into her office, on the pretext that he wanted to see David. Gloria knew very well that David was out that afternoon! Stella guessed that Gloria had also known very well that George would prefer to meet David's secretary. Well, she had no complaints about Gloria on that score, at least. George had seen her, George had liked her looks, and it hadn't been long before his phone call had come, asking her if she'd care to have dinner with a lonely old man. Stella had known that George Cox had been married at least three times and wasn't exactly lonely for female companionship, but the fact that he had asked her out was flattering—and he was such a rich man!

Behind her desk was a window that looked out over the city. Stella loved her view of all the white buildings that seemed to glimmer in the sun when the fog went away, and the faint crescent of blue in the distance that was San Francisco Bay. She had hated Los Angeles, but the first time she had seen San Francisco she had felt as if she belonged here. Perhaps, she mused, it was because here, for the first time, she had been really free, and able to choose her own friends, make her own life. Thanks to contacts she had made through Mim, she had been lucky enough to land the legal secretary job at H. H. & B.

Mim, whom she hadn't thought of in months, started a whole new train of memory. Mim led to Kevin, and the thought of Kevin, hateful even now, reminded her of herself as she had been just a few years ago—a naive, uncomplaining child-woman, Southern small-town style. Brought up to believe in church and marriage and a life just like her parents had led, raising lots of kids. Well, she'd been lucky that there had been no children. Some kind of trouble with her ovaries, the doctor had said. No children for her ever unless she wanted to stand some kind of operation that might even be risky for her. A good thing Kevin had wanted to wait.

Kevin Maynard. She didn't like to remember now that she had once been Mrs. Kevin Maynard. Married to her high-school sweetheart, the only boy she had ever dated, because he had been the only one her parents approved of.

He had been a quiet, ruggedly handsome man, and she had believed herself deeply in love with him. She had taken secretarial training while Kevin did his hitch in the Army, just so that she would be able to help him when he started back to college afterward.

They had been married soon after Kevin got his discharge from the Army, and Stella settled down to the routine of a working wife while Kevin studied hard— he was ambitious and she had admired and encouraged his ambition. And she had even found keeping house kind of fun, at first.

Being a conservatively brought-up Southern girl,

Stella had never questioned the fact that she didn't really enjoy doing "that" with her husband. She wasn't *supposed* to, was she? It was something a woman submitted to, when the man was her husband. Kevin was kind enough to her, and this was what she had expected from marriage. She did not question the fact that he never tried to caress or arouse her—just rolled onto her and off her, and then they'd both fall asleep. The only time it had hurt was the very first time, and of course she had expected that.

They might have gone on that way forever, except that Mim happened to them. Kevin's big sister, the one his family hardly ever talked about because she had run away from home to make herself a *somebody;* landing a job on TV, making herself a home somewhere on the West Coast. Mim had become something of a legend in their hometown.

Mim just happened to be visiting the city where Kevin attended college, and what could be more natural than her staying with them? If Kevin's acceptance of Mim was a trifle stony-faced, Stella had thought nothing of it. Kevin had always been the quiet type, and of late he seemed to have become quieter than ever—in fact, she hardly ever saw him anymore. She worked all day, of course, and he was having to study very hard so he could get good grades—this was the *only* reason he spent so much time at the library. She must fight back that devil-instinct that suggested to her that the blonde assistant librarian might have something to do with it.

Then—Mim. An invasion; perfumed, long swinging hair, pale face with big made-up eyes. Kevin became quieter than ever and stayed away more after Mim arrived, but Stella blossomed. Stella loved Mim, loved to hear of the life Mim led and the people she met in Los Angeles and San Francisco.

Mim was beautiful, fascinating. Stella felt she could listen to Mim talk for hours, watching those expressive eyes and hands, loving it when Mim's soft fingers touched her arm or cheek fleetingly. Even when she was in bed with Kevin she was aware of Mim's presence on the living-room couch, wishing she could be out there talking to Mim or just *listening*—sitting on the rug as they sometimes did, with their shoulders touching.

It was very hot that particular summer, a moist heat; and their apartment had no air conditioning. Stella fainted at work one afternoon, and they sent her home early. She thought she was going to faint again when she walked into the hot, sticky little apartment.

Miraculously, she found Mim there. Mim had planned to go shopping, meeting some people she had to interview, but it had turned too hot, and so here was Mim lying on the couch, reading—wearing the briefest bikini she possessed.

As Stella came in the door, half-staggering, Mim caught her—made her get undressed right down to her bra and panties. Then, because the bra was so tight, Mim took that off, too, in spite of Stella's shy, half-hearted protests.

"Come and sit over here, baby—I've got the fan turned so the breeze hits the couch, see? There's just *us* in here! You've got such lovely breasts, Stella. Bet Kevin loves them all the time. . . ."

Mim's soft hands stroked her lightly, and Stella felt a sudden, *different* kind of thrill shoot up through her whole body. No—Kevin never did *that* to her. Mim talked soothingly to her, soft fingers tracing patterns on Stella's gold-tinted skin. Oh, it felt beautiful! Mim's hands cupped, molded, teased. . . . Stella closed her eyes. They were lying on the couch together now, and it was really too hot to move. Besides—did she really want to move?

"Take your panties off, too, luv—let's get you all cooled off, huh?" Mim's voice had gurgles of laughter in it—or was it something else? Stella lifted her hips, letting Mim slide the panties down and off her body. How cool it felt now; how cool Mim's fingers felt against her skin.

"Let me massage your shoulders for you, Stella; you look too tense. Turn over—yes, like that."

Mm, that was good! Did she say the words aloud? Afterward she thought she might have. Why else would Kevin have jumped to the conclusion he did, walking in on them lying that way?

Suddenly, the apartment seemed to explode with his anger and the words he flung at them both.

"You! Dirty lesbian! I thought maybe seeing that doctor had cured you by now, turned you into a normal woman, but he didn't, did he, and now you—and you, you bitch, my wife! I always did guess there was something wrong with you, Stella, I knew it. No one could be as pure as you pretended to be. You were a virgin for me because you preferred making out with the *girls*, isn't that it?"

His voice had an ugly, hysterical ring. Now he grabbed for Stella, jerking her off the couch and onto the floor, and then back up onto her feet, holding her arm with one hand while he slapped her mercilessly.

"No, Kevin, no!"

Both she and Mim saying it at the same time, making him even wilder.

"Dirty, cold, frigid les! Never giving, always lying there, stiff. And I tried to be patient with you, gentle. What a laugh! I'm going to give you something to remember, now—both of you. Because you're going to watch, Mim, dear. Else I'll spread the story of what I just saw as far as it will go. Your career will be finished then, sister—*you'll* be finished."

Her head throbbing and spinning from his slaps, her face starting to swell, Stella could do nothing to stop him as he pushed her ahead of him and into their bedroom. She felt him shove her roughly onto the bed and tried to struggle, sobbing hysterically. Again she heard Mim crying out for him to stop.

"Liars—lying, unnatural bitches, both of you! Just don't scream too loud, or everyone's going to find out what's been going on between you two while I've been working my ass off," Kevin advised, his voice rough and hoarse.

Stella had to lie there and watch him as he took his pants off, took the belt out of them. She turned over as she saw him coming, muffling her screams of fear and horror, and then he was beating her. She wrapped her arms around her pillow and stifled her pain-filled screams in it while her body struggled and twisted, trying to avoid the blows that kept coming and coming mercilessly until she was in an agony of hurt, throbbing and stinging all over.

When he was through beating her, he threw the belt at Mim, who was kneeling crouched in a corner of the room, sobbing, her hands over her eyes. Only half-conscious now, Stella felt him turn her over; she lay there not able to move as his weight came down on her and he raped her, pulling her legs apart and upward. He seemed bigger than he had ever been, she was dry, and she could feel him tearing his way up inside her, battering into her vitals. She screamed out loud, and his hand slammed down across her mouth, cutting her lip and loosening her teeth. She could feel herself bleeding, and that must have made it easier for him because soon he discharged himself inside her and at last she felt him leave her.

From very far away Stella heard his voice, threatening, cruel.

"Be out of here by the time I get back—both of you. You got two hours, that's all. And you better not contest the divorce, bitch. Get out—and I don't want to hear anything from either of you again, understand?"

She heard him go stamping out of the apartment, but

she couldn't move, couldn't stop her own cries of pain.
Oh, God, what pain!

Mim washed her protesting body gently. Mim kissed
her all over, stinging her cuts with salty tears. And Mim,
her mouth and fingers so very gentle, gave Stella her first
orgasm, there on Kevin's bed.

Afterward, leaving most of her clothes behind, Stella
let Mim take her away. They went to Los Angeles first,
and Stella became beautiful again as the bruises healed.
Mim taught her things she hadn't dreamed about, even
bought her books to read, and gradually she began to
understand about Mim and about herself.

Never again would she let a man touch her, never!
She didn't care what they called her; she was going to
be like Mim, accepting herself for what she was, accepting her own needs.

That's what she thought at first, until the ugliness of
the looks and sly little innuendos and the feeling of
merely existing on the fringes of life began to get
through to her. Stella still wanted no part of men, but
she did want to be accepted by other people. After
months of protests and tears and arguments, Mim said
at last that she understood; and it was Mim who had
helped her get the job. "I suppose I owe you something,
after what I caused," Mim said, her big eyes sad and
pleading. Somehow, from somewhere, Stella had found
the strength to resist that pleading. She had grown tired
of Mim, in any case. Never again would she let someone
dominate her completely.

CHAPTER SIX

THE TELEPHONE RANG, sending shock waves through Stella's body. She closed her eyes for an instant before she answered the insistent ringing. This was the *present;* both Kevin and Mim were tucked safely in the past. She picked up the phone, hoping it wouldn't be Marti.

But it wasn't Marti; it was David Zimmer.

"Stella, I won't be in this morning—looks like we're going to be tied up in court for quite a while yet. Be an angel and get my correspondence all sorted out, would you? Answer whatever you can, leave the rest for me."

"Yes, Mr. Zimmer. Will you be in this afternoon?"

"I expect to be, sure. After lunch, though. Hold the fort, honey."

She hung up and looked quizzically at the phone. David was being very free with expressions of endearment lately. Could that mean—well, why not? He had told her frankly some time ago that she was a beautiful woman, and he liked to be around beautiful women. Maybe he was leading up to asking her out. God, Marti would go crazy with jealous anger. And Eve—oh, Eve would almost die.

Stella wondered if Eve knew that *she* was the one who'd confided to David that Marti had once made love to Eve. *Once*, only once, Marti had said. And that had been very long ago, almost in the nature of an

experiment—never repeated. She had pretended to
David that she was jealous because of Marti, but really
—really it had been because she was mad at Eve. Eve
had acted like a snotty bitch, and it served Eve right.

The trouble with Eve was that she was dumb and not
experienced enough in the fine art of playing games.
Eve had allowed herself to fall in love with David, and
that made her vulnerable. Loving was one thing; being
in love was another. Being in love was being weak, letting someone else get the upper hand. That wouldn't
happen with Stella. No one was going to hurt her again,
not *ever*.

Stella rolled a sheet of long paper into her typewriter
and started to type. Might as well get this will out of the
way and have it ready for David to read through when
he came back in.

A few minutes later, she was glad that she had been
busy, because her door opened without any preliminary
knock and Gloria Reardon walked in, carrying a magazine and some papers.

"Hello, Stella. David must keep you awfully busy.
You're always working, and always so *quiet!*"

Stella smiled up at Gloria, but her mind worked fast.
Gloria was up to something, but what? Had she heard
anything? Had David said anything? David was the
only person who knew about Marti. . . .

"I have some files here that Howard wants David to
look over. I'll just leave them on his desk where he can
find them, shall I?"

Gloria went through the door that led into David's
office without waiting for Stella to reply; and a few
seconds later she came sailing out again, a smile on her
face. Stella noticed again, with a stab of envy, that
Gloria really was quite beautiful. And her clothes! They
were the most expensive that Stella had ever seen anyone wear, close up. Not only did Gloria dress beautifully; she had quite a figure as well. It was no wonder

that Howard Hansen was said to have more than just a
business relationship with Gloria. How, Stella, wondered, did Mr. Hansen take Gloria's obvious fondness
for David Zimmer?

Stella would have been surprised if she had known
that this was exactly what Gloria intended to discuss
with Howard Hansen.

Hansen was a tall, slender, man with piercing gray
eyes and sparse blond hair. In his late forties, he was
soft-spoken and rather gentle in manner until he stood
up in a courtroom, and then he could cut a witness to
pieces with the lash of his voice and words. He had
once been told that he should have been an actor;
diffidently, Howard had replied that the practice of law
brought him more money and the knowledge needed to
invest it.

Howard Hansen had been a man of few weaknesses
until he had met Gloria, the young English widow of
an ex-client. Recently widowed himself, Hansen had
been on a European trip to dispel his loneliness, when
he met her. They had found several things in common.

After he had gotten to know her well, he had discovered that she was not only willing but happy to cater
to all his secret sexual desires, thus obviating his regular
hiring of highly paid call girls. She had introduced him
to the orgy scene in London, Rome, Hamburg—she had
even taught him a few things he had never heard of. He
had wondered why she had not turned her talents into
the channels to which they were best suited and become
a courtesan, but she had told him, laughing, that she
preferred the cloak of respectability, of anonymity.

Howard had brought Gloria back to California with
him—she had said London had begun to bore her.
Neither of them felt ready for marriage yet, so Gloria
had been given a position in Howard's office, which
gave her an excuse to be a part of Howard's life. They

understood each other and had very few secrets from
each other. It made for a very satisfactory arrangement,
generally.

After she left David Zimmer's office, Gloria came back
to Hansen's plush office and, without asking, fixed them
each a martini. Very dry. She saw Howard raise an eyebrow at her, but he said nothing, waiting for her to tell
him whatever she had on her mind.

After she'd brought the drinks over, Gloria arranged
her body on the couch that ran the length of one wall.
Every movement she made was deliberately seductive,
but Howard knew that at this moment she was not
trying to seduce him—she had practiced the rites of
seduction for so long that they had become second nature with her.

"I left the latest issue of *Stud* on David's desk. It had
his girl friend's picture in it—centerfold."

With Howard, Gloria was herself, direct and abrupt.
And he was glad of it.

"I thought she was an ex-girl friend, thanks to you.
Or to us, I should have said."

"Howie, you know damned well he's still carrying a
torch! Why else would he have gotten so mad at her,
just because he found Archer in her bed? My God, you'd
have thought she was his wife, the way he fussed."

"So you didn't expect him to get quite that upset.
You just thought he'd be annoyed enough to play 'what's
sauce for the goose is sauce for the gander.' Does it matter at this point?"

Gloria sat up, her eyes gleaming.

"Baby, of course it matters! You know how I am till
I'm sure I have a new man all tame and on a leash.
David isn't, and he won't be as long as he's still jealous of
Eve. So we'll see how he reacts to the picture."

"She certainly has a lovely body. A shame she didn't
prove more cooperative, or I'd have enjoyed a sample
of her charms myself."

"Which way, baby—doing or *watching*?" Gloria waved her hand impatiently to signal that he needn't answer. "It doesn't matter. In spite of her job, Eve Mason is too naive to hold a man like David. The way she kept begging him to listen to her, to *understand*, made me sick. How could David continue to want her?"

"Maybe she has something you're not able to recognize, my dearest. Maybe she was flattering to his ego. Have you stopped to think that he might actually be in love with her?"

"That's it—she flattered his ego. David's not in love with her; David's not the type. I think he's going to be hard as nails when he finally grows up. Like you, Howie. And like me. But as it is, I don't like competing with dear Eve's ghost."

Watching her over his martini, Howard said dryly, "I can hardly see *you* having to compete with anyone, Gloria. Ghost or not. There are very few men who can resist you. Why bother with David? Wait until he grows up, as you put it, and then sample him."

"I hate waiting for anything—you know that. And in a few weeks I'll be tired of David. He'll be all yours then."

Howard raised his eyebrows.

"Gloria, my love, you know I never play with the hired help. Besides, David is a damned good attorney. As you so perceptively remarked, he's going to end up with no illusions, like the rest of us, and then he'll make an even better lawyer. So when you're through with him, don't be too hard. Try to part friends with him; it'll make everything much easier."

"Darling, your advice, as always, is excellent, and I'll take it." Gloria had finished her drink, and now she put the glass down on the table decisively. "However— there's *now*. Would you mind if I dragged David away from the office a little early and took him down to the house? I feel like a swim."

"Go ahead. But sweetheart, if you plan on doing your lovemaking *out*doors, be sure the servants aren't around, hmm? I'll try to come down myself, but I'm not sure if I'll be able to make it or not—I have to meet with Senator Tidwell in about a half hour."

Gloria's smile was mischievous.

"Don't forget the binoculars, darling, in case you do come down in time for the fun."

After she had left, Hansen let a slight smile come to his lips. How well he and Gloria understood each other! He was lucky to have found a mistress who was as understanding as she was.

Gloria stood in her own office looking out of the window, and now she was not smiling. She was thinking about David Zimmer, who had made the mistake of being hard to get. If he had shown himself aware of her initial, exploratory flirtation with him, she would probably have forgotten all about him by now. But he had *pretended*—and when she'd asked him down to Howard's big country house for a weekend house party, he had asked if he could bring his girl friend along. Stupid David! Or was it clever David? Had he played hard-to-get on purpose, to intrigue her?

Gloria had a devious mind; Howard had often said so. Devious or not, she was usually pretty good at figuring other people out and finding their weaknesses. It had been her spur-of-the-minute idea to have David and Eve allotted different rooms, and then to have Archer go to Eve, playing drunk. Everyone switched partners at the weekend house parties. Everyone knew this except the two newcomers—David and Eve Mason, his date.

As Gloria had hopefully anticipated, Eve had not put up a fight at all, until she had suddenly realized that the man in her bed wasn't David. And then all she had done was whisper to Archer to get out, she was the wrong girl. But by this time Archer, who wasn't a slow worker by any means, wasn't about to stop what he was doing. And it was this pretty scene that David had walked in on. . . .

He was supposed to act sophisticated about it, shrug his shoulders, and go off with Gloria, who was standing right beside him. She wouldn't really have minded if they could have joined them on the same bed. But David had flown into a rage and had made a terrible scene. In the end Archer had had to take Eve home, and although Gloria did succeed in luring David to her bed after he had had far too much to drink, the party had turned out to be something of a fiasco. And David, drunk, hadn't been very good in the sack, either.

Well, she was going to give him a second chance, which was more than he deserved—more than she gave most men. But Gloria had a kind of sixth sense about men, and this feeling told her David could be very good if he was really trying—very exciting. So, lucky David— today she'd give him a chance to seduce her. Impatiently, Gloria waited for him to return.

CHAPTER
SEVEN

WHEN DAVID ZIMMER ARRIVED in his office after a late lunch that hot afternoon, the first thing he noticed was the latest copy of *Stud* magazine lying in the center of his desk.

Frowning, David rang for Stella on the intercom. Her voice came over from the next room, quiet, ladylike.

"Yes, Mr. Zimmer."

"Stel, did you happen to leave a magazine lying on my desk?"

"Why, no, Mr. Zimmer, I didn't."

"Well, has anyone been in here since I went out to lunch?"

There was an almost imperceptible pause at the other end. Then Stella's voice said primly, "Gloria Reardon was here. With a memo from Mr. Hansen."

In spite of his annoyance, David repressed a half-smile. None of the other secretaries knew quite how to refer to Gloria, who was Howard Hansen's mistress as well as his "administrative assistant."

"Thanks, Stella."

David sat down before he reached for the magazine. If Gloria had left it here for him, that meant there was something in it that Gloria wanted him to see. "Bitch" was a word that described beautiful blond Gloria perfectly; and already, even before he started flipping through the pages of the magazine, David half-suspected what Gloria meant him to discover.

In spite of his lunch and the two martinis that had preceded it, he started to get a hollow feeling in his stomach. Eve wouldn't—she couldn't have, not even to spite him! But she had, and, mixed with his rising anger, David could not help the unwitting, unwilling tightness in his loins.

She had a four-page spread and the centerfold. The title was "The Many Faces of Eve," photography and story by Tom Catt.

"It took a challenge thrown at her to persuade Miss Eve Mason, San Francisco's loveliest answer to Barbara Walters, to pose for this magazine. Eve, an ex-model who has never agreed to pose for so much as a lingerie shot before, was stung when we suggested to her that all models are toothpick-thin and would never qualify to make the pages of this particular magazine. . . ."

There was more, but David didn't want to read it. He looked at the pictures, shots of Eve from various angles and in various outfits. Making a TV commercial, Eve working—looking very businesslike—Eve and her roommate Marti fixing supper in their apartment, Eve at the opera on the arm of a pompous old man with a potbelly. Curled up with a book, reading—her face devoid of makeup but still flawlessly beautiful.

His fingers shook when he came to the centerfold. Unlike most of them, this one could almost qualify as a work of art. Tom Catt, alias Jerry Harmon, alias the "Body Merchant," had really outdone himself with this picture.

A waterfall in the background, a real one, with its spray creating a misty effect. Shrubs in the foreground, wet green leaves. And Eve. Half-smiling, minute drops of water standing out on her body to give it a sheen (how could he not remember how the perspiration looked just so after they had made love?), the leaves barely covering her. No mistaking that this model, at least, had a real figure. "I'm one of the fortunate few who photograph skinny, darling," she had told him once.

The pain in his groin was almost unbearable, but then, so was his anger—a rage intense and primitive.

How dare she? How dare she do this, knowing how he felt about the kind of woman who would put her body on exhibition for everyone to see?

He raged at her silently, fists clenched. Hypocritical, lying bitch! All those tears she had shed, begging him not to leave her—all those times she had told him how much she loved him, that he was the only man she had ever loved, could ever let love her again . . .

The telephone rang, startling him. He knew it was Gloria and didn't want to answer it, knowing all the same that he had to. It was the direct "hot line" from Howard Hansen's office, and Howard was the senior partner of Hansen, Howell, & Bernstein, attorneys-at-law—"H. H. & B." as they were known in the city. Mostly, only Gloria would call him, but sometimes it would be Howard. It rang again, insistently, and David picked it up, taking a deep breath before he did.

"Darling, did you get your thrill for the afternoon? Now I *know* why you were so hard to get. Quite a body under those skinny-look dresses!"

"All right, Gloria. You know damn well Eve and I are all washed up. I couldn't care less if she went in for porno movies next. If it's advertising she needs, *I* could provide that, for that matter." He caught himself, realizing he'd let his irritation show through.

Gloria chuckled; it always gave her a kick to needle someone.

"You must tell me *all* about it, lover. When you're through making noises like a jealous boyfriend, that is."

The phone clicked in his ear as she hung up.

In spite of himself, David went back to *Stud* and the feature story on Eve. Of course, he knew why she had

done it. To make him mad—to make him realize what
he was missing. Eve wouldn't have done it except to
spite him. She was a bitch all the same, and he longed
to tell her that.

Somehow, he knew that right now, right this minute,
she was thinking about him. Feeling the same way he
did. "Our damned ESP," she used to call it.

Without stopping to think, not *wanting* to consider
what he was doing, David dialed Eve's number. Of
course, she wouldn't be home. She worked hard all day—
hadn't she told him that often enough?

He heard two empty rings then hung up, disgusted at
himself for his own weakness. Why couldn't he forget
about her, let her be? It didn't matter to her whom she
went to bed with—man or woman. When poor, unhappy Stella had told him about Eve and Marti, he had
not wanted to believe it, but when he'd seen Eve with
that other man, a *stranger*, he'd felt sick to his stomach.
Why did just her picture give him a hard-on?

There were letters on his desk that had to be
answered, a brief he should be reading through. But
David didn't feel like working this afternoon. Why not,
he could almost *hear* himself think, why not Gloria? At
least she wanted him and made no bones about it. And
he still had something to prove where Gloria was concerned. . . .

He picked up the telephone and called her extension.

Gloria's body was beautiful, almost perfect, except for
the overlarge breasts. But they were high and firm, and
very lovely—sexy, too, with the shiny drops of water
standing out against the slight oiliness left on her skin
by the tanning lotion she had used.

David's anger made him almost aggressive. Gloria
wanted him—she had certainly been obvious about letting him know it. Why in hell should he hesitate, waste
time?

He put his hand out and touched a breast, and she didn't move. Then, very deliberately, he lifted it out of the barely confining bikini top and bent his head, his tongue stabbing greedily against Gloria's already hardened nipple.

"Ohh, baby, yes!" her voice breathed as she turned against him and the other breast came loose, too, pressing against his bare chest while their hands fumbled at wet swimsuit bottoms.

She was easier to reach than he, and she was ready for him. He pushed her backward and down, uncaring now that they were right out in the open where anyone might surprise them. His fingers explored her, gauging her readiness before he plunged into her and felt her tighten wetly on him—swallowing, sucking him inside her.

The sun gleamed off her blond hair, reflected off each individual golden piece of fuzzy down on her body that proclaimed proudly she was a natural blonde. She was lying half on and half off the pad she had been sunbathing on, her head back, her eyes closed against the blinding brilliance of the afternoon sun.

"That's the way, lover—that's the way!"

Her legs clamped around him, and he felt her fingers digging into his buttocks, pulling on him, grabbing at him. She was a big golden-haired bitch squirming under him, wanting it, grabbing for it. A bitch like every other woman—like Eve—only Eve was more of a bitch, a lying hypocrite. What or who did they think about when they got screwed, the bitch-women?

Gloria's eyes were still closed, but her half-open mouth emitted sounds of pleasure and words that spurred him on. Gloria knew *all* the words; she was taking him on a mad, wild ride on her bucking, writhing body. He got one hand underneath her and rammed a finger up her ass, enjoying her yelp of pleasure and the way she came up to meet him with new fervor.

All right, bitch, he kept thinking, all right, then, get it, grab yourself one, and hurry, damn you, hurry, because I'm going to shoot my load all the way inside you any moment now!

Out loud, his voice prodded at her, urging her, "Come and get it, get fucked, baby," and she started to moan, and then she was saying, "Yes—God, yes!" and the last "yes" was a kind of scream.

He felt her start to contract convulsively around him, and that did it for him, too; there was no holding back now, and he had to let it go, to let the explosion of himself happen—the eruption into warm, tight, woman-cunt, not caring who or what the woman was; and it didn't even matter that his hands were hurting her and his mouth was bruising hers; she was taking it, wanting it, screaming for it.

"That was *very* good, lover," she said minutes later, her voice sounding only slightly breathless. "But get off me now, there's a good boy. I'm finding it hard to breathe, and besides, someone might come."

"That's a good one! All of a sudden you start to think about someone surprising us. 'Someone might come'!" he mimicked her cruelly, but at the same time, he did as she demanded—rolled off her body and reached for a cigarette before he reached for his swimming trunks.

Gloria, unlike Eve, ignored his sulks. Carefully, and quite daintily, she was slipping her bikini back on, fussing with the top.

"After *that*, I could use a drink. I'll ring for Hill, shall I?"

She pressed the bell-button that was set into the low table beside the pad where they now lay again, quite decorously.

Against his will, David was impressed by Gloria's coolness and the composure of her manner. Who would guess, looking at her now, that she'd just fucked like a great golden beast? Their eyes met for an instant, and she chuckled, a throaty, sexy sound.

"Don't try to figure me out, David, darling. It's a waste of time. I've tried analysis for a whole year, and even my analyst couldn't figure me out for sure—no one can!"

"Not even Howard?" he said spitefully, unable to help himself.

She chuckled again. "Especially not Howard, although he tries the hardest. He does come the closest to understanding me, though. In fact, he's *very* understanding. He knows little Gloria needs her fun—and variety, too. He doesn't mind, as long as I screw him, too, as often as he needs it."

Gloria slipped on her sunglasses and lay back on the pad.

"Tell Hill I'd like a long, cool daiquiri, would you, lover? I think I'll catch some shut-eye until he gets back with the drinks. I certainly *do* feel very good and relaxed. You perform much better when you're not too drunk, darling. Do remember."

He had to bite his tongue to keep from saying something that would have sounded spiteful. Damn her barbed tongue, and damn the way she thought she could just turn him on and off like a fucking robot built for her pleasure. He'd have to teach her different—Gloria could learn, too.

He saw Hill walking toward them, his white duck trousers reflecting the sunlight, and tried to appear as relaxed and nonchalant as Gloria did.

Quite unbidden, the thought of Eve came into his mind. The last time he'd been down here, Eve had come with him. Suddenly, he wished that she were lying beside him now.

CHAPTER EIGHT

Eve HAD BEEN WORKING all morning with a cameraman and two assistants interviewing demonstrators who were protesting the tearing down of an old apartment building. It was fortunate, she thought, that her assignment that afternoon was outdoors, close to the waterfront, and the cold, salt breeze blowing in across the bay had cleared her head. When she'd called the answering service on her return to the apartment, the girl who handled her calls had given her Peter's message along with the rest.

"Your doctor called—he said he could squeeze you in tonight if you called him right away."

She couldn't suppress a smile, even while she wondered what had prompted Peter to call her on a weeknight. Maybe he wanted her to make another tape for him! However, once she had taken her shoes off and cleaned the day's makeup off her face, she was sufficiently intrigued to call him back.

Peter wanted her to go with him to a party, a big one given by a well-known rock singer. He wanted someone ornamental to take with him, he told her, apologizing for the last-minute invitation.

"I really hadn't intended to go," Peter explained, "but Ray called me this afternoon and went *on* about it. Used to be a patient of mine, and he wants me to meet his latest girl friend."

To bribe Eve, he mentioned cunningly that there were bound to be photographers present in droves, and she'd get her picture in the *society* pages for a change. He added significantly that it might make David sit up and take notice, and that was what decided her in the end. Peter was right; let David see that she was circulating and perfectly happy without him.

Peter arrived in his English sports car to pick her up in exactly an hour, and Eve decided that he was really quite a fun escort when she could get him away from the dark little restaurants he loved to frequent. He was the perfect escort in public—attentive, handsome with his clipped David Niven mustache and Pierre Cardin clothes, and he had a dry sense of humor and could make her laugh, too. So what if he had his little quirks and perversions; they only made him seem more human, and, after all, who didn't have hang-ups?

After they had arrived at the party, and following the introductions and naming of drinks, Eve and Peter joined a small knot of people gathered under a graceful arch in the enormous living room of the new house. It was a housewarming, thrown to celebrate an architect's achievement and the completion of the famous singer's San Francisco town house. And Eve agreed, along with everyone else, that the house was not only well designed but beautiful inside.

Peter started talking to the singer, and their conversation was low-voiced and intimate and excluded the rest of the group. Eve stood there fiddling with the thin stem of her martini glass, looking around her for familiar faces. So far she had spotted quite a number of celebrities, but no one she knew personally.

Her eyes wandered, then came back with something like shock to one particular face—the kind of face, the kind of man that any woman would stare at. At the back of her mind was the feeling that she had seen him somewhere before—not in the flesh, perhaps, but in a newspaper or a magazine; perhaps even on TV. Who was he? He stood slouching carelessly, looking bored in spite of the attentive-seeming inclination of his head, listening to something that the singer's girl friend was saying to him, her hand touching his arm. He was surely the best-looking man that Eve had ever seen, and she found it hard to believe that such classical good looks existed. She found herself trying to place him—a male model from out of town? Or maybe even a movie star come up from LA for the party?

The recognition, the feeling of having seen his face somewhere before was an elusive, intangible thing, and she caught herself watching him while he talked, looking almost unconsciously for a gesture, a certain kind of shrug that would mark him as one of the gay crowd.

Jerry Harmon, who had done the *Stud* pictures and article on her, walked up to the man and said something in his ear, ignoring the singer's girl; and she clutched more tightly to the golden man's arm, demanding his attention. Eve had named him that already because of the way he looked, and she watched now the somehow intimate way his gilt head bent toward the other man's dark one, even while his eyes continued to watch the woman who stood so close to him.

He was all bronze—face and arms and throat—contrasting with the bright bleached gold of his hair, and he was dressed so casually it was almost insulting—open-neck shirt unbuttoned halfway down his chest, thick gold chain about his neck, teamed with tight, faded blue Levi's and sneakers. He looked as if he'd been out sailing and didn't give a damn about his appearance, and if he *was* gay, that was unusual. His hair was long enough to curl at the back of his neck, giving him the look of an Edwardian satyr. Still staring, unable to help herself, Eve decided there was something about

the slight flare of his nostrils, the mocking, somehow
cruel curve of his chiseled lips that reminded her of an
animal scenting prey. But whatever he was, satyr or fag,
it was obvious the woman with him wasn't going to let
go easily.

Eve realized suddenly that both Peter and the singer
had ended their conversation and were following the
direction of her gaze.

"Good-looking bastard, isn't he?" the singer murmured, watching his girl start stroking the blond man's
arm. "I guess I'd better rescue Margo. He's the type
who would swallow a little thing like her up like an
hors d'oeuvre and then spit her right back out."

Eve thought that Margo looked neither little nor helpless; nor did she act as if she needed or would welcome
her impending rescue. No polite, curvy redhead with
Margo's good looks deserved pity, anyhow. But the
singer obviously thought she needed protection, and he
moved away purposefully.

Peter smiled warningly at Eve after the singer had
left them.

"My pet, that's one man I'd advise you to stay away
from. Ray isn't right about too many things, but he *is*
right about Brant Newcomb."

"*That's* the notorious Brant Newcomb?" Eve looked
over at him with renewed interest, this time mixed with
a cautious kind of horror. "I've read all kinds of nasty
things about him. He sounds too bad to be true, almost.
Is he really?"

Peter caught her hand and swung it between them,
smiling his superior, knowing smile.

"He is, indeed! But I realize that by warning you to
steer clear, I've probably madly intrigued your delight-
fully feminine mind, Eve darling. So I shall let you decide for yourself. Just try not to let yourself get too
shocked or too excited by anything he says."

Eve felt like pulling back now, but Peter was already

tugging her along with him and was halfway across the room when Brant Newcomb turned away from the singer and his pouting lady and noticed Eve. His eyes met hers briefly, moved away, and then came back to her, raking down the front of her dress quite openly and insolently, with no civilized attempt to disguise what was in them. And while she hated the way he had looked at her, she could not help noticing that his eyes were the brightest blue she had ever seen—so blue and thickly lashed they seemed opaque.

He began walking to meet them, and even his manner of walking was junglelike—an animal stalking its prey.

"Well, well. It's been quite some time since we've run into each other, hasn't it, Pete baby? And that's a lovely creature you have by the hand there. Is she yours, or only borrowed?"

"I'll lend her to you for a few minutes if you'll swear you'll bring her back. I think she's curious about you, and I want her to find out."

Eve listened to them talk at each other—light, fencing words that showed they knew and disliked each other. Already she regretted having let Peter lead her into this.

Brant Newcomb was saying, "I'll be sure this charmer finds out anything at all she wants to know, sweetheart. I like girls who look like her—all autumn tones. She looks warm. *Are* you warm, honey?"

Eve tried to return his somehow mocking look levelly and coldly, but she felt uncomfortably as if his eyes were not looking *at* her but into her, eating through her clothes. Suddenly and unreasonably, she was frightened and didn't want to be left alone with him. Her fingers tightened around Peter's. She didn't want him to leave!

"I'll be back in just a few minutes, Eve," he said, smiling at her urbanely. "I'll just get us some refills at the bar, and Brant here will look after you for me until I get back."

Peter winked at her, pulled his hand away firmly, and

left her there with Brant Newcomb. Who was *the* Brant Newcomb? Money and women were his specialty, and dangerous sports. If she remembered right, he'd been in a few spectacular wrecks, automobiles and motorcycles. He was the kind the magazines called a playboy, the kind of man she despised.

Already she hated him, and so she looked back at him defiantly, letting her dislike show.

"Peter's always playing psychiatrist, even if it's after office hours. I'm sorry."

"No—no, don't be. Tell me, Eve Mason, are you his plaything?"

If she was amazed that he knew her name, she refused to show it.

"That's really none of your business, is it? Or is rudeness one of your habits?"

She had made her voice icy, but he only laughed, catching at the hand that Peter had dropped so unceremoniously.

"Ah, I can tell you've heard all the bad things they say about me, and believe them. Well, luv, they're true. But you're not the type who's easily scared off, are you?" He squeezed her hand meaningfully. "I think—I just have the feeling we might like the same kind of things. Why don't you come home with me tonight and find out? I'd really like to fuck you, Eve. And Jerry would, too, wouldn't you, Jerry? I mean, you really owe him one for that really great picture of you he did for *Stud*."

The dark-haired photographer seemed to trail Newcomb everywhere he went, Eve thought contemptuously, even as she felt her insides coiling up with anger at his words. She ignored Jerry Harmon and fixed her cold gaze on Brant Newcomb.

"Why don't you just fuck each other instead?" she said politely. "I mean, I'm sure it wouldn't be the first time."

She pulled her hand away and started to walk, hearing their delighted laughter behind her.

Eve could feel her cheeks burning with rage and humiliation as she kept right on walking. She was furious with Peter, too, for leaving her alone with that *monster* of a man.

Brant Newcomb had caught up with her and was walking beside her, still laughing.

"All right, Eve Mason—touché! No sharing with Jer, even if he *is* my best friend. But I want you, so let's not play games. Name your price, baby—anything you say."

"Oh, God, you have a nerve! I'm not for sale. And now will you please leave me alone?" Her voice shook with rage as she tried to brush past him, but he moved in front of her, thumbs hooked into his belt in a kind of deliberate caricature of a Western movie villain.

"*Everyone* has a price, Eve. And one way or another, I'm going to find out what yours is—one of these days. I almost always get what I want in the end, luv, and I'm patient. I can wait."

Before she could move or retaliate, he had patted her face lightly and almost absently, and then he turned away from her and was gone, mixing with the crowd. Eve continued to walk toward the bar, her knees feeling suddenly weak. It took her a few moments to realize that she was actually *frightened*. Where on earth was Peter? Suddenly, she wanted to go home.

CHAPTER NINE

MARTI WAS SITTING up late again when Eve let herself into the apartment. She waved the drink in her hand at Eve.

"Hey, you're early. Want to help me drown some sorrows?"

Eve was still preoccupied, her brows drawn together in a frown.

"Marti, do you know a man called Brant Newcomb? You know more people than I do, and he's not the type you'd forget easily. A big blond guy; reminds me of an animal. And I get the feeling he is one. I—"

Marti was sitting up straight, her eyes suddenly alert.

"So you finally ran into him. Every girl in town runs into dear Brant sometime, and senses the same thing. Women are a kind of hobby with him, you might say— among other things."

Eve shuddered. She flipped her shoes onto a chair and walked over to the small portable bar.

"Suddenly, I could use a drink myself. I met him this evening, and my stomach's still revolting. Tell me more about him—is he just another professional rake who counts on the shock value of the things he says, or is he something more? Marti, I sensed a kind of *danger*, I'll swear. It ruined my evening. I was actually scared!"

"And you were right, baby. He's pure poison, and I

mean that. He's the type of guy any woman should stay away from; the unfortunate thing is that many of them are attracted to the bastard because he's rich and so damned good-looking." Marti looked at Eve with sudden concern. "You didn't make him mad, did you, baby? Because he's dangerous—I mean, in every way. Even physically. The thing is, he doesn't give a damn about anything or anyone. And because he has all that money, he gets away with practically anything he pleases."

Marti was actually looking worried, and because Marti wasn't the worrying type as a rule, Eve felt her unreasoning sense of fear come back. She brought her drink over and sat on the couch beside Marti.

"What did you mean, you hope I didn't make him mad? He was quite horrible in his nasty, sneering way, but he didn't exactly strike me as a psychopath, either. You're trying to warn me about something, Marti, and that's unusual!"

"Sure it is—I try to mind my own business! But you're a good kid, Eve, and I wouldn't want you to get hurt. Brant Newcomb's the type who could do it if he felt like it."

"Don't worry, it's not likely that I'll ever run into him again. I intend to stay as far away from him as I can get! Honestly, Marti, I never thought I'd meet a man who could really scare me, but he did. Afterward, I got to wondering if most of it wasn't just my imagination."

"No, it wasn't just imagination. Don't ever dismiss Brant that easily, because he's—a very ruthless person. And he doesn't have feelings, not the kind other people have."

"You sound as if you *know* him."

Marti's voice changed—the slightly slurred quality was gone—and Eve could see that she had tensed.

"I know him too well. I should say *knew* him, because all these years I've tried to stay out of his way. He doesn't come to this city too often—lucky San Francisco!" The sound Marti made was short and bitter, not really a laugh, although she meant it for one. She looked at Eve, her eyes measuring.

"Eve baby, I'm in the mood to talk. I've been sitting here all bloody evening trying to get drunk, waiting for the goddam phone to ring, hoping Stel would call and tell me she changed her mind. But she didn't, so—no, don't waste your pity on me, Eve," Marti warned, catching Eve's look. "If there's one thing I despise it's pity. But we were talking about Brant. And I've a story to tell if you're interested. Perhaps you'd better listen and learn."

"That sounds rather ominous!" Eve tried to make her voice sound light, but Marti's mood and solemn words had depressed her.

Marti said sharply, "Eve, I'm not kidding! Listen, I don't usually tell my life story to anyone, but this part concerns Brant Newcomb, and I'm just drunk enough to want to tell you enough so you'll know he plays rough. You want to hear it or not?"

"If you're sure it won't upset you," Eve began, but Marti interrupted her sharply.

"Nothing can upset me more than I am right now— and this all happened a long time ago, anyhow. Funny how you try to forget things, put them firmly out of your mind, and then something happens and it all comes back like a goddam movie or something. God! I can almost see myself as I used to be in those days. Stupid ingenue trying to play it cool and sophisticated."

Marti had begun to turn her glass around and around between her palms as she spoke, her voice curiously husky.

"I guess it's an old story, really. My parents—they were so damned rich and such damned snobs! They had to send me to a private school. Public school wasn't good enough for their only daughter—I mean, little Martine might meet poor kids with lower-class morals, and that wouldn't do, would it? So I was sent to Miss Dietrich's Academy for Young Ladies. Boarding school—which meant I was safely out of their way. They enjoyed traveling a lot and they were always partying, and I suppose having a kid was inconvenient. I was quite young when they first sent me away. At least, that's how it seemed to me at first, until I learned how to fit in." Marti looked up at Eve and smiled mirthlessly. "Yep— you could say that that's where it all began. The way I am now, I mean. I started young, and I had really en- thuiastic teachers. And you know what? I *enjoyed* it! For the first time I knew what it felt like to be wanted and loved. I had my first crush on a girl when I was only eight. She was much older than I, but she loved me back, and she was mother and lover and teacher all in one. I took to the life like a duck takes to water. Craving for love, my analyst called it. Perhaps! But it felt *good*— it still does."

Marti shrugged lightly, almost defensively.

"To cut a long story short, I was one of the few kids who really *enjoyed* Miss Dietrich's. But after I gradu- ated I tried the 'normal' kind of love the other girls had moved on to—the heterosexual route. I wasn't bright enough for college, you see, and my parents were eager to have me married off, I suppose. They 'brought me out' in a hurry and shoved me on the marriage market. God, they must've wanted me out of their way real bad— we were like strangers! Anyhow, I tried to please them; they teach you respect and obedience at Miss Dietrich's. I guess I was curious, too; all the girls I'd been with seemed to enjoy boys just as much as they'd enjoyed each other during our cloistered years. I had a lot of freedom; I mean, what my parents didn't realize was that our set was really pretty wild, especially the younger crowd. Try anything for kicks was our motto. And some of the guys, for instance, had traveled all around the world with their folks and had picked up all

kinds of sexual expertise. I'd go out on decorous dates
and end up in some Greenwich Village pad, maybe; or
in someone's beach house. Sometimes alone with one
guy, and sometimes with the rest of the gang. And I'd
lie there and let them do it to me because I felt it was
the done thing to get laid. But inside I felt nothing. And
I hadn't learned to pretend too well, so some of the guys
I ended up with would get damn disgusted at me because of my lack of enthusiasm. Word got around that
I was too aloof—cold."

Ice clinked emptily in Marti's glass, and she blinked
down at it as if she were surprised. She drew a deep
breath, and Eve heard herself sigh, too.

"Oh, well—I'm nearly through, in case you're starting
to wonder. Well—then I just happened to meet Brant.
He'd come up to town for a few days to inspect the current crop of debs—that was the way one reporter put it.
We met at a party—by chance, I thought—and I was
even flattered that he singled me out, but a girl friend
told me afterward that some of the guys had been talking about me. Miss Iceberg, they called me, and they
thought he'd be the best one to teach me a few things.
They picked well, I suppose. Brant's a good teacher!"

Something in Marti's voice made Eve want to reach
out her hand to her, tell her she didn't have to go on
talking, but at the same time she felt she wanted to hear
what Marti had to say. Maybe it would help Marti to
talk about it. Maybe, as Marti had intimated, it might
help her to hear. After a slight pause, Marti continued
speaking, her voice low and somehow harsh.

"Brant asked me out. My parents *knew* about him—
they at least had heard all the wild stories about him,
but he was richer even than they and a bachelor, so
they nagged at me until I accepted his invitation.

"I was supposed to be one of a party of six, including
a chaperone, that would cruise to the Bahamas and back
on Brant's yacht. Well, I was one of six, all right, but

he'd lied about the chaperone, and the other five were all men." Marti shivered slightly.

"We were away for a week—ten days—what does it matter? They brought some other girls aboard, in Jamaica, I think. They were black—high-breasted, with proud, outthrusting buttocks. They were really something, those girls. And that was the only time I was able to reach orgasm—to come, over and over, with those girls—I was past caring by then that all the guys watched. After that, they had me pegged for what I was —am—and they didn't bother me too often on the cruise back. Brant even took me to see a doctor before he escorted me back to my parents' house. He advised me, on the way, to stick to my own kind from now on, that I'd be happier and more contented that way, and I followed his advice. It's always better once you adjust to knowing yourself. Ever since then, I've accepted the fact that I am what I am."

Eve, her eyes filled with shock and horror, could hardly contain her angry reaction. Dear God, poor Marti!

"But—didn't you tell your parents? Surely there was something they could have done to have him punished? I mean, what he did to you—that was horrible, unforgivable! A man like that ought to be locked away somewhere. I'd have tried to kill him if I could!"

Marti's eyebrows lifted.

"Sweetie, I thought about it. But he was careful. And he had my parents figured out. They're the type who are more afraid of gossip than of God Himself; and dear, careful Brant took lots of pictures, especially of the scenes with the girls. It was actually Brant who suggested afterward that I ought to become a model. He said I didn't have the talent to learn to act, but I should do well at modeling, and he was right. So you see, Eve—"

"I see. God, Marti, if I ever set eyes on him again, I think I'll *run*, not walk, to the nearest exit."

"Don't get me wrong, though, Eve. Brant can be very, very charming when he wants to be. I've seen him that way, too. But underneath—if there's anything underneath, it's rotten. Maybe he's some kind of misogynist; maybe he's a closet queen trying to prove something. Whatever he is, he's all evil."

Eve got up and walked over to the bar again.

"I need a drink after that. I hate Peter! *He* was the one who introduced us. I guess he knew what would happen, the kind of proposition the man would make. Ugh!"

Marti came over to join her and started to pour herself some vodka. Her eyes were unreadable.

"By the way, David called. I didn't tell him where you were, just that you were out."

Her casual, offhand statement caught Eve by surprise and acted like a jolt of electricity.

"*David?* Oh, Marti! What did he say? What time was it? Did he want me to call back?"

Marti shrugged. Obviously her talkative mood was over and she was withdrawing into herself—something Eve had noticed about Marti since the advent of Stella.

"He didn't say much, just asked for you. But then you know he doesn't like me." Almost violently, she added, "Why in hell do we have to fall in love with the people who are *worst* for us? Look at you, getting starry-eyed because David calls out of the blue—and after the lousy way he's treated you. And me—not able to play it cool with Stella, waiting for a damned phone call that I know damned well isn't going to come!"

Marti turned away so abruptly, she spilled part of her drink. But she didn't bother to wipe it up.

"I'm going to my room. I have a shooting at ten in the morning, and I'm going to feel like hell and look worse."

After she left, weaving slightly, Eve finished her drink
and thought about David as she stared at the phone. She
was still in a state of shock. David had called. Out of the
blue. What did it mean? Of course it had to mean that he
still wanted her. That he loved her, even if he never had
admitted it. Oh, damn, damn! Why hadn't she stayed
home tonight? Now David would think— Well, she
shouldn't care about what David might think. Forget
David. Wasn't that the name of the game, the name of
the project she'd been concentrating on all these
months?

She should forget about David. Not talk to him if he
called again. But her hands were shaking and her knees
felt weak. David, David, David. Please God, let him
call again!

CHAPTER TEN

HE DID CALL AGAIN, after all—at six in the morning—and she felt, groping fuzzily for the telephone, as if she'd just barely fallen asleep. As usual, he sounded crisp, alive, and wide-awake. And just as if nothing had ever gone wrong between them.

"Eve? I'm sorry if I woke you up, but you're very difficult to get hold of these days. Listen, I'd like to see you. To talk to you."

"Who . . . David?" Eve sat up in bed, the sheets falling away from her body, her head starting to spin. "David, it's only six o'clock!"

"I know." His voice had a chuckle in it. "Time you were awake—the sun's up already. You shouldn't party so late."

"I didn't— You have some nerve, David Zimmer! Calling me up at this ungodly hour, telling me I shouldn't party so late. Is that what you—"

He interrupted her smoothly, his voice changing, becoming warm and intimate, making her cheeks flush.

"Eve—baby—I'm asking to see you again. I've missed you. I tried like hell, but I haven't been able to get you out of my mind. So I'm a coward, asking you on the telephone, but I want you to be my girl again. Eve?"

She held the phone to her ear and felt her eyes close. Her hands were shaking. He was asking her to see him again, to be his girl. Oh, God, you *must* be real, you heard me!

"David—" Her voice came out as a whisper, and she had to swallow hard before she could say any more. "Oh, damn you, David! Why'd you have to catch me by surprise this way? Just when I was starting to get over you, too. After everything you said, the things you *thought* about me—oh, David, I just don't know what to say!"

"Say you'll have dinner with me this evening. That'll do for starters. You don't know how much I need to see you again, baby, or just how much I've missed you. Lisa keeps sending her love, too. Every time I go down to see the kids, she keeps asking for you."

"You rat! You *knew* how that would get to me. I shouldn't even be talking to you. . . ."

In the end, though, as they both knew she would, she agreed to meet him right after the location shots she was doing that afternoon.

"Just give me enough time to take my makeup off and change," she warned him. She remembered he didn't like her to wear makeup when she was with him and they weren't going out anywhere in particular.

After he'd hung up, David wondered again why he had called her. Sheer instinct, sheer—what? Was it weakness? He had sworn, both to her and to himself, that he was through with her. But he wasn't—that was the hell of it. He still needed her—that much was true. Contrasted with Gloria or any of the other women he'd been seeing recently, Eve was all woman. Loving and giving, soft and yielding. And not asking for his soul in return for a fuck. Gloria was a ballbreaker and too damned possessive. Let her see that he could still have Eve. It was something that *he* needed to find out, too.

Thinking about Eve and seeing her again tonight

gave him an erection. Gloria was a tease, and Eve
wasn't. In bed, Eve gave all of herself—she was warm
and wild and wonderful, and she'd made him think it
was all for him, that she'd never been this way with anyone else. That was why seeing her in bed with that grinning, fatuous-faced playboy had been such a shock.

He'd been thinking about that, too, having second
thoughts. Frowning, David walked over to the small
stove his kitchenette boasted and poured himself his
fourth cup of coffee for the morning. Now that he knew
Gloria better, he wouldn't put it past her to have en-
gineered the whole thing, just to get him in the sack
with her. And perhaps Eve's stammering, almost incoherent attempts to explain and excuse had been genuine,
and it had been a misunderstanding after all.

"I love you, David," she had wept. "Doesn't that mean
anything to you, anything at all? Do you think I'd be
crawling to you now, without pride, if I were really as
cheap and as easy to make as you think?"

He hadn't listened. At that point he hadn't wanted to
listen, much less have to look at her again. Later,
through the window of Gloria's room, he had watched
Eve drive away with the man she'd been in bed with,
and had been certain then that she'd been lying to him.
She was like any other predatory, lying cunt, he'd
thought then. Pretending to be something special so she
could trap him into marriage; playing around on the
side.

And now—he wasn't certain at all. Except of the fact
that he wanted her. God, how he still wanted her! Eve,
naked, in bed with him. Beads of perspiration standing
out on her skin like the drops of water in that damned
photograph. Crying out to him as she made it, calling
his name, telling him she loved him. She made him feel
good, and their loving never left a bad taste in his mouth
—the kind of feeling he had after screwing Gloria. Well,

the hell with Gloria. Tonight he'd have Eve. Again. And again, and again.

There was nothing David derived more enjoyment from than making love—except, perhaps, preparing a brief that he knew was perfect and without any flaws or loopholes. He often considered that in many ways it was a good thing his parents had brought him up to believe that the *mind* should control the emotions, not the other way around. The emotions were there, yes, but to be practical was much more important.

He had been taught from his youth, during all those early years of being his parents' only child, their *son*, to be strong and in control of himself; that emotions were there, yes, but to control them and to be practical was much more important. A man is rational; he can control the physical side of himself and those dangerous emotions that could carry him away. He was taught to be dispassionate rather than passionate, to think rather than react blindly and unreasoningly.

Ambition, too, was one of the legacies that his parents had left him. That, and a sense of responsibility toward the younger children who had come along so suddenly and surprisingly in his parents' middle age. He often thought that it was as if they had somehow known, had expected what might happen. Dying together—just as they had done everything else together. Somehow, David was never able to picture his parents singly; his memory captured them always as a unit, standing or sitting close together.

David had been in his teens when he discovered the deep and passionate sexuality of his own nature. Even then, he had had the appealing good looks that always had and always would attract women to him. David was only a sophomore in high school when he let Dee, a waitress at the hamburger stand the crowd frequented, seduce him. The other guys were constantly ribbing

Dee, trying to make out with her, even taking bets on who would get in her pants first. She'd kid back and forth with the others, but David started to find that her eyes strayed to him, watching him, wondering about him.

Dee was the first woman to discover and to encourage the deep and passionate sensuality that lay beneath his quiet and unemotional exterior and polite manners. Dee was not too much older than he was; she had dropped out of high school early and had a child to support. But she knew what she was doing in bed, all right, even if she'd made mistakes with her life all the way around.

David never talked about Dee to any of the other guys, and she knew this and was grateful. Grateful enough to let their relationship continue even when she discovered he was dating other girls. David filled all her needs, and she in turn provided him with the abandoned, uninhibited kind of lovemaking he was beginning to crave—the kind the other girls couldn't or wouldn't give him. He kept seeing Dee steadily until he went away to college, and in the meantime, without any fuss or locker-room talk, he had also seduced most of the prettier and sexier girls in school.

By the time he'd finished collecting his degrees and started working at the profession he'd chosen, he'd discovered how easy it was to control women while avoiding all commitment. He could not settle down with one woman because he felt he needed them all. He *enjoyed* women—needed their bodies and their dependence with an insatiable kind of lust that he sometimes despised in himself. One side of him was sober, conservative, and responsible—he was the kind of young and ambitious man that people instinctively expected to make good. But the darker, hidden side of him was a passionate rakehell of a fellow who could not live without women—symbols, to him, of the satisfaction of his desire for their bodies.

Someday, David knew, he would marry. Because it was expected of him and because it would help him form and mold the facade he expected to present to the world. But the woman he would marry would be carefully picked with his head and not with his loins. A suitable wife—*suitable* was the key word. Well-bred and intelligent, but not too intelligent. Not too astute or worldly-wise. Because there would always be other women—this he'd already realized and accepted.

Fighting the usual city traffic on his way to the office, David found himself thinking again about Eve. In a way, he was almost glad that something had happened to make him furious at her. He had been infatuated with Eve soon after he'd met her and gone to bed with her, and suddenly, his carefully thought out plans hadn't seemed to be important any longer.

He remembered how they had come together with a kind of joyful abandon that was completely uncalculated and had taken them both by surprise. Eve was an unexpected person, and she had made him feel that he was the only man who had ever penetrated the brittle shell of knowledgeable sophistication she presented to the rest of the world. She was as sensual and as uninhibited in bed as he was, yet there was a kind of tenderness in her, a sort of small-town friendliness and openness that he was unused to in women. In spite of the fact that she was obviously not inexperienced, and had been a model, there was even a kind of purity about her—or so he had thought. Without her "face" on, with her hair pulled back, and wearing jeans and an old shirt, she was like the girl next door he hadn't had time for—a happy, understanding companion who sensed his moods and feelings with some uncanny sixth sense. But at the smart cocktail parties to which he'd sometimes taken her, Eve could transform herself into a regal beauty he was proud to be with. Of all the women he had known, she could best change herself to fit his moods, his needs.

Although he had told her casually in the beginning that he was far from ready to settle down or make commitments yet, he had begun to think of her as "his"— even, after he saw the way she loved and understood Lisa, to wonder how she would be as a mother. That was why he had not reacted at all when he'd found out suddenly but unmistakably that she was interested in him.

When Gloria had had Howard Hansen ask him to that weekend house party (an invitation extended only to people Howard liked and trusted), he'd responded by telling Howard he'd already made plans to see his girl that weekend. Howard, as affable as ever, had insisted that he bring Eve along.

Goddam, David thought suddenly, slamming to a stop as a light changed just as he got up to it, why *had* he taken Eve? The practical side of his nature took over then, and he found himself rationalizing, telling himself it had happened for the best. He'd been getting too involved, in too deep. Now he'd take Eve back on *his* terms, and those terms didn't include marriage. He'd make her understand that. After all, he'd watched another guy screwing her. Whether it had been her fault or not, how did she expect him to forget?

But there were other things he couldn't forget, either. He remembered that she'd told him once that her sexiness wasn't real, it was part of a facade she'd erected for herself; but God, in bed (or out of it, for that matter) she'd prove herself a liar over and over, in the most wonderful ways imaginable.

Yes, he thought. That was the way he wanted Eve. In bed. As a mistress, not as a wife. He wondered if he could make her understand that things would be different. Although while he'd been seeing Eve he hadn't wanted any other woman, he intended not to lose any chances this go around. No possessiveness, he'd tell her. Let's play it by ear and see what happens. She'd go along with it. Sixth sense, ESP—whatever it was—he knew she'd go along with anything he wanted.

He wanted Eve. When he picked her up in the parking lot behind the studio, he felt he couldn't wait any longer. Just having her sitting beside him in the car again, smelling her perfume and feeling her warmth, made him want to groan with desire. And he could tell she didn't want to wait, either. They knew each other so well—they wanted each other so badly, why wait for all the preliminaries that didn't mean a damn thing?

He started to drive aimlessly, feeling the pressure of her fingers—first over his, and then along his thigh. Her apartment was out of the question; Marti would be there, and quite possibly Stella. They were in no mood for other people tonight. His apartment was all the way across town, far too far away.

In the end, they drove to a motel on Lombard Street, the first they came across. He registered, and as soon as they were in the room, he took her, with her dress pushed up over her thighs. No preliminaries—the only words short, brutal, seeking, describing. What he felt, what he was doing with her, what she wanted.

At the moment of his coming he said, "Good God, you bitch! You witch-woman, Eve!"

And she, only: "I love you David, I love you!"

CHAPTER ELEVEN

THEY WERE BACK TOGETHER, but nothing was quite the same as it had been, except their lust for each other.

Eve felt that their coming together again was such a tender, tentative thing, their new relationship so fragile, that she went around scared all the time—torn between the wonder and the bliss of having David back again and the horrible tearing pain that might be lurking in the background to destroy and engulf her all over again. She wouldn't lose him again! She had to try to pretend that it didn't matter, that things were still the same between them, *exactly* the same, when they were not.

David wanted her—but he wanted other women, too. ("Let's try, Eve, but no jealousy, no commitments this time, huh, baby?") He didn't call her every day, and there were nights when she called him and heard his telephone ring and ring and she knew he was with someone else. And then jealousy would tear at her and she would want to kill him, to hurt him just as much as he was hurting her.

She continued to see Peter, to date other men she really didn't give a damn about, just to prove to David that she, too, could play games, that men desired her. She told herself that she would be a whore and flaunt it in his face, and then she would despise herself for letting him do this to her. But David was her drug, and she was hopelessly addicted to him. All he had to do was call her, tell her he wanted to see her, *wanted* her, and she was happy again—unreasoningly, unquestioningly so.

She would lie in David's arms while he made love to her, and think desperately that she couldn't live without this. In bed, at least, they communicated without words. Like a ritualistic ballet, the movements of which only the two of them knew, they would shift from one position to another, from mountaintop to valley and back to mountain peak of passion again, their hands and mouths and bodies touching everywhere, their movements fluid and beautiful, making whatever it was they shared beautiful and right, too.

At such times, Eve thought that *this,* at least, would never end. She could sense that David craved her body as much as she craved his. And yet for her, at least, it was not just the way he made love, it was *him,* David himself. She loved him; there was nothing she could do about it except hope that he wouldn't hurt her too badly someday.

They made each other jealous, they quarreled, and then they made up in bed.

"David—oh, God, what's happening to us?" she asked him once, despairingly.

"I don't know. Maybe we're trying to find whatever it is we really want," he told her, and she had to be content with that.

THE SECOND TAPE:

Thank you, Peter. I guess I should try to afford you professionally—I must need help. Even Marti is disgusted with me—I sicken myself. You're the only one who hasn't condemned me for my lack of pride and practicality, Peter dear, but then, you have your own ax to grind, don't you?

I wonder if David knows about this—about us.

You never did tell me. Never mind, I don't think I want to know. Any more than I want to know who David is with tonight. I think it's Gloria. I think he sees a lot of Gloria, but of course I'm afraid to ask. And then there's Stella—I'm almost sure he's screwed Stella. Something about the way she avoids my eyes, something about the triumphant, sly look she wears when she thinks I'm not watching her. I hate Stella!

Oh, not because I feel (shit, I know) that she's been to bed with David, but mostly because of what she's doing to Marti. Blowing hot and cold. Swearing George is just a convenient front and things haven't changed between them, when they have. Poor Marti! She and I are in the same boat. Both loving, both wondering, both afraid to open our eyes too wide in case we discover something we don't want to see.

You don't mind if I talk about David, do you, Peter? No, of course you don't. You're nice that way. At least I know where I stand with you. I don't feel as if I'm on trial, as if I'm constantly being tested.

Sometimes I wonder what David really wants of me. Not just me—of any woman. What does he expect? What does he need? I'd be anything he wanted me to be, if I only knew. It sounds so sloppy, doesn't it? Like something out of one of those old, corny movies from the thirties. Where did I read that clichés only become clichés because they are the oft-repeated truth?

Never mind. Whatever the cost to my ego, to my pride, I'm going to try to hang onto David for as long as possible. I have this feeling (all right, so maybe it's really wishful thinking) that, after all, I'll become necessary to him—a habit, if not an obsession. All I have to do is hang in there, try not to make too many jealous scenes, and wait until he makes up his mind. And in the meantime— Oh, God, sometimes I feel that he's making me into a whore, a tramp—the kind of woman he keeps saying he despises. He told me once, "I can only love a woman I can respect. The kind of woman I can be sure of, the kind who won't whore around the minute my back is turned." And when he said it, he looked at me with contempt. He was telling me he knew about the other men—about you, Peter pet. And the others. Did you know there were others? Before David, I used to be selective, I was careful even about the guys I just dated. Now, when I go out, and go to bed with someone I don't really know and don't give a damn for, it's only because I feel I have to. I have to prove something to myself—what's sauce for the gander is sauce for the goose. Peter, am I turning into a nympho?

You're beginning to sound quite overwrought, sweets. Perhaps this isn't too good for you at this point. The tape, I mean. And you're asking questions again.

I know, I know! But Peter, I need help. Honestly I do. What's happening to me? I wake up at night and ask myself that. I'm scared—and yet I'm more scared of losing David—or whatever crumbs of his time he allows me—than of anything else.

I might have known. Why do I get drawn into analyzing the females I fuck? All right, Eve. Tell me. Is David very different now from the way he was when you two first started going together?

He's different; I'm different. I'm at a disadvantage now, you see—he knows I'm in love with him. God, I can't help saying it; the words seem to slip out. And he takes advantage. He treats me so casually now, like a possession. And I am his possession, I suppose, only he wasn't supposed to know that.

Just the other day, when we were together in his apartment—I don't even know if I should be telling you this—

Don't stop just when you were starting to get me so interested, darling. Go on—you know what I like to hear.

I suppose it doesn't really matter—you know we fuck, David and I. And that's what we were doing, right on the couch, with our clothes on. He likes doing it that way sometimes.

It was a Saturday, and he'd just picked me up at my place—he was expecting his family, the three kids, you know, to come up to the city for the day, and he was in a hurry. We—we try out new positions sometimes, and—well, he had me lying with my shoulders braced against the rug while he sat on the couch with my legs up on either side of him. And he was moving me onto him. It was—it was really kind of wild. Like the look on your face right now, Peter.

But anyhow, quite suddenly, right in the middle of it all, the damn doorbell rang, and he dropped me—pushed me away from him on my back onto the rug as if what we were doing had suddenly become—dirty—just like that! And suddenly he was standing up, zipping himself back into his pants, and looking down at me with a kind of distaste.

He— Know what he said? "Get up, for God's sake, Eve. You look like some cheap whore, lying there that way."

And in that moment I hated him—God, how I hated him! But not as much as I hated myself for being there and for letting him treat me like that— use me and then shove me aside.

So what happened?

Nothing. I got up and disappeared into the bathroom to repair my makeup and get hold of myself.

While he let the kids in. Did I say kids? Mistake. Francie is no kid. That's Dave's sister, the older one. She's seventeen, and when she's around David, she acts even younger. But she—I swear, Peter, that she knew what we'd been doing. I could actually feel myself blush when she looked at me.

And then, to make things worse, David suggested that I take her out shopping. For something suitable. Poor Francie, she's outgrown most of her clothes, she needs a new dress.

"Eve has such good taste, I'm sure she'll help me pick out something really cute," she said.

I tell you, Peter, that girl is a woman when it comes to getting the darts in. And David's dumb where Francie is concerned. He thinks she's just a sweet, innocent kid, and it's like she hung the moon.

I had to take her in my car. David took Rick and Lisa to the zoo. And of course, once she was alone with me, Francie forgot about her act. For openers, she asked me what I thought about David's performance in bed. And while I was still trying to come up with an answer to that, she went on to say sweetly that of course I'd have to be passable in that department myself because, quote: "Dave likes to fuck, and of course he's always had women chasing him." Unquote.

She sounds like a sweet child.

Oh, she is! She really is! I tried to freeze her into shutting up, you know? And I did tell her that she needn't think she was shocking me, because I had already noticed how precocious she was—I didn't exactly consider her a child, everything she said so cute.

"But Dave doesn't think that way. Dave thinks I'm still a kid, and I'm a woman. Bet I know a lot more than you do." Her very words. And then she

*added, grinning, that she knew I'd really like to
sock her, and why didn't I?*

"At least I'm honest about things. I hate you,
and you know I do, don't you?"

*I really did want to hit her then. We finished the
shopping in a state of armed truce. She wanted a
new dress, and she had to have me along to help her
pick one out. We argued about that, too.*

*Oh, shit! The things I put up with for David!
We didn't talk much after that, but at least she did
bring it out into the open, the way she feels. . . .*

Did you tell David?

*Of course I didn't—how could I? He's so damned
sensitive about his family, and particularly about
Francie. He says she needs lots of love and attention, and he's so proud of her because she's pretty
and a good student. He has a live-in housekeeper,
but he thinks Francie really runs the house. He
keeps saying what a good wife and mother she's
going to make someday. How can I disillusion
him? He wouldn't believe me, and he'd hate me for
it. He might even think I was jealous—or worse,
that I disliked her. And then . . . But it all comes
back to one fact, doesn't it? I can't stand to lose
David. If I can help it, I won't let it happen. Peter?
What the hell am I to do?*

Sorry, luv, your hour's up. Time for you to turn
into a pumpkin.

Peter pumpkin-eater! Is that what's on your
mind?

Now that you mention it, luv, it sounds like fun.
Is that what you want? Let's try it David's way,
shall we? Let me just slide you down . . . there!

*Goddam you, Peter! No—stop it—no, please—
ohh. . . .*

END OF TAPE.

CHAPTER
TWELVE

FRANCIE ZIMMER STOOD on the corner waiting for the
lights to change. She touched her hair lightly, assuring
herself that her sexy blond wig was still in place. She
wanted to giggle when she thought about the looks
some of the girls in school had given her when she'd
put the wig on in the locker room, carefully making sure
that no strands of her own dark hair showed to give her
away. Those little bitches had really acted cold, whispering to each other, but the guys had really flipped
when she went outside, telling her she looked just like
Farrah Fawcett. Several of them had offered to drive
her home, but she'd turned them all down, acting
mysterious and hinting that she had a date already and
he'd be picking her up.

She'd started to walk home—casual, cool—and, sure
enough, it hadn't been long before some old guy driving
a late-model Caddy had stopped and offered her a ride
to wherever she was going.

He'd brought her all the way into the city, and if not
for the carefully pinned-on wig, she might have thought
about letting him stop off at a motel along the way and
ball her like he wanted to. But she'd spent too much
money on that wig, and too much time and care getting
it on just right; also on her makeup—she couldn't let
him ruin the way she knew she looked. So she'd played

with him a little and let him play with her, opening her
legs and letting him discover she wasn't wearing panties, which seemed to drive him wild—Christ, for a few
moments she'd thought he was going to drive through
the guardrail and end up in the bay! She'd promised to
meet him later in the bar he'd named—she had this
really important appointment right now, she'd explained. She smiled to herself now. He'd have a long
wait, wouldn't he?

Francie crossed the street briskly, quickly, her heels
clicking on the pavement. She hadn't really been lying
—she *did* have an appointment of sorts. And after she'd
come all this way, she just knew the man wouldn't turn
her down—he couldn't.

She walked four city blocks, ignoring the looks and
leers from the men she passed, her hips swinging pro-
vocatively. Another time, maybe, she'd let herself get
picked up, just for laughs, but right now she was in a
hurry. She didn't mind the walking, though. Just to be
walking on her own in San Francisco was a kick; she
enjoyed the free feeling, the sights and sounds and
hurrying people all around her, feeling herself part of
the scene.

The studio was located in an unexpectedly plush
apartment building—a high-rise with a view of the
bridge and the bay. She'd expected a run-down, sleazy
little place on Market Street or the Haight-Ashbury—
maybe even the Fillmore District—over a shop that sold
adult books—but this place was something else!

Francie patted her hair again, thankful she looked
older than she really was. This joint had class, and that
meant this photographer friend of Eve's must be successful in order to make enough bread to afford something like this.

He had to pick her for the assignment—he just had to.
She called up to his apartment from the telephone in the
lobby, opening the door when the buzzer sounded, tak-

ing the quiet elevator. His voice had been deep and interesting; she wondered what he looked like. He'd sounded slightly surprised when she'd first called him up, asking about the job; fortunately, she'd called soon after she'd overheard Eve talking to Dave. She was sure he hadn't had time to advertise yet, or ask around. He wouldn't have asked Eve to pose for pictures if he'd already had someone else lined up, would he? Eve— she was a stupid cow, anyhow. Always trying to justify herself to David. And what *did* Dave see in her, anyhow? She was too skinny, and her boobs weren't that big. Maybe she made up for it by being bitchy in bed— Dave would enjoy that.

Francie moistened lips that were already shiny with gloss before she knocked at the door, and when it opened, she looked unwaveringly into the face of the man who stood there, wearing a loose Mexican-style shirt with full sleeves and embroidery down the front, tight white Levi's, and sandals. He was looking her over, too, and she forced herself to be just as slow and insolent in her appraisal of him. Finally, he smiled at her and stood aside to let her in; and she felt suddenly relieved —she'd passed the first test, at least!

She walked nonchalantly into the carpeted room, pausing to kick off her shoe. She dug her bare toes into the carpet. Wow, it felt so soft!

"Oh, bravo! Such a charming gesture, and so well done, too. I really like your style, sweetheart."

Francie spun around quickly to look in the direction of the other voice, the slightly mocking, teasing one.

This second man was dressed even more casually than the first. His thin cotton shirt was open all the way down to his waist, and he had not even bothered to tuck it into his pants. He sat with one leg thrown carelessly over the arm of a Spanish chair, and his very bright blue eyes were undressing her already.

Francie found herself checking him out just as closely, even while the photographer, Jerry, was introducing them offhandedly.

"Brant Newcomb—Frances . . . Frances . . . Ah, heck, who gives a damn about last names, anyhow! If you don't mind if Brant here looks on, Frances, I'd like to get started right away. I have a deadline to meet.

So he'd decided to let her have the job after all—fantastic! She had to hang onto her cool, though. Brant Newcomb was still watching her with a kind of amused insolence, and somewhere at the back of her mind was the nagging thought that she'd seen his face somewhere before—maybe in a magazine? He was good-looking enough to be a male model or a movie actor; maybe that was it.

Francie kept thinking about him when she went into the bedroom Jerry showed her to change from her clothes into the short hapi coat he'd left lying across the bed. Jerry Harmon was okay, he was a good-looking dude, but Brant Newcomb really got to her. He was one of the handsomest men she'd ever seen, and she liked the way he looked at her, not trying to hide it. She didn't usually go for blonds in a big way, but this particular blond guy had something about him that reached out to her and made her tingle. *He* knew it, too.

Emerging from the bedroom in the short Japanese robe, Francie let her hips sway a little, kept her head high. She'd tied the belt around her waist, but had let the robe stay open down to there. Let them see that she had a cleavage and nice boobs. And at least she had hips to swing under a guy's nose, unlike that skinny bitch Eve!

There was a kind of improvised platform, doubling as a couch, running the length of the big windows—brightly colored pillows scattered along its padded expanse. Jerry gestured toward it. He was playing with his camera equipment already, and there were wires strung out all over the floor, and lights that hurt her eyes when he flicked them on.

"I'm going to start off by having you pose out here against the windows, sweetie—use the tall buildings and the sky as a backdrop. Afterward—well, we'll take it from there."

Francie threaded her way through all the scattered equipment, meeting Brant Newcomb's eyes head-on for an instant. She climbed up onto the soft platform, waiting for Jerry to tell her what to do next. She felt a tingle of excitement shoot through her—it had begun, she was going to be a model at last. Maybe they'd want her for a *Stud* centerfold someday—wouldn't that just *frost* big-brother David?

Jerry was squinting through the viewfinder of the camera, adjusting the lights, turning them so they impaled her with their brilliance and heat. She couldn't see the other man now, but she felt his presence there, and she had finally remembered where she'd seen his picture. It had accompanied an article in *See* magazine, called "The New Breed of Playboy." He was very, very rich, she recalled, and he raced cars and grooved with movie stars and skiied and gave fabulous, wild parties. He really fascinated her, and she was determined to make him notice her—*really* notice her.

"Okay, luv, drop the robe now. That's right. Just kick it aside and stand there turned sideways so I can get a profile shot. You really have a gorgeous pair of knockers, you know that?"

Trembling slightly—was it from cold or excitement? —Francie dropped the robe.

After about a half hour, when her body had become so stiff that her muscles screamed their protest every time he made her move, changing her pose, Jerry told her she could take a break while he changed film— that Brant would fix her a drink if she needed one.

Still blinded by the brightness of the lights, but de-

termined to show her poise and nonchalance, Francie
didn't bother to look around for the robe. She walked
over, almost groping her way, to where the blurred
shape stood waiting for her.

Francie asked for a Scotch (Eve's drink—it sounded
sophisticated), and while he fixed it, she could feel her
eyes getting used to the ordinary light again.

"How did I do?" she longed to ask, but that wouldn't
be cool—better to stay silent and let *him* make the first
move.

He handed her a glass and let his eyes run obviously and openly over her body. She felt herself grow
warm. The Scotch warmed her insides, too. He'd made
it very strong, and it took a real effort on her part not
to grimace over the first swallow.

What a *gas*, she kept thinking. This dude is a *billionaire,* and he's in the same room with me, looking at my
body. He can't hide the fact that he wants me, either. . . .

It was true—there was that familiar look in his eyes
now, the look she had seen before in the eyes of other
men. He put his hand out and cupped one of her breasts
casually, for just an instant.

"Nice. They feel real, too. I don't know how much
Jerry's paying you for his pictures, but whatever it is,
I'll double it for one special one, just for me. One without the blond wig. You'll be twice as pretty with your
dark hair, won't you? I pick the pose, and you get a
bonus for being so sexy and cooperative." His eyes
crinkled at her, although she could recognize no
laughter in their depths. "Are you going to be cooperative, Frances?"

Her breast still felt all warm and tingly from his touch,
and the Scotch was making her stomach burn and kind
of vibrate in the same way it did when she thought
about the four guys in her freshman year who had "initiated" her. Somehow, just the way Brant Newcomb was
studying her with those bright blue eyes made her re-

member all the things they'd done to her—the things they'd made her do for them.

He was waiting for her to answer him, and just then, she felt Jerry come up to stand behind her.

"Looks like you've propositioned her already, Brant. Heck—I haven't had a chance to get my pitch in yet."

"Maybe Frances will give us *both* a chance. What do you say, baby?"

It was exciting—Francie had never felt more *alive* than she did now, standing here nude between two guys while they talked about making it with her in such casual, polite voices.

The photography session began again. This time, the pictures were a little more suggestive, more explicit in what they showed of her. Francie kept wanting to giggle. Wow, if *David* ever saw one of these pictures! The thought of his reaction, of what he'd do to her afterward, made her whole body glow and get kind of weak. It gave her face a sensual, pouty look that seemed to drive Jerry wild—he kept telling her she was a natural.

When he'd finished what he referred to as the "official picture-taking," Francie went into the bedroom with both Jerry and Brant, pulling off the blond wig as her long dark hair cascaded around her shoulders. She let Brant tumble her on the bed and make it with her while Jerry took more pictures—zooming in for lots of close-ups.

When Brant was through with her, Jerry took his place on the bed, and Brant took the pictures this time. Afterward, they all had drinks and sat together looking at some of the pictures they'd taken with a Polaroid camera. They were wild and pornographic, and they turned Francie on so much that she began clawing at Brant's groin with her hands until he tumbled her down onto the floor and began screwing her again, taking his time this go around, laughing all the while at her eagerness and wildness.

His laughter seemed to mock at her, and she got so
mad that she began to bite and claw at him; then he
slapped her hard, slapped her coldly again and again
until her anger and viciousness subsided and she was
clinging to him, begging him in a choked voice to do it
to her again, quickly.

"You're one of *those*, are you, you little hellion? You
dig being hurt. Okay, honey, I'm willing to oblige. Sometimes it even turns *me* on, you know? Especially when I
do this to a woman."

"This" turned out to be sprawling her across his knee
and spanking her bare and wriggling ass while she
gasped and whimpered and rubbed herself lewdly
against his leg, needing the contact of his flesh against
hers.

When he was through beating her, she continued to
wriggle and squirm across his thighs, the tears pouring
from her eyes. But there was a sly triumph in her voice
when she spoke.

"I'm really yours now, you know? You just made me
yours. You can do anything you want with me, anything
at all, I wouldn't mind. Do it to me, Brant, do it! Screw
me, fuck me, make me crawl, use me. . . . I'm *good*—
all the guys tell me I'm the best. And I'll do anything
for you, everything you want me to, you'll see!"

Without wasting words, he took her again, bending
her over the bed this time, ramming himself into her
violently and painfully and satisfyingly while Jerry took
more pictures. And then it was Jerry's turn again. . . .

Brant actually offered to drive her home afterward.
Sitting beside him, snuggling into the softness of real
leather seats, Francie was in heaven. She'd finally found
a guy—a *man*—who could give her everything she
craved. And she was going to make him need her, too.
He was definitely interested; she could tell—why else
would he be taking her home?

Francie told Brant Newcomb that she lived with a

very jealous and uptight guy, so he'd better drop her off a couple of blocks away. She wondered if he'd believed her, if he'd ask her any questions, but he only shrugged as if he couldn't care less. He intrigued her—everything about him intrigued her, including his money. She'd never ridden in a Jag before, either; it was neat. And she was glad that he drove fast and rather carelessly—who wanted to live without some risk and danger to make things exciting?

Snuggling closer to Brant, Francie put her hand on his thigh, running it up and down his crotch until she felt the sudden hardness there. She smiled. It was easy to give a guy a hard-on; she'd learned that real early.

"Shall I blow you?" she asked him eagerly, already bending her head down to him.

With one hand on the wheel, he pulled her up by the hair.

"Not now, baby. Later. You'd better learn not to be greedy."

His eyes studied her for an instant before they went back to the road. She couldn't read anything in them.

"I'm going to give you a phone number, doll. Call me sometime when your jealous lover is out of town, and we'll party, okay?"

He was full of surprises—just when she had begun to pout, fearing that he was bored and done with her for good, here he was suggesting that she call him. He *was* interested in her, then. Francie couldn't help wriggling in anticipation of the next time, another wildly exciting time with this strange and fascinating guy.

Even after he had dropped her off, she continued to think about him. Walking the two blocks back home, she was already planning for their next meeting. She wanted Brant Newcomb. She'd make damn sure he'd never get tired of her.

CHAPTER THIRTEEN

FRANCIE CALLED BRANT NEWCOMB two days later. It was a Saturday morning, and Dave had already called to tell them that he was unavoidably tied up this weekend and couldn't come down to Albany. That means another weekend alone with the kids—Saturday was Mrs. Lambert's day off, and she would be expected, without any question, to take over and baby-sit the kids. Well, this time she wouldn't do it! Why should she? Didn't Dave realize she was seventeen and entitled to some life of her own? Dave was selfish and overbearing and she hated him, but Rick would take care of things. He was really a good kid—quiet and dependable. One good thing about Rick and Lisa, they loved her and they'd never tell on her. She'd tell them they could stay indoors and watch as much TV as they wanted, and she'd make sure there were plenty of sandwiches and snacks in the refrigerator. They'd be okay, they wouldn't even miss her, and she'd be back in plenty of time. . . .

Her hands shook when she dialed his number, hoping desperately that he'd be there. It rang for a long time before he finally answered, his voice sounding sleepy and mad at being awakened. She told him who it was, wondering suddenly if he'd remember her. There was a pause, and the tone of his voice changed subtly, carrying a kind of charged, challenging amusement as he told

her to come up soon after noon, by which time he'd be
wide awake enough to enjoy her company. He gave her
the address and hung up abruptly, leaving her still holding the phone, her knuckles white with tension and excitement.

Getting away from the house wasn't quite as easy as
she'd thought it would be. Rick asked her where she was
going and acted sullen because she'd promised to pitch
for him that morning.

"I'm tired of sitting around in this dumb old house,
too," he complained. "If *you* can't do it, then maybe
Bob Fields's dad might. He said he might the other day,
when I told him I didn't have anyone to pitch for me—"

Francie cut him off short, trying to hang onto her
temper. It wasn't easy because Lisa, sensing tension and
anger in the air, had already begun to cry silently, her
face hidden in her hands.

"Look—look, you guys, this is really important to me.
I mean *really*. I swear. Otherwise I wouldn't be leaving
you, would I? But look at some of the other girls *my*
age—they're out driving their own cars and going on
dates, and Dave expects me to hang around *here* all the
time. It's driving me nuts!"

Rick looked uncertain, and she dropped to her knees,
holding his shoulders.

"Rick, please? I'll give you five dollars. And—and no,
wait, I'll give you a couple of bucks and I'll call Cheryl
right now and ask if she'll come over and watch you till
I get back. How's that? She doesn't have a steady guy,
so she'd be home anyhow, and she was complaining
just the other day she needed some bread. . . ."

Francie usually got her own way in the end. Even
with Cheryl. It took twelve dollars out of the money
Brant and Jerry had given her the previous day—money
she had already hidden away to start what she called
her "getaway fund." But twelve dollars was worth it,
even when she had to add on the bus fare to the city

and a taxi from the bus depot over to the address Brant
had given her.

She was glad that she had taken a taxi when she got
there—it was quite a distance away from the bus depot
and the crummy downtown area. Even the air here
smelled different, and there were trees and beautifully
kept lawns and even gardens that blazed with color.
She looked up at the tall row house almost reverently
after the taxi driver had left. Yeah, he'd have a place
like this. Just like the kind of house that got featured in
Better Homes or *American Home*—all the way up at the
top of one of San Francisco's snobbier hills, view of the
bay and all. He could have anything he wanted, she
supposed, with all that money and his looks. And he
wanted *her*—he must want her, or she wouldn't be here.

Now she wished she'd bought herself something
really expensive and sexy to wear for him. But thinking
about it, she suddenly giggled. Shit—what was the
point? It wasn't her *clothes* Brant was interested in; it
was her body. Still giggling, Francie rang the doorbell.
A disco tune ran through her head, and she swayed to
the rhythm, waiting for him to let her in.

Brant, by himself, was a perfect, polite host. Feeding
her caviar and champagne out on the terrace because
she'd confessed she'd always dreamed about tasting
caviar and drinking champagne with it. He'd wrinkled
his nose at the thought of champagne, but he'd opened
a bottle for her and poured out some chilled white wine
for himself. And afterward, bringing out two little pipes,
he let her smoke hash with him. It was wild—the smoke
made her feel kind of loose and high almost at once.

She wondered what he would do with her this time,
and when he would make his move, but he was taking
his time—toying with her, only occasionally, as if to
remind her why she was here.

Then, at last, he took her into his playroom, with its

mirrors and its enormous bed, and he showed her the
movie and sound equipment that was concealed everywhere. He could even take pictures in the dark, he told
her, using infrared lighting.

Without waiting for him to tell her to, she started to
take her clothes off, watching herself in the mirrors, and
he laughed.

"How do you know I'm ready for you yet?" he mocked
her.

So she knelt in front of him and unzipped his tight
sky-blue pants and began to give him head. After a few
seconds, he pushed her away.

"You need to take lessons, baby. That's a delicate
instrument you're handling so carelessly down there,
not a hot dog!"

He moved back, his cold eyes watching her.

"But I've forgotten—you're the one who likes to be
hurt and then screwed, right? Or is it that you like to be
screwed so it hurts? I forget easy, but I do remember
that's why you're here, isn't it?"

Her pride smarting, she squatted on the floor, staring
up at him.

He was jeering at her, playing games with her, and
she didn't like it.

"You—you bastard. No guy ever complained about
the way I give a blow job before. What do you mean,
I need to take lessons?"

"Talking's a waste of time, baby. You came here to get
screwed, and now I'm ready for you. And you do need
lessons, but I don't have the time or the inclination to
give you any. Now get on that bed and get yourself
ready while I shuck my clothes."

Something in the contemptuous tone of his voice, the
studied cruelty of his words, got through to her, and
suddenly she didn't care if he screwed her or not.

She stood up, her face flaming with rage.

"Don't talk to me like that, Brant Newcomb. I'm no whore!"

He hit her across the breasts, and the pain and shock made her yell.

"Sure you're a whore, Francie. Every woman I've ever known is a whore—for some man. Get on the bed and spread your legs—real wide."

She backed away from him, her eyes studying his face warily. Suddenly she was no longer sure of herself, and she was scared of this man—there was no feeling in him.

Her breasts ached and stung, and her eyes blurred with tears. She saw him reach out and flick a switch; then she heard a whirring sound.

"You're—you're going to take pictures?"

"Movie, Francie. My friends and I make some of the best skin flicks you've seen—no *acting*, either."

His eyes moved over her; they were without depth, like glassy blue marbles.

"Hurry up, Francie, or you'll get me mad again. Or is that what you're trying to do—make me mad?"

His pants were flung aside—she noticed that he had not bothered to wear shorts under them. He came to her, and she felt him push her backward with what was almost a kind of relief. He hit her again, and she heard her own groan of pain, but she continued to lie there with her eyes tightly closed and her legs open, feeling the familiar tickle of desire begin to grow and expand in her.

The hash was working on both of them now—he seemed to move in slow motion as he made her pose for him, contorting her body grotesquely, hitting her when she was too slow in obeying him or seemed reluctant. And in the end he turned her over on her stomach and beat her across her ass a few times with his belt while she rubbed herself against the silky sheets and screamed for him to fuck her, get on with it—anything—just make her come.

He came into her savagely, fingers twisted in her hair; and almost immediately, Francie could feel herself start to climax—a never-ending spiral of feeling that took her up, up, her body arching and jerking under his until he exploded into her.

Afterward, lying beside her on the bed, he acted as if the violence and passion that had erupted between them had not touched him in any way. He was cool, remote, even polite. It was hard for Francie to imagine that just a few minutes ago he had attacked her like an animal.

He poured wine into a glass for himself—champagne again for her.

"You didn't even put a hand up to cover your face when I hit you, you stupid little bitch. I could have really marked you up. Don't you have the normal self-preservation instinct?"

He confused her.

"I don't know," she answered him honestly. "All I care about is being able to come, and when you hurt me and beat me, it's like you're telling me to feel, you know? Like you're telling me you know I'm here, you want to put me down, you're doing something to me, and that means you want me."

"I don't know if I really do understand, but so what, if it turns you on. How old are you, by the way?"

His question caught her by surprise, so that she stumbled over her lies, her voice uncertain.

"I'm—I'm twenty."

He slapped her hard, knocking her off the bed and onto the floor.

"You're a lying cunt. Now tell me."

"Okay, okay, so I'm still nineteen."

This time, he got off the bed and pulled her to her feet by her hair, walking her over to the far corner of the room, where he calmly proceeded to wipe off all her carefully applied makeup with tissues dipped in cold cream.

Francie wriggled and cried and called him all the filthy names she could think of until he smacked her a few more times across the rump. Then she begged him to stop.

"I'm seventeen," she sobbed. "Really, I swear it. But I'll be eighteen this year, soon after I graduate. Honest, Brant, I'm not lying this time."

Like an alley cat, she rubbed herself up against him, touching him eagerly, licking at his skin with short, urgent jabs of her tongue. Suddenly he began to chuckle, his anger gone.

He carried her back to the bed and taught her how it felt to have a guy go down on *her*. Always before, it had been the other way around; she'd never had this happen to her before, and the sensation was wild and exquisite. Francie thought she'd go crazy with joy.

After a while, he moved his body alongside her, sixty-nine–fashion, and she tried to reciprocate, being more careful, gentler this time. But what he was doing to her felt so good that sometimes she forgot what she was supposed to be doing, and then his teeth nibbled at her clitoris until she screamed. Nothing she had ever experienced before could compare with this. . . . Francie thought she would never stop coming.

Suddenly he rolled onto his back, pulling her with him, making her ride him until he climaxed inside her. Aside from the way he seemed to swell and start to throb in her, the only indication Francie had that he had made it was the way his hands tightened around her sore hips, making her cry out. Through it all, his face remained bland, cold, uncontorted. She decided he was the strangest guy she had ever met, and then, without warning, he lifted her off himself and tumbled her backward off the bed and onto the soft carpet, ignoring her as if she had suddenly ceased to exist for him.

Francie could tell, just looking at him, that already he was bored with her. Those blue eyes of his still seemed to glitter coldly, but he had shadowed them with too-long lashes.

"Do it again," she begged him, still squirming on the floor where he'd let her fall.

"Why?" His voice sounded pleasant, but his words stung. "Even if I could, I don't think I'd want to. You forget, there's no mystery left to you, Francie. I know all your secrets now; there's nothing to find. And that sadomasochistic bit can be a drag; it's no new kick for me, anyhow."

"I don't care! Brant—please, please be nice to me! Don't you understand? I really do dig you. Nothing before has been this good for me, this far out. I dig your scene—all this. Let me stay, and I'll do anything you want me to—anything—you know I will. Brant, please?"

He stood looking down at her, still nude, still bored. Annoyed by his indifference, she reached up between his legs, her fingers like claws. But he was quicker than she; his hand slammed into her face, knocking her backward onto the carpet with her head ringing.

"Fucking bastard! You *hurt* me!"

"But you *like* to be hurt, baby—remember? And remember, while you're about it, that I *don't* dig being hurt."

He just stood there watching her, his face unreadable, and she began to sob with her mouth open, bawling like a child—all mouth and screwed-up eyes.

"Oh, shit, what a stupid little cunt you are! Your tears don't affect me one way or the other, Francie, but you are beginning to bug me. What in hell are you looking for?"

"If you won't let me stay, can't I at least see you again? Please, please let me keep coming. I swear I won't bug you, and I'll do anything you tell me to do. . . ."

"If I let you come back, you bet you will, baby. Heck,

who knows, maybe some of my friends might get a kick out of your kind of thing."

He smiled at her, but there was no mirth in his smile.

"Just remember—no complaints or whining afterward. You'll have to act like a big girl and look out for yourself—and you'll have to do as you're told. You on the Pill yet?"

"I've been on the Pill since—since I was a freshman. Oh, Brant—thanks!"

Brant grimaced into his drink. He wondered why he had let her have her way. Sometimes, when the wrong mood hit him, he wondered about everything—his whole way of life. Why did he *bother?* Always looking for new kicks, new women, new entertainment. What was it his shrink had told him? Something about the rich constantly needing to be entertained? He'd told him something else, too—that he had a subconscious death wish, that he was trying to destroy himself, as well as other people. But then even psychiatrists didn't know everything. No one knew anything. Men kept creating new gods, when the only *real* power was there already, inside themselves. But what the heck, this was no time to indulge in introspection.

He watched Francie over the rim of his glass. She was sitting up now, rubbing her knuckles childishly into her eyes. She looked like such a kid without all that makeup on and her dark hair falling around her face. . . . But then, there was the surprise of finding out that she wasn't—not by any means. Maybe Francie, too, in her own peculiar way, was hell-bent on self-destruction, just like he was. Maybe that was the common bond between them. Whatever it was. . . . He kept studying her.

And then he told himself with a mental shrug to forget it. What did he care what her hang-ups were or how she had acquired them?

CHAPTER
FOURTEEN

BRANT HAD NEVER BEFORE met a chick who was a complete masochist, who really *dug* being hurt the way Francie did. Sure, there were plenty of women who went around asking for it, who craved it subconsciously; but then when you gave it to them, they squalled. And then there were those others who'd do it for money. But this one, this chick really *enjoyed* it; he suspected it was the only way she could come, because to her, sex had to be mixed up with pain. And maybe she'd prove a new kind of kick for the crowd, at that.

He walked over to the phone and began to dial.

"Get over here and make it big," he told her harshly.

She crawled over on her hands and knees, her eyes suddenly bright. Just as if he'd offered her some kind of treat to stop her from crying.

"Jerry? About the party tonight. Yeah, I know. But I've got this bird I'm bringing—Frances someone—remember her? Yeah—that's the one...."

His voice went on, without a pause in it, a hesitation that would show she was getting to him. But Francie *knew* she was because she could feel him getting bigger, harder already.

Still talking, he grabbed her by the hair, bringing tears to her eyes, and pushed her mouth onto his cock. He filled her mouth, hurting the soft part at the back of her throat, making her gag. But she could take it! Anything Brant did to her she could take, because she loved him. Yes, she did, she really did! She clasped his body with her hands, feeling the hardness of the muscles in his buttocks under her palms.

He was still talking on the phone to Jerry as if nothing were happening, but she didn't care.

He was happening; he was big for her. No matter what he did or how he acted, he did want her. It reminded her in some weird way of the times when she was little and Daddy beat her—the times before the accident that had killed him, and mother, too. Her eyes closed, Francie remembered.

First—yes, it had always started with the trip down to the cellar. He'd make her go ahead of him, and he'd be right behind, the belt swinging from his hand, swishing in the air. And she'd be crying harder and harder, begging him not to beat her, to give her one more chance to be good for him, but he wouldn't answer. The stairs going down to the cellar always seemed endless to Francie. And then, when at last they'd reached the bottom, she'd cry even harder and louder, beginning to squirm already.

"You know you've got it coming, Frances," he'd say sometimes, his voice sounding sad and very deep. "I don't understand why you keep doing these things, telling so many lies. After all the promises you've given us, after all we've told you and given you, your mother and I. Why, Frances, why?"

But sometimes he'd be so mad at her he wouldn't even trust himself to speak. He'd just make her bend over the old pickle barrel in the corner and pull her skirt up, and then the belt would come whistling through the air and the pain would explode across her body—making her scream and yell her promises not to be bad anymore, to listen to Mama and her big brother and to stop her stealing and lying. But Daddy wouldn't stop beating her until his arm was tired, she guessed, and her behind felt like it was on fire. All the time he was beating her, she'd have to stay bent over, and she'd rub herself up against the roughness of that old barrel while the belt made her squirm and dance with pain. And then the pain would get mixed up with something else after a while—and when it was over and she was held in Daddy's arms again, sobbing, and he'd tell her how much he loved her and that he only beat her for her own good, *because* he loved her, why even then, Francie knew she'd go and do something bad again real soon, and it would all start over. . . .

After the accident, Dave had been the one. Dave, her big brother, so many years older than she that she'd always been in awe of him. It hadn't been easy at first, making him mad enough so he'd spank her. He'd told her once he'd always been sorry about the way Daddy used to beat her—he thought they should have tried psychology on her, instead. But after the time he'd come home to find she'd deliberately cut up one of Mama's fine linen tablecloths to make herself a sundress, he'd given up on the psychology crap. He'd spanked her on that occasion, and from then on, he'd do the same whenever she did anything he didn't like—sometimes just because her grades were poor.

Dave never did take her down to the cellar to do it, like Daddy used to, but somehow, with Dave, it was even more exciting. Especially the feel of his bare hand on her buttocks while she pretended to squeal and beg him for mercy.

Without quite realizing what she was doing, Francie had one hand between her thighs, touching herself.

Brant hung the phone up abruptly and began to chuckle.

"Goddam, but you're a horny little animal, aren't you?" he said. Francie couldn't make a sound in reply, but it didn't matter.

"You're going to have lots of excitement this evening," he told her, his hand in her hair hurting her just enough to make her whimper and wriggle. "Now, take your fingers out of your cunt—I want you to be good and hungry for it when the time comes."

She clutched at him again with both hands, enjoying the sensation of servicing him, obeying him, belonging to him. God, but he was big! So big her throat ached and her jaw muscles hurt from holding her mouth open to take all of him.

Now that he was off the phone, he came quickly, his hot juices spurting down her throat. She hadn't swallowed a man's come since the very first time, the time when she was fourteen and it was her first month in California—her first month in school, as a matter of fact.

Dave had moved the family from the small Midwestern town she'd been born in to the West Coast because he'd been told the job opportunities were better—and then he started leaving them on their own most of the time, with just the dumb old housekeeper to watch them.

Thinking about it—about herself then—Francie could not help grimacing. She'd been so damned green in those day that no one would have believed it, and then those four boys who thought she was just a prick-tease had taken her one day into the old house that everyone said was haunted, and had raped her—first one by one, and then two at a time. She'd sure grown up in a hurry then!

Francie told Brant about it later, while they were taking a shower together. She was feeling very, very good—she loved him more than ever, and she wanted him to know everything about her. Brant, in spite of his offhand manner and his sudden cruelties, was being nice to her now—he'd even sent his manservant out to buy her a dress to wear to the party, after letting her pick the style from one of the magazines he'd had lying about.

Head back, letting the water stream down on her closed eyelids, her hair, her nose, Francie told Brant, in her little-girl voice, exactly what the guys had done, what they had said, and how she had reacted.

"At first, you know, I was scared shitless! I mean, no one had bothered to explain anything to me, for God's sake, and they said I was too young to date—you dig the irony of the thing? I used to wear these tight, tight dresses when Dave was away in town, and I knew even then that my body was pretty good, but I sure as hell didn't know what it was *for*. Until they showed me."

Francie laughed shortly and moved, letting the water have her back this time. Brant smacked her bottom sharply and saw that his fingers had left red marks over the weals she already sported.

"Ouch!" she yelled.

"Go on, your story's got me fascinated," he said.

Shrugging, she continued, doing a kind of sensuous dance step now, raising her arms over her head and swaying her body while she almost crooned the words.

Brant wondered idly if the hash she'd persuaded him to let her use earlier was acting belatedly.

"After the first guy, the first time, it didn't really hurt too bad, but oh, man, was I scared! So scared I peed in my panties and they joked about that when they pulled them off me. I was so damned terrified I kept struggling and trying to scream until they clobbered me a few times to shut me up, and then they took turns. While one was doing it, the others would hold me and feel me up—they hurt my boobs something terrible, I had bruises all over afterward. And I got screwed. I mean, well and truly! And you know what? After a while, I stopped fighting them because what was the point? There were four of them, like I said, and they told me they wouldn't hit me again if I let them do what they wanted. One of them, Lonnie, he was on the football team, a senior, big deal, and I'd always kinda followed him around, you know? I didn't think he'd even noticed me, and here I was, getting fucked by him. He was the one with imagination, and he thought up everything they were going to do with me next.

"That was some scene, I'll tell you! I used to dream about it afterward and wake up all wet. They even gave it to me in the ass, and man, before then I hadn't even dreamed that guys would want to use you that way— I mean, that *really* hurt! But Lonnie, he wanted it, and he did it to me after he'd smacked my butt a few times."

Frances paused, her body still gyrating slowly under the steamy-hot water—the bathroom was murky and cloudy with steam by now, and Brant felt, with a kind of surprise, his penis become rock-hard again.

Francie giggled, and he jabbed it up against her, between the plump, firm cheeks of her ass.

"You stupid little cunt. How did you survive a gang-rape? It's a wonder they didn't screw you to death."

She realized that she had almost succeeded in shocking him, and giggled again, bending slightly to give him better access to her.

"They weren't as big as you are, not any of them. You make it feel like the first time when you do that to me—ow!" Her delighted wriggles belied the complaining tone of her voice.

"Do you want me to go on? You do, I can tell."

She moaned softly because he was big and he filled her, making her feel as if she would tear any minute. But he was fucking her, hard, his hands slippery on her hips, and she loved it, even the pain. She came up to meet him halfway, pushing herself against him.

He didn't speak, but his breath rasped against her neck as he bent over her. She closed her eyes and let

him do whatever he wanted. He was enjoying this—
enjoying her. He wasn't bored any longer, and she was
going to make sure he never became bored with her
again. She loved Brant Newcomb, and she loved the
thought of all his lovely money and the things it could
buy. He could take her places, make her really free, if
she played her cards right. No more brother David
keeping her locked up, telling her it was her responsibility to look after the kids.

She remembered Dave's shocked, angry face when
she'd come back home after the rape, and wanted to giggle again. Poor Dave! He'd had to carry her up to bed,
and he'd had to call a doctor because she was bleeding
all over the place. All she'd done was sob hysterically
and tell them both that it had been dark and the men
were real tall and had worn stocking masks over their
faces. She knew David wouldn't call the cops—reliable
David! No scandal, he kept saying—for *her* sake, of
course, and the sake of her future. And the doctor finally, reluctantly agreeing to say nothing, either—for *her*
sake. Balls, she'd thought, even then. Dave just wanted
to keep it out of the newspapers because of his job.

She hadn't talked. And afterward, when she was back
in school with a letter from the doctor to say she'd had
the flu, she'd walked right up to Lonnie after the first
day of classes, as bold as brass, asking him to drive her
home in his new car.

And Lonnie? He'd done just that. Gone with her,
leaving his girl flat. He'd taken Francie out into the
hills someplace, and they'd screwed over and over, with
her wild and willing this time, and eager to learn much
more.

After that, it had been Lonnie, and his friends, and
his friends' friends, too, as word got around. One of
them got her a prescription for the Pill, and she had it
made.

Remembering became all mixed up with the present, and the pleasure and the pain of what Brant was doing to her.

"Hurt me, give it to me!" Francie heard herself scream as his fingers dug deeply into her flesh and he seemed to swell inside her. It was better than it had ever been for her before.

CHAPTER
FIFTEEN

EVE HAD NOT been able to help noticing that Marti was getting quieter and quieter and drinking more. But now she did her drinking in the privacy of her own room or in the more fashionable gay bars, where she would go soon after her afternoon's work, returning home very late.

Sometimes Stella came over, and then Marti would smile again, but not for long, for Stella was seeing a lot of George Coxe these days, and not bothering to hide the fact any longer. Already in the society pages of the newspapers, their names were being linked. Tycoon George Coxe and attractive legal secretary Stella Gervin. Stella *was* attractive, especially in the new clothes that suddenly appeared in her wardrobe. There was a certain shy reserve about her that her new admirer found irresistible—he was used to women who succumbed to him easily, and this Stella would not do.

"I'm afraid I'm old-fashioned," she would smile. "After my unhappy marriage, I really haven't cared to date too often, George. If you want someone easy, why, I'm sure there are hundreds of women who would be more than glad to accommodate you."

George was finding out, though, that it wasn't the other, easy women he wanted—it was Stella. And the most she had ever allowed him to do with her was kiss

her goodnight. She was frightened—he could sense that
sometimes, when he held her too close or too tightly.
She'd as much as admitted to him that her husband had
been a sadist who had taken pleasure in giving her pain,
beating her badly. How could he blame her for being
afraid? The possibility that there might be a different
reason for Stella's reticence had not even entered his
mind.

She was not as reticent with David, who had become
her confidant and adviser as the affair with George pro-
gressed. David had never liked Marti or quite approved
of Stella's relationship with her. Now he encouraged
Stella to keep seeing George, reminding her that here
was her chance to make something of her life.

What started off one day as a routine dictation session
ended up in the end as a kind of encounter group—
for two.

"Stel, you're really a lovely woman; there's no reason
for you to settle for life in the half-world. *Keep* George,
and if you really want to, and can be discreet about it,
keep your other women on the side."

Stella wondered fleetingly if this was David's own
philosophy that he was quoting to her. It probably was.
She knew, via Marti, that Eve was far from happy these
days. And she also knew about Gloria.

"I—I really need someone to talk to, you know,"
Stella faltered, looking across at David. Gathering her
courage, she admitted that the one thing that *really*
scared her was how she'd react to George's embraces
when the time came.

"He's been hinting about marriage. And he's being so
darned nice to me, so sweet, that I can't keep him at
arm's length forever. What shall I do? I don't know if
I can make it with a man—or even if I'll be able to pretend well enough."

"There's one way to find out, if you don't mind my
being blunt. Go to bed with a man."

Stella could feel herself blush. Did he mean what she thought he did? She found her boss attractive; she always had. And it had piqued her in the beginning that he hadn't tried to make a pass at her. He'd been friendly and informal, and she'd trusted him enough to tell him about Marti, even take him to the party where he'd met Eve. But why hadn't David shown some interest in her as a woman? And was he trying to make up for that now?

David got up and walked around the desk to her. Suddenly, Stella was glad that Gloria wasn't around that day. She and Howard had gone to Tahoe with friends and wouldn't be back until the beginning of the following week.

"Stella, I really meant what I just said, you know. It's something you should at least *try*, for your own sake. Christ, you don't need a psychiatrist to tell you that. You're an intelligent woman."

He put his hand on her shoulder, and she felt its warmth through her thin blouse. David was really a warm person, she felt. And he *was* interested in her; he had always been her friend. Of all the men she'd known, David came the closest to making her feel— Stella looked up at him and felt his hand tighten. He was so good-looking—there was no mistaking that. And she had the feeling that he could be very gentle and tender —and discreet. They both had a lot to lose if anyone found out.

"I—I think you're right, David. I have to find out."

They separated after work that evening. She left her car in one of the city's big parking lots, and he picked her up there in *his* car. His apartment was warm and friendly—like David himself.

Stella didn't feel any guilt when she thought about Marti, or even about Eve. Marti was acting kind of cold and withdrawn these days, anyhow; and Eve—Stella knew Eve went out a lot. Not always with David, either. But this wasn't the time to tell him.

This was the time to find out if she could respond to a man or not. She wondered how it would feel, how he would begin. But David, she discovered, believed in taking his time. And when it finally happened, what with the wine and his very gentle caresses that led up to what happened later, Stella couldn't imagine what she'd been afraid of.

The first time, before he entered her, he went down on her. And before that, he explored every inch of her body with his tongue and fingers, making her writhe and moan as she begged for release.

David himself enjoyed this part of lovemaking as much as he enjoyed the final explosion of himself in a warm, tight cunt. He had the gift of being able to detach himself and yet enjoy what he was doing—the squirming and the sighs and the opening up for him; the stage where a woman lost her reserve and control and let go, crying out with pleasure and begging for more.

Consciously and carefully, he acted as if Stella were a virgin, and was very slow, very cautious with her until she began to relax, and then at last to give in to her own body's reactions. She had a really lovely body, beautifully proportioned for her size, and he enjoyed making love to her, although he had to be very careful not to go too deeply into her because she was so small and tight.

The second time around, David taught Stella how to go down on him. By now, the wine they had been drinking had made them both high and very relaxed with each other. He found it terribly exciting to actually teach a woman *how*—God, he thought, had he ever had a woman who had never done this? He felt like some sort of a teacher as he explained to her that he had to be gentle, and told her what tricks could excite a man almost to bursting point.

After her initial reluctance, she proved a good pupil. She told him she hadn't read any of the sex manuals like *The Joy of Sex*. She knew how in theory, of course, but. . . .

"It's really not as bad as I thought it would be," she admitted honestly. And then, blushing again, "I mean. . . ."

David laughed, pulling her back up against him. Still holding her gently, he began to excite her again with his fingers, enjoying the way she opened her legs for him after a while and began, quite involuntarily, to rub her breasts up against his chest.

"You're really a very sensual woman, Stella," he whispered to her. He turned her on her side so her back was to him, and then entered her again, lying spoon-fashion. This way, he could play with her breasts while at the same time his finger, pressing on her engorged clitoris, excited her so much that she began to tremble and then to move wildly on him.

Stella wondered why she had never before realized that a man's penis inside her could provide so much pleasure. Or that a man's hands could be just as clever and knowing as a woman's.

At the same time, she was sensible enough and pragmatic enough to understand that this thing with David was merely an experiment for both of them and hardly the beginning of a love affair. But she was also grateful to him for being so patient, so gentle with her.

Stella hoped that George, when she decided to give herself to him, would also be gentle and considerate. But now she felt more confidence in herself. David told her that she could manage George and teach him subtly how to please her—that older men were much easier to handle than younger guys.

She was glad she and David were friends. Perhaps some other day they would come together like this. Why not? All she had to be was very discreet.

David had Stella back in her apartment by nine-thirty. She was expecting a call from George, who'd had to go out of town. He had a feeling almost of affection for Stella. Poor kid, she'd had a tough life, and she deserved a break. If that Marti female left her alone, she'd be much better off. Perhaps he could hint as much to Eve. He wondered, angry at himself, why just the thought of Eve could give him a hard-on, even after he'd been with another woman.

Damn Eve—why was she acting so stupid? She was turning into some kind of a tramp, and whenever they quarreled now, she'd try to put the blame on him. Why couldn't she realize that women's lib or not, the old double standard still existed? A guy could sleep around and no one thought the worse of him, but a woman who did was soon labeled. Why was he so damned jealous of her still?

He remembered suddenly that they'd had a tentative kind of agreement to see each other this evening, and wondered if she'd still be up, waiting. He stopped the car by a telephone booth and called her.

Her voice sounded as if she'd been crying, but she was mad, too.

"Goddam you, David! Where have you been?"

"Busy, sweetheart. At the office. I just got through. Still want to see me?"

There was a silence at the other end of the line, and then: "I wish I didn't." He heard the small sigh that escaped her. "Oh, David! Why couldn't you have called?"

"Stop making wifely noises, Eve. I didn't call because I kept thinking I'd be finished early. And then, when I noticed what time it was, I couldn't believe it. Can I come over?"

"I—oh, I guess so! Marti's in bed, so don't ring. I'll leave the door unlocked. David, will you be spending the night?"

It had been a long time since they had spent a night
together. Why not, he thought. She usually had to be
up early, and that would give him time to get back to
his apartment before the traffic got too heavy.

"Okay, baby. Look, I'd better hang up now, so I can
be on my way. Wait for me."

"Don't I always?"

Was there a trace of bitterness in her tone?

Marti heard David come in, and knew who it was.
She wondered why Eve put up with the kind of treatment he had been giving her recently. She *loved* him,
Eve said. But was a love that made you crawl and beg
for crumbs, forgetting all pride, all reason, really worth
it?

Not for me, I'm stronger than that, Marti vowed to
herself, turning restlessly in bed. The drinks she had
had earlier had given her a headache, but she couldn't
be bothered getting up and going to the bathroom for
water and aspirin.

The drinking had to stop. Pat, from the agency, had as
much as told her that outright. She guessed they'd heard
rumors. Who hadn't? She hadn't tried to hide her feelings for Stella from anyone, nor her reactions to Stella's
gradual withdrawal, her betrayal. What the hell, Marti
thought, there are other women in the world. No use
crying over what was already, in effect, lost to her. Why
should she have to be content with being Stella's hidden, backstairs lover?

Suddenly, Marti thought of an offer that one of the
photographers she had posed for a few times had made
her. Movies. The underground kind. There was a great
demand these days for slim, beautiful women—the
public was tired of the obvious whores, the usually over-
plump and *older* women who played in the skin flicks.
Since *Deep Throat* and *Behind the Green Door,* the
business had gone almost respectable.

She didn't have to be much of an actress, he'd told
her persuasively; they had a really great young director
lined up, a guy who was destined to go places. And
these movies his company was going to make would be
a cut above the usual run-of-the-mill pornography.

"We're going to show them that fucking is fun—and
something of an art. Baby, we already got distributor-
ships lined up all over the country, and in Europe, too.
Art movies, these will be. Sophisticated porn, aimed at
the more educated and discriminating section of the
public."

To shut him up, Marti had told him in the end that
she'd think about it, let him know. Now, lying sleepless
in her bed, Marti thought about it some more. Knowing
what she was, what she liked, he had told her about the
other girls he had recruited. Young and lovely and eager
to learn. Many of them aspiring starlets. There was
much demand for lesbian films these days, as well as the
S and M variety. Marti could practically have her pick.
Of course, it would mean moving to Los Angeles eventually, and she didn't care for the climate there or the
constant rushing. But what the hell? She'd think about
it. That couldn't hurt, just thinking about it. It was a
damn sight better than lying here thinking about Stella
and wondering what she was doing. With George.
Lucky George!

"Well, at least I'm not going to sit around feeling
sorry for myself—just waiting around in case she calls.
No more crying jags, and no more booze. I managed
okay before Stella, and I'll manage now. My way. Me
for me, just like the old days. It's the only way to survive,
and Eve had better learn that, too."

CHAPTER
SIXTEEN

EVE HAD BEGUN TO FEEL, tentatively, as if she could at least start *thinking* about being happy again. It was a feeling something like being able to release her breath after holding it for a long time. She had started to be afraid that she was becoming hooked on talking into Peter's little tape recorder, just for the sake of trying to sort out her feelings; but now, suddenly, she'd begun to feel as if there might be a chance for her to make it with David.

Since he had spent the night with her a couple of weeks before, he'd been more like the David she remembered—more attentive toward her, more spontaneously affectionate. She didn't know why, and she didn't dare ask. Whatever had caused the change, David was being much nicer to her these days. They had talked for hours that night he'd stayed over at her apartment, and he'd confided in her how concerned he was about Lisa, his little sister. Lisa really missed Eve's frequent visits and asked for her often, he said. And he had added:

"We ought to do more together than just screw, angel. I want you for my friend again."

David knew just the right words with which to get under her carefully constructed defenses! That night she had been prepared to have it out with him, to demand to know, once and for all, if there was another woman he was seeing. But he'd disarmed her—as usual. The thing about David was that he always seemed so damned *sincere*. And then there was the way he concentrated on her in bed, giving her endless, limitless pleasure. When they were in bed together, it was as if no other woman existed for him. She always forgot her jealousy and her insecurity and loved him all over again then.

David started to take her down to see the family more often. He couldn't spend too much time with the kids as it was; mostly he went down over a weekend, and occasionally on a weeknight. The two younger children, particularly Lisa, needed adult supervision—more concerned, *loving* adult supervision. Mrs. Lambert, the housekeeper, seemed a motherly kind of woman and fond enough of the children, but Eve still felt her own instinctive mistrust of Francie that had been there from the beginning, when she first encountered the girl's cold, too-knowing eyes.

She felt that Francie, these days, seemed really quiet —almost withdrawn. Usually she'd try to show Eve in some sly, secret way that she only had David on loan, so to speak. But recently Francie spent more time in her room—studying, she said—than she did downstairs. It was almost as if she were staying out of their way—out of *David's* way. Eve couldn't figure it out. But she didn't try too hard, because of Lisa, whom she really loved and enjoyed cuddling, and David, who acted happy and satisfied in her company again. She guessed that she should be relieved that Francie was behaving, for a change. Maybe she was actually growing up?

Francie's studied avoidance of her big brother was really due to her new, secret status. She was Brant Newcomb's latest plaything—the current kick he of-

fered his friends at the parties he was always throwing
when he was in town.

Since Brant had discovered her secret weakness,
Francie found herself obsessed—both with him and
with her own body and the sensations he could evoke
in it. There was nothing at all that he could not make
her do and enjoy doing; and, after a while, almost nothing that she had not done.

She was leading a double life, Francie would think
with smug satisfaction. Still a high-school senior and,
on the surface, a normal teenager. But her other, hidden
self attended all of Brant Newcomb's wild "partouzes"
and those of his jet-set friends. She was the far-out chick
they all wanted, who'd do anything for kicks.

Two months after she had first met Brant, everything
had become old—even turning on. One wild night,
she'd even tried acid after everyone had gone and Brant,
who had forgotten about her, had discovered her tied
spreadeagled on the bed in the game room.

"Jesus God, why didn't you yell?" he asked her, half-
amused and half-annoyed that she was still there. And
then, as he looked down at her, he'd begun to laugh.

"You dumb little cunt! But okay, baby, since you're
here and I'm really not that sleepy, want to trip on acid?
They tell me you shouldn't use it alone. Want to see if it
does anything for either of us? The last time for me"—
she saw his frown—"I didn't really remember too
much."

As he untied her, he spoke to her like a real person,
a human being, and she loved it—most of the time he
either ignored her or treated her like some strange kind
of insect he'd discovered.

Brant turned on some outlandish, weird-sounding
music he said was Indian, and then he turned *her* on.

Francie never forgot her first acid trip. It was the
most beautiful experience of her life up until then, she

thought, and it was made even more beautiful because
Brant was sharing it with her. They lay holding each
other close on the big bed and watched the night and
the music unfold in shapes and colors around them; and
then they made love, and it seemed to go on endlessly
in slow motion.

Francie often wished that he'd do it with her again,
but he never did; he'd brush off her suggestion with a
shrug or a laugh. She couldn't understand Brant—she
spent whole nights thinking about him and wondering
how she could possess him the way he possessed her.
She had to become important to him—she just had to!
And so she took enormous risks just to be with him and
his friends, slipping out of the house at all hours and
sometimes returning at dawn. She knew that Mrs. Lambert knew whenever she sneaked out, but neither of
them ever spoke about it. Mrs. Lambert drank a lot, and
she needed the job badly; she knew she'd better not
snitch on Francie or she'd be out on her ear!

Because she was wild and freaky and would do anything at all, Brant had started having Francie on tap at
all of his parties. She provided a new and kicky type of
entertainment for the jaded appetites of his guests, and
some of the movies she let them make of her and various
other members of the crowd were much in demand, as
was Francie herself. Some of them were almost in awe
of her capacity for punishment, even some of the experienced call girls who were also regular "guests." She
was still so young, and yet more perverse than any of
them. Francie was a sadist's dream come true—the perfect masochist. She would let anyone do anything to her.

At various times she had been whipped and ravished
in every conceivable fashion—tied down, stretched out,
or suspended by her arms; exhibited naked and open,
to be used by anyone who wanted her. Nothing was too
wild or far out for Francie.

She told herself that she did it all for Brant, to prove

to him that she loved him. Just like the girl in that book, *The Story of O.* She was his slave, his plaything, and she would give herself and abandon herself just as slavishly to anyone he "gave" her to.

But after the first few times, when he used her as regularly as any of the others, the only attention he paid to her was to have her fitted with an IUD. She told herself that he was testing her to make sure she could take his kind of life; she wanted him to know she could take anything *his* woman would have to take.

Once, Brant had to stop a group of fast-rising young rock musicians from literally screwing her to death between them. But Francie herself had not protested against anything they'd done to her. When Brant asked her, his voice hard and old, why she hadn't tried to stop them, or at least called for help, she'd whimpered, "But you told them they could have me, that I'd do anything they wanted me to."

"Oh, shit! Sometimes I wonder about you! You have to be sick to let them go that far and not try to stop them. Damn it, they could have killed you!"

Nevertheless, in spite of his disgusted manner, he'd called up one of his doctor friends, who'd come around and given her some shots that made her feel better and stopped the bleeding. And afterward, Brant had taken her home himself, letting her rest her head against his shoulder as he drove.

After that particular incident, however, Brant didn't call her for quite a while, and when she'd call him, he'd tell her, in that bored, aloof voice, that he felt she ought to get herself quite healed up inside.

"But Brant, I am, I promise I am!" Francie insisted, almost crying with frustration. She glared at the phone in her hand. "Brant, please, I'm so horny I can hardly stand it! Let me come—I'll be good, and I'll be more careful, I promise!"

This was a Friday, and he usually gave a party when he was in town Friday night. Why couldn't he let her come?

"I'll think about it, baby. You can call me again this evening. And in the meantime, if you're that horny, why don't you use that vibrator I gave you?"

She heard the click in her ear as he hung up and slammed the phone back into its cradle. Goddam Brant Newcomb to hell!

Like a caged animal, Francie paced around her room. On her bulletin board, right next to her Mick Jagger blowup, she'd pinned a small picture of Brant, cut out from a magazine. She wanted to tear it to bits, but she stopped herself—it was the only picture she had of him, after all. And something told her she'd be going to more parties—he'd have to see her, he was going to need her, miss her!

Oh, shit! Was there time to call up one of the guys she sometimes screwed around with in school? Probably not—they were usually out with their straight girl friends until late in the evening, especially on a Friday. And—the sudden thought stopped her as she reached out for the telephone—Dave might be coming down this evening, just to check up. He sometimes did, when he planned to stay away the rest of the weekend. He'd blow down early Friday afternoon and return to the city after supper. Oh, godammit, she wished he wouldn't come. He'd probably have that dumb Eve with him, unless they had been fighting again. Thinking of Eve and David reminded her of fucking. They must do a lot of it, she figured. And with no one to interfere. Well, Dave was a damn nice-looking guy, even if he was her brother. He had quite a body, too—one of her girl friends had said once she'd sure like to get screwed by him because he'd probably know what he was doing. She bet he did, too.

A slow smile started to spread over her face, making

her look suddenly much older and wiser. That was a thought. *Dave!* Big brother David. Why not? She'd learned from being with the fast crowd that nothing but nothing was forbidden, not even a brother and sister making it. Or a father and daughter, for that matter. They did it all the time, those laughing, glittering people she'd met. Didn't think anything of it.

Wow, Francie thought, starting very slowly to take her clothes off. What a kicky trip that would be—to see if she could seduce Dave. Maybe he wasn't as uptight as he pretended to be.

And in the meantime, since she *was* horny, she might as well get out her vibrator and watch herself in front of the mirror while she used it....

CHAPTER
SEVENTEEN

DAVID WAS FURIOUS. Francie thought smugly that she had never seen Dave quite this mad before. It was good to know she could still make him react to her. She could almost giggle right into his red, angry face as she thought of the look he had worn when she had walked down the stairs wearing just her briefest panties and a T-shirt that did nothing to hide her curves. And she'd made her face up so she looked older. Let David really notice her, for a change.

He'd already dismissed Rick and Lisa, and had banged the door shut. Now he turned back to face her, and she could not help smiling—a smile that mixed defiance and impudence.

"Francie, I don't know what's gotten into you suddenly, but by God, I'm going to show you that you're still young enough for some good, old-fashioned discipline! I'm not going to see you turn into a little tramp, blatantly advertising everything she's got."

Deliberately provoking him further, she ran away from him, stopping to face him defiantly from across the length of the room.

"You'd better not touch me, David! I'm too old to be spanked like a baby. I'm going to start doing as I please. I'm almost eighteen now, and you can't stop me."

"Oh, can't I? We'll just see about that, shall we?"

He almost sprang across the room at her in his rage, and she felt him grab her wrists painfully as he dragged her over to a chair and across his knees in the old way. She fought him just hard enough to make it more interesting, and to make him madder.

Then he was doing what she craved—his hand coming down hard and efficiently on her wriggling buttocks while she struggled and yelled and felt her nipples burn as she rubbed them again the arm of the chair.

David was so angry he'd lost control. He hit Francie as hard as he could, even though his palm started to sting. It was only after his head had cleared and his arm was starting to tire that he noticed how her short T-shirt was hiked up above her waist, and that her transparent panties hid nothing. When and why had Francie bought herself anything like that? With a sudden uneasiness he noticed that her buttocks, already red and inflamed-looking, kept jerking almost enticingly, even though the force of his blows had slackened. She had a woman's backside, shapely and well formed—but Christ, he thought, this was his *sister!*

He stopped spanking her so abruptly that Francie, on the verge of orgasm, lost her head. Still squirming on his lap, she begged him to go on, not to stop *now*.

"You bastard, you bastard!" she sobbed. "Don't you stop now; don't leave me hanging! I was almost there, d⁻mn you!"

David felt that this couldn't be happening, this wasn't Francie, he couldn't be hearing right.

With a movement of instinctive revulsion, he let go of her wrists and pushed her away from him. She fell onto the rug and lay there, still squirming and sobbing, her eyes glaring hate at him.

"Go up to your room, Francie. *Now*. My God, you must be— You'll see a psychiatrist tomorrow. Right now, I don't want to look at you!"

David's voice was dull—he wasn't strong any longer;

he was really kind of pitiful, he was so square! He wasn't *her* strong Dave—he was Eve's, Francie thought viciously, still lying there. Eve had made him weak and stupid. She despised him now—he'd never dare spank her again, and they both knew it.

"Make me go, David," she taunted him. "*Make* me, why don't you?" She pulled the T-shirt up, putting her hand between her legs. "Since you're not man enough, want to watch me make myself come first?"

He wanted to be sick, looking at her, seeing what she'd started to do to herself.

Like a parent he thought, God, where did I go wrong, when did this happen? He couldn't let her lie there doing what she was doing. She must be *sick*—why hadn't he noticed?

"Francie," he said, his voice cold, "either you go to your room this minute, or I'm going to have the juvenile authorities pick you up. Take your choice. Whatever you think you're doing, you can finish it in your room, not here."

Something in the remoteness of his voice stopped her, froze her hand in midstroke, and she stared at him measuringly. Yes, he did mean it. She'd driven him too far this time. And she didn't want to be taken away and locked up somewhere, because she had to see Brant, she just had to, now! Maybe she'd better pretend to knuckle under. . . .

She pulled the T-shirt down and scrambled to her feet, her head hanging so Dave couldn't see the calculation in her eyes, her long dark hair hanging like a curtain over her face.

"David, I'm sorry, I don't know what happened, but suddenly everything seemed to go dark. . . . It's just that I'm a *woman* now, and you treat me like a kid." She came close to him, and he couldn't help recoiling. For a moment he thought sickly that she might *touch* him, and he didn't think he could stand it.

"Francie! Just get out! Go on up to your room and stay there. I'll have supper sent up. And remember, I don't want you leaving your room, and I don't want you talking to the kids or using the telephone—do you understand? Maybe by tomorrow morning we'll both be saner and cool enough to talk."

"Dave, I'm really sorry. Don't stay mad at me! I'll do anything you say. Don't be mad anymore?"

He couldn't respond. His lips tightened, and he turned his head away from her. After a few seconds, he heard her leave the room and run upstairs. But he stayed there a long time, his hands clenched together, until he felt able to walk and move and talk normally again.

Tomorrow morning, things would look different, and he'd know what to do. Tomorrow, he'd come down early, bring Eve with him. Lisa was bound to be upset; she seemed to sense it when things weren't right around the house, and she'd go into one of her silent, autistic moods. Only Eve could talk and love her out of her spells. She'd need Eve when he took Francie away.

But when David came down to Albany with Eve the next day, Francie wasn't there. No one knew what time she'd left, or how. Mrs. Lambert had discovered her room empty, her bed not slept in, just a few minutes before David had arrived.

The woman was almost hysterical; obviously, she'd been fond of Francie.

"I didn't want to wake her too early," she kept repeating. "She always did like to lie in bed late of a Saturday morning!"

In the end, after David had sent her to her room to lie down, he'd started to search through Francie's things impatiently, clumsily. There had to be something that might tell him where the little tramp had gone! Maybe an address book, a diary—did girls still keep diaries? Eve was downstairs with Lisa, keeping her calm. Thank God he'd brought Eve!

Suddenly, David noticed that Rick had come in and was standing silent in the doorway, watching him. He looked up to tell the boy to go away; then he saw Eve behind him, her face worried.

She came in quickly, hardly noticing Rick.

"David, I think we have something—it was Lisa. Suddenly, out of the blue, she announced, 'Francie's gone to *stay* with Brant this time; she'll never come back!' Do you know who—"

"He's the guy in the picture—she said he was her boyfriend."

Rick's voice froze them both, and their eyes went to a magazine clipping on Francie's bulletin board—one of many other pictures and clippings, so that no one had really *noticed* until now—following the direction of Rick's pointing finger. The man was blond and sunbronzed. He was on a yacht, leaning against the mast and holding onto some rigging. His shirt was open to the waist, and one could almost see the bulge in his brief white shorts. He was beautiful and decadent-looking, and Eve knew him at once, with a shock of recognition.

"Oh, God, not *him!* How did Francie ever meet him? He's— Oh, David, he's really *evil.* That's Brant Newcomb!"

Standing there watching the color recede and then flow back into David's familiar, sharply angular face, Eve suddenly felt sick—for him, her love. The story Marti had told her came back, as well as her own unpleasant experience with the man. Obviously, even David had heard things about him—the look on his face told her that. Francie was *seventeen;* in spite of her vicious tongue and sneering eyes, she was just a kid— and David's sister, after all. She wanted to protect him, to hold him....

"Oh, David! What will you do? There must be *something—*"

"I know, Eve, I know. I have to *think*. I must be clear-minded and rational about this, as if Francie weren't my sister, as if— We can't have a scandal, something that might get in the newspapers—that much I'm sure about."

"But David, how can you find her unless you tell the police? She could be *anywhere*. We're not even certain she *did* run away to Brant Newcomb."

He made a sudden, impatient gesture that silenced her.

"Eve, you don't understand! If she did—Newcomb's not only a billionaire, he's a client of ours. Howard Hansen handles some of his oil interests—and Howard won't have scandal attached to anyone who works for him. Don't you see? They're even talking about a partnership for me—I just can't afford to have Francie's name, *our* name, dragged through the mud. We have to be sure, we have to find out if she's with him, get her away—to a psychiatrist—"

"David!" Concern for him sharpened Eve's voice. "David, listen. You can't let him get away with it, if she's with him. Please listen to me, he's—he's a terrible man! But he's not above the law, is he? I mean, maybe the police will agree not to make it public. After all, Francie's still a minor—they can't put her name in the papers, can they?"

"No, Eve! No police. No. I have to find her, but I can't use the police. God, if I only knew someone who *knows* the man. . . ."

A sudden recollection made Eve put her hand on David's arm, stopping him in mid-sentence.

"I just thought—David, he's giving some kind of a party tonight. Tony Gonsalves was in to do a commercial yesterday, and he was talking about it. In fact, Tony wanted me to go with him to be his front for the evening because he's gay, you know. But I was thinking, maybe *you* could go? You could mix with the guests— no one ever checks on who's invited and who's not at parties like that—you could look for Francie—"

"No, no, I couldn't, baby. I can't get mixed up in this thing because if Francie were there and I saw this guy, I'd—God, I'd probably want to kill him! I don't have that much self-control that I could stop myself from throwing a punch at him. There has to be some other way; there has to be." Slowly, his words dragging, then pausing, he turned away from the picture he'd been staring at so blankly, his eyes widening as they looked into Eve's. She somehow knew, before he even started to speak again, what he wanted her to do, and her hands came up in a warding-off gesture.

"No, David! No, don't ask me. I won't do it!"

It was exactly as if he hadn't heard her.

"You're the only one who could do it, Eve. The only person I can trust. If this gets out, you know how bad it would be for me, for Francie, for all of us. They'd say she was neglected, that I didn't have sufficient control over her. It would look very bad." He caught her hands, held them tightly as he looked into her face. "Baby, can't you see? You're the only person who can help me. You could go to that party as a guest, not as a gate-crasher. You could find Francie if she's there, reason with her. She'd never listen to me in the mood she's in! And if you had to, you could talk to *him*, tell him her real age—I'm sure she's lied about it. Sweetheart, you've got to do this, please!"

Oh, she thought helplessly, letting him pull her close, oh, what a treacherous, underhanded bastard he was! He was taking advantage of her, of the way he knew she felt about him. Damn him, damn him! She felt his hands move up her arms, heard his voice become tender, cajoling.

"Eve, you'll do it, won't you? Because it's so damned

important to me, because there's no one else I can turn
to, and you're my girl. Honey? I know Francie's been
a little hellion and she hasn't always been nice to you—
I can see that now—but she's just a *kid*, dammit, and
she needs help. I'm asking you to share with me the
responsibility of seeing that she gets it."

She leaned against him, shaking her head.

"Oh, stop it! You don't know what you're asking me
to do, David! I met Brant Newcomb once at a party,
and—" She bit her lip quickly, knowing how David reacted to her mentioning the names of other men she'd
met at parties. He thought she'd been to bed with all of
them.

And now, predictably, she felt him release her and
take a step backward.

"You *know* him? And all this time you didn't even
mention it? Why, Eve? Was he one of the guys?"

"David, please! No, he wasn't. I—I was introduced to
him and I didn't like him, and that was all. Please
don't keep tearing me down just because I did a lot of
stupid, foolish things to get back at you. I *love* you,
David!"

There, she had said it again—it was as if she couldn't
stop herself from saying that to him, from betraying
herself. But at least it had made him soften, and when
he held her close to him again, she trembled inside with
relief.

Without shame, without pride, she let his arms enfold
her, melt her inside their warm, charmed circle. Her
knees became familiarly weak as he pressed her against
him, his mouth so sweet, so tender on hers that she
knew she would give him anything, do anything at all
for him, just to have him go on kissing her this way,
as if his tongue would scoop out her very soul. Her
hands clung to him for balance, and her thighs, with
their own kind of radar, parted slightly as he started to
swell against them. He moved his mouth to her ear.

"God, Eve! I want you. Whenever you're this close to me, I can't help it. You're still my girl, aren't you? All mine, only mine. Say it, baby. I want you to say it!"

This was David the way she loved him most—part satyr, part little boy needing reassurance.

"I'm your girl, David. You know that already. I love you so much, I hurt sometimes because of it!"

He held her even more closely.

"I'll never hurt you again, sweetheart, never! I know I've been a brute and a rat sometimes, but that's only because you have the power to make me so damned jealous! And that's it, Eve. That's what keeps me coming back to you, wanting you. It's your strength, your love for me, the way we understand each other's thoughts and needs without words."

His hands moved over her body, and she shivered, closing her eyes. Why did she have to be such a fool for this man? And what was there so special about him that he alone, of all the men she'd ever known could turn her into a cringing, crawling slave? Her fingers tangled in his crisp-feeling dark hair, traced the firm line of his jaw. He was her guy, and he needed her!

"Listen, Eve," he was saying seriously, "no matter what I do or say, promise you'll stick with me. I need you so much, and you know it, too, with that ESP of yours. Stick with me, luv, and in the end we'll make it, you and I."

It was the closest he had ever come to committing himself to her, and Eve felt a surge of hope and happiness go through her. He loved her—her instincts had been right all along! He'd marry her someday—of course he would! He was just the type of man who was cautious about marriage, and why not? Wasn't she glad some other woman hadn't snapped him up before?

David felt her melt against him and could almost hear the pounding of her heart against his chest. He hadn't lied about wanting her, nor even about needing her, because he did. Damn the fire that burned between them, that kept him after her like a dog after a particular bitch. No one, not even Gloria, was as exciting to him physically as Eve was—and she loved him, she'd do almost anything for him. It was exciting enough just to look at the lovely woman in his arms and to know that a million guys must lust for her when they saw her on the television screen, but she was *his*.

"Shut the door, baby. Lock it."

His voice sounded harsh as he shoved her away from him, his fingers fumbling for his belt. Eve understood his harshness and felt that she could not stand another moment without Dave's hands on her. Desire rose and stirred in her like a storm.

Not taking her eyes from him, she backed to the door and slammed it shut, locking it with shaking fingers. He was undressed already, waiting for her. God, how much she wanted him, how much she loved him!

She got on her knees in front of him and started to caress him in the way she knew turned him on the most. It was marvelous to feel the way he responded to her, to hear his groan of pleasure.

This was the first time he'd ever shown his need for her in this house, and this was one time that neither of them should be thinking about sex, but she didn't want to *think* right now—not about Francie nor about the party she had to attend tonight. She wouldn't let David think, either.

He fell backward onto the bed, pulling her up and over him, his hands urgent on her body.

"Get your damned clothes off, Eve! I want your warm, bare flesh against mine!"

It was like the early days of their love, when the urgency was always there and they had felt, both of them, that it was too good between them to last.

She shivered with delight and excitement as she felt his fingers fumble, helping her undress. Everything was flung aside and onto the floor, even her brand-new de la Renta dress, bought to impress him.

He made love to her for what seemed like hours. The world seemed to be compressed into their bodies and the narrow circumference of the bed they lay upon. And the only sounds in the world were their soft lovewords, their ragged breathing.

David made her reach orgasm over and over again, with her vagina contracting each time in spasms that excited him beyond measure.

"Oh, Eve! Oh, sweetheart, you're so wonderful!" he said almost savagely when he allowed himself to climax at last. He kissed her, kept kissing her, while she moaned under the possessiveness and fierceness of his mouth.

He lay inside her and over her for a long time afterward, and she thought that somehow his taking her this way on Francie's bed sealed his possession of her, his need for her. He loves me, he really does, she thought. And the thought of that would make everything else turn out okay.

CHAPTER EIGHTEEN

BRANT NEWCOMB. Cold, icy-blue eyes burning like frost under glinting gold hair. Michelangelo's *Eros*—cruel, decadent, corrupt.

Eve shivered under those eyes, feeling beneath the swift, flickering look he'd just given her as if he'd lifted her skirt with his eyes and looked between her legs. Which was, she knew, exactly what he had wanted her to feel.

"Hi, Eve Mason. Glad to have *you* here tonight, luv. Francie has told me a great deal about you. In fact, Francie talks about you quite often—don't you, Francie honey?"

Francie's high, childish voice sounded vicious, almost hysterical. Eve noticed how abnormally bright her eyes seemed, and wondered what kind of drug she had used.

"If David sent you, you're wasting your time. I'm never going back, and he can't make me—can he, Brant? So why don't you just fuck off. Make her go, Brant!"

"Now, Francie! That's no way to talk to one of my guests. You ought to know better. I'll bet you're just begging to be punished, aren't you, baby? Melvin, why don't you take Francie into one of the bedrooms and slap her a few times? Or spank her, if you prefer. That's what *she* prefers, isn't it, luv?"

141

A tall, skinny man who had been standing by grabbed a suddenly cringing yet obscenely excited Francie by the arm and started to drag her away, while Brant Newcomb stood there, smiling thinly. Francie grimaced at Eve over her shoulder like a kid making faces, and Eve wanted to run after her, but Brant stood in front of her, a drink in his hand.

Tony Gonsalves had already disappeared somewhere into the depths of the room with Richard, who was his current lover, and here she was, forced to stand with a polite smile feeling frozen on her face as she thought of Francie and what might be happening to her now, right now, in this same house.

"Have you met everyone yet? Here, this is for you— you did say Scotch, didn't you?"

Brant Newcomb was being vaguely polite to her— the Devil transformed suddenly into bored host—and she had no choice but to go with him, play his game, loathingly aware of the light pressure of his hand on her arm.

He was introducing her to some of the people who stood in the farthest corner of the enormous living room, talking about the theater and TV. They seemed to know what they were talking about. In the same group, Eve recognized Jerry Harmon and the two girls with him. They were new in town, called themselves models, but did mostly nudes and seminudes. That was Jerry's specialty, anyway. They called him the "Body Merchant"—he was always introducing new talent to the skin magazines and moviemakers. Jerry was smiling at her, showing his really beautiful white teeth, his smile somehow both knowing and mocking.

"Why, Eve baby! Such a nice surprise!"

"You'll look after her, won't you, Jer? Make sure she has enough to drink and meets everyone. I want Eve to feel at home. Have fun, Eve, and I'll see you later."

Brant Newcomb walked away then, and she was

filled with a sudden, unreasoning feeling of relief. One of the girls with Jerry Harmon tugged at his arm and whispered something to him, taking his attention from Eve. She stood there silently, holding the drink in her hand and wishing desperately for David. Please, please come to me, David. Please let this crazy plan work, let me go home safe! She realized she was being childish, but she was afraid, unreasoningly so. Someone, noticing her silence, had asked her a question, and she forced herself to answer lightly, sipping at her drink now, at last. It gave her at least the appearance of being a part of the group, without a care in the world—did people at parties always have to wear the same look? She was trying to pay attention to the conversation, in case someone asked her another question, but it wasn't possible to stop her mind from going back to Francie—how to get to Francie, how to make her *listen*. It had been stupid and foolish to allow David to talk her into this ridiculous position—she was the last person that Francie would listen to! Still, she was here, she had promised, and she had, at least, to *try*.

Wild jungle music—all drums and flutes—began blasting out through concealed speakers, and people were starting to dance. Suddenly, Jerry was grabbing at her hand, and she was being forced to go with him— to stand with her body a few inches away from his, moving automatically in time to the beat of the music.

"You're some dancer, Eve," Jerry said admiringly, flashing that white grin at her again. "I dig the way you move your body, baby. Sure wish you'd relent and pose for some of those pictures I was telling you about."

"Jerry, I'm sorry, but I've already told you I don't go in for that kind of modeling."

"That's okay, baby. Just keep dancing, keep moving, you're great!"

She wished she could stop this farce and go home. Why did she have to stand here and move her body to that sensuous, thudding beat, when she felt nothing but dislike for the man she danced with? She made herself smile, as if the cameras were on her, as if she were enjoying every minute of it. Normally, she enjoyed dancing, loved this primitive-sounding music. Maybe if she just let it take her along with it, stopped thinking . . .

She didn't know how long it was before Jerry finally tired and led her off to one side. She felt tired and thirsty, and he brought her a drink, being very attentive. With a feeling of relief, Eve saw one of the girls Jerry had been with earlier come up to him and pull at his arm.

"Come on, baby, c'mon!" she pouted. "Don't you like me with my clothes *on*?"

Jerry shrugged, rolling his eyes apologetically at Eve before he let the girl lead him back to join the dancers.

Eve looked around, trying to get her bearings. Someone had turned most of the lights off; the few dim lights that had been left on seemed to waver like flickering torches—what a weird effect! She could smell the acrid, burned-leaves odor of marijuana—it seemed to hang in the air, stinging her nostrils. Didn't anyone smoke *cigarettes* anymore? Eve noticed suddenly that the fat, machine-rolled sticks of the weed lay blatantly piled up in silver bowls on every table, alongside smaller, silver-chased antique goblets that were filled with a fine white powder. Oh, God, surely not cocaine? Obviously, Brant Newcomb didn't have to be afraid of police raids. Maybe he just didn't give a damn!

Francie—she had to find Francie. Maybe now was the time, while everyone was occupied and it was so dark you could hardly see. The dancers were becoming more and more uninhibited—some of them looked as if they were making love right in the middle of the floor. Those people who weren't dancing were just as oblivious of everyone else; they either talked with their heads together or were silently entwined with each other.

Eve started to pick her way through the crowd, trying to make herself as inconspicuous as possible. She *had* to find Francie without making her efforts seem too obvious, although by now she had begun to wonder despairingly whether it would do her any good to try talking to the girl. Francie hated her; she always had. Goddammit, why had she let David persuade her into this foolishness?

She wandered through the room clutching her drink in one hand like a talisman and smiling mechanically at anyone who looked at her. Quite suddenly, she caught a glimpse of Francie, just a few yards away. The girl was obviously high on something, and she was giggling foolishly and loudly. Her thin silk dress had been torn, baring half of her torso, and there were purple marks on her back and upper arms. Shocked, Eve started forward quickly and instinctively, but the crowd suddenly seemed to swell, and there were too many people between her and Francie now, all pushing in the same direction. A tall young man with long, shaggy hair, a full beard, and wearing leather-strung turquoise beads swinging against his bare chest, shoved his way past her. The music was suddenly muted, so that the silence seemed to beat against her eardrums.

Now she could see Francie again, standing on one of the heavy, elaborately carved Spanish coffee tables with Brant Newcomb and Jerry Harmon half-supporting her.

Brant was speaking, asking everyone to shut up. Francie started to giggle again, and he slapped her lightly across the rump. Eve couldn't help but notice how the girl pressed her body backward against him immediately, her head twisted around so that she could peer into his face.

"Will you all shut up and listen a minute? Maybe some of you might dig this scene. It's like this chick says she's in trouble with her family and she wants to blow this town; only she needs someone to look after

her, give her some bread. Francie here really digs
money—she says she'll go anywhere with whoever bids
the highest for her. Any takers?"

There was a wild cheer; someone clapped delight-
edly.

"A slave auction—yeah!"

Other people took up the clapping, and Francie began to laugh. Her face looked swollen and vapid, and
Eve wondered miserably if she were capable of realizing what was going on. God, this couldn't be happening!

Brant Newcomb's hair glinted like dull gold as he
moved closer to Francie, his hand ripping away what
was left of her blouse to expose her breasts—large and
ripe for a girl her age.

"Guess most of you here know Francie already—
she's quite a chick, ready for anything. Those who don't
know Francie can come up here and take a close look.
Remember, our girl's up for grabs this evening. Any
one of you can have what she's got to offer, so let's hear
the bidding!"

Jerry, laughing, whispered to Francie, and she began
a slow weaving of her body, beginning to slide her skirt
down over her hips. Eve gasped with outrage when
she saw the welts on the girl's buttocks and thighs.

"I bid fifty," someone said hoarsely.

Brant must have tired almost immediately of the
game he had started.

"Done—and she's all yours, Derek buddy," he said
quickly, his voice sounding bored. "Don't forget to give
her the dough after you get her out of town, but be
sure she earns it first."

Someone began to titter, but Francie's voice, shrill,
hysterical, cut through all the other sounds and voices.

"Hey, no! No, that's not enough bread. Goddam you,
anyway, Brant Newcomb, I won't go with him. Told
you already, I'm going to stay with you."

"I'll throw in a couple of thousand extra myself, sweetheart, and you go with Derek here like a good, *quiet* girl. He'll take you to his commune in New Mexico, and you'll find it's a whole new experience for you—won't she, Derek?"

Brant had moved back, grinning, and the bearded young man who had pushed past Eve caught Francie by the waist, pulling her off the makeshift platform.

"Hell, no! I'm not going off to any old New Mexico—I'm staying right here. Let go of me!" Francie yelled, her nails raking at the man's face.

He slapped her, the blow sounding like a small explosion. It knocked her backward onto the coffee table, where she lay sprawled out, her legs outspread obscenely. Eve could hear Brant laugh as he threw a wad of bills at Francie, heard the girl scream curses at him even as she grabbed for the money, clutching it to her bare breasts with greedy fingers.

Derek pulled Francie to her feet, and someone handed him an Indian blanket. In spite of her struggles and screams of rage, he began to wrap it around her squirming body, pinning her arms against her chest, as if it had been a straightjacket. Some of the other men who stood close by helped him. Eve could hear their laughter and their coarse comments.

It had all been like something thrown from a projector onto a movie screen—it just wasn't possible that this was really happening, here in the same room with her! Suddenly recovering from her disbelieving, frozen immobility, Eve began to push and fight her way through the crowd of people that seemed to hem her in.

"This isn't true, any of it!" she exclaimed aloud, and a man glanced at her curiously.

"You never been to one of these 'partouzes' before, doll? Stick around and we'll make even wilder things happen, you and I. . . ."

His hands reached under her skirt, pawing, but she

managed to elude him, almost running now. She could see Francie again, being carried out of the room by Derek, half-smothered by the blanket, but still struggling. There was a flurry of cheers and lewd remarks as one of Francie's flailing bare legs knocked another man off balance.

Another minute and Francie would be gone—she'd never catch up with them. How could she, with not even a car to follow them in?

Eve forgot everything but her own anger at what she had just witnessed, and her frustration at not being able to do anything about it.

"*Francie!* Bring her back in here, you crazy, irresponsible fool!"

She screamed it as loud as she could, not caring who heard, hoping only that the man would hear her voice over the yells and catcalls of this gang of maniacs.

Eve grabbed at the arm of someone who loomed in her way, shutting Derek and Francie out from her view.

"Please, stop them! Francie's only seventeen—and anyway, it's nothing but kidnapping, and he'll get in trouble, too! Please . . ."

Her words trailed away as Brant Newcomb's fingers closed around her arm, stopping her, freezing her.

She felt suddenly isolated on an island alone with him —encapsulated within the sea of faces and voices that swirled like a rising and falling tide around them.

He had said nothing. His mouth smiled at her without humor, and his eyes stayed cold, chilly blue, showing neither feeling nor emotion.

"Will you let me *go!*" she whispered to him, without knowing why she felt impelled to whisper. "You must be insane to think that you—even you—can get away with something like this. Francie is—she's a *human being,* or don't you understand that? You can't just auction her off as if—"

"But I just did, sweetheart. And it seems as if I did

it at the right time, too. You know her, what she's like. Can't you see that she'll be better off with Derek in New Mexico? Now, suppose you and I talk about it quietly and *alone,* while Derek takes Francie away, hmm? You don't have to worry; Francie will like him, and he'll be good for her. He might not look the part, but Derek's a psychiatrist and he's into social work. He knows about Francie and her hang-ups, and he's worked with kids like her before. So why don't you come along with me now, baby, and we can talk about *your* hang-ups. You know our little talk is long overdue, don't you?"

His grip on her arm was unrelenting, and she thought that his speech sounded almost imperceptibly slurred. As if— God! she thought frantically, is everyone here stoned right out of their minds?

She tried to pull away from him, her eyes starting to search desperately for Tony, for any familiar, friendly face. His grip tightened, hurting her, and she found herself forced to move along with him.

And Marti's words, Marti's warning came back to assault her mind with their terrifying implications. . . .

CHAPTER
NINETEEN

BRANT NEWCOMB TOOK HER to the bar and held out his hand to the bartender, his eyes never leaving her face. He took the drink the man gave him and handed it politely to Eve, still holding her arm with his other hand. Automatically, without will or volition, she took it from him, glad of a respite of some kind. His fingers continued to dig into the soft flesh of her arm, hurting it. It took an effort not to wince with pain.

"Let's drink, Eve Mason." He took the glass that the bartender slid across to him and lifted it in a formal and somehow mocking toast.

"Let's drink to a pleasant conversation—the one we're going to have presently. And you'll tell me all about your concern for Francie, and for Francie's big brother —the one who gets his kicks beating her ass. And I'll tell you—no, maybe I'll *show* you, instead. I think I'd enjoy that more."

She held her glass with suddenly nerveless fingers. He touched the rim of his against it, nudging it upward toward her lips.

"Drink up, Eve. I'm starting to get impatient."

His voice was soft and slow and so polite—and all the while, his fingers kept digging into the vulnerable flesh of her arm, forcing tears into her eyes.

Because she was left without an alternative, she

151

drank quickly and sloppily, not stopping to think about anything except getting away, *escaping* from this soft-spoken maniac. Marti had been right, and Peter had been right. Brant Newcomb was dangerous, and she was very much afraid of him. The melodrama she was involved in had suddenly become very real, and she had to do something to save herself—and Francie, too. For after all, what could he do to her—*kill* her? No, of course he wouldn't dare go so far, but he could hurt her in other ways. . . . Eve shuddered; her drink spilled as she drained the glass and set it down on the counter, trying to be defiant.

Politely, he wiped the front of her dress with a clean napkin. She could not help flinching away from his touch, bringing a slight, mirthless curve to his chiseled mouth.

"What's the matter, Eve? Don't you like being touched? And don't tell me you're shy—I couldn't quite believe that, coming from a *Stud* centerfold. Or am I the wrong sex? Is that what it is, baby? Let's see—you're Marti Meredith's roommate, aren't you?"

"You—you—" Eve couldn't speak coherently for the rage that suddenly filled her, obliterating her fear and even the thought of Francie.

"Save it for when we're alone, Eve. You can call me all the names you can think of while I'm fucking you. And I've waited a long time to do that. Why don't you come with me now and show me what you can do, huh?"

He was already taking her with him before the impact of his lightly uttered words sank in, making her suck in her breath with anger.

He took her through the crowd, and people moved aside to let them go—some of them staring curiously, and others too busy with each other. Eve moved with him, helpless. She could make a fuss, she supposed, with a detached part of her mind, but that would only serve to put her on exhibition, like Francie. She wouldn't give in.

He led her through a door that she hadn't even noticed before.

"I apologize for the room," he murmured behind her. "I realize that it's a trifle overdone—a kind of Frank Harris daydream come true—but it does impress a lot of people and actually helps get rid of a lot of inhibitions. Francie calls it the game room—I suppose you might say there are a lot of games played in here."

Eve had stopped, staring around her with a kind of disbelieving horror. She almost forgot the pressure of his fingers around her upper arm, the steely, painful pressure that had brought her here with him against her will.

At first sight, it was a functional kind of room, all stark blacks and whites, with mirrors everywhere to catch the reflection of the enormous bed from all angles.

The lights that blazed from the four corners of the room were photographer's lights, blinding-bright when he turned them on; and apart from the bed, the only other furniture was a heavy, leather-covered desk in one corner of the room with a single hide-upholstered chair behind it. Large cushions lay huddled in an untidy pile against one wall.

Eve stumbled as he suddenly propelled her forward, feeling terror like a sudden weight in the pit of her stomach when she heard the door close behind him. She had the feeling that she was caught up in a nightmare, that this wasn't really happening to her—she couldn't have let Brant Newcomb bring her here with him like a wooden puppet to this horrible, nightmarish room. It wasn't possible either that he was now turning her body around so that she faced him.

"Why don't you take your clothes off now," he told her quietly, his very bright blue eyes on hers. His voice was polite and quite casual, just as if he had merely offered her another drink, and for a stunned moment she couldn't believe that she had heard him right.

Anger washed through her again, drowning the fear.

Eve tried to make her voice cold and firm, but she could not stop it from shaking. Even in her own ears, it sounded pitifully weak.

"This—I can't believe it! And it's gone far enough, too. You said you were going to tell me about Francie. ... I'm leaving now, do you understand?"

"Ah, Eve, you disappoint me! You're putting on an act and *pretending*—I had expected better from you. You struck me as being—well, intelligent, at least." As an afterthought he added softly, "I didn't invite you here tonight, sweetie, remember? You came of your own free will. And I got to thinking—now, why else would you come to my party except to get laid? Especially after we'd already discussed it at our last meeting."

He ran the fingers of one hand gently down the side of her face, and she shuddered with distaste, pulling her head back sharply.

But at the same time, she felt herself almost hypnotized by his cold, empty eyes, unable to speak. Sensing her turmoil and taking it as a kind of surrender, he began to smile.

"You *do* want to get screwed, don't you, Eve Mason? That's why you came, isn't it? There's no need to act embarrassed about it, baby—I don't mean to boast, but this kind of thing has happened before. *You*, however— I've wanted you, too, for a long time. But hurry up now, I have other guests to attend to."

At the back of her mind, she realized that he seemed to be deliberately taunting her. She heard herself stammer, "I won't—I don't," and wondered dimly why, when she tried to speak, the words wouldn't come out right.

His fingers tightened, drawing a stifled cry of protest from her.

"You will, and you do. You'll want it, Eve. And I'm going to have you in any event—you already know that, don't you?" His voice hardened as he continued, "Stop playing silly games, doll. Let's forget all the pointless preliminaries for a change. Or are you Francie's type? Is it rape you desire? Perhaps you enjoy being hurt first, is that it?"

He had her by both arms now, pulling her toward him. His eyes seemed to burn into hers like blue frost-fire, but his voice remained even and polite, heightening her feeling of unreality.

"Stop it," she whimpered. "Let go of me! You can't— I won't let you touch me. You're wrong, *wrong!* I'm not like Francie!"

Her words sounded pitifully inadequate even to herself, and he laughed, tightening his hold on her arms until she winced, crying out.

"Ahh! Stop hurting me!"

He made his voice exaggeratedly patient.

"Eve, it's too late to stop anything. If you want it to be rape, then I guess I can oblige you. If you won't take your clothes off by yourself, then I'll rip them off your cringing body. Will that turn you on, honey? Is that one of the things you enjoy having done to you?"

Inexorably, ignoring her struggles and her protests, he forced her closer to him while his hands slipped down her arms until one was clamped around her waist, pulling her up against his body. She felt stifled, suffocated! With his free hand under her chin, he forced her face up to meet his and began to kiss her brutally and thoroughly, his cruel, hurtful fingers pressing on either side of her mouth now until he had forced it open and she felt his tongue ravage it.

Sobbing, whimpering, Eve tried to push him away from her, but he was like a rock—obdurate, hard, and unyielding—and she was compelled to endure his kissing with her head strained back, her mind starting to whirl strangely so that she thought back with sudden panic to the drink he had given her earlier. God, suppose he'd had the bartender put something in it, some kind of drug that was now making her dizzy, taking the strength away from her arms and legs, leaving her weak and helpless? She felt as if her head were floating in space, detached from her body. She felt the taste and texture of his tongue, his lips, his teeth pressed against her lips, hurting her.

Suddenly and silently, while he continued to kiss her bruised and open mouth, Eve felt his hands go up to the neck of her dress and rip it downward.

She tried to cry out against the pressure of his lips and plundering tongue. She felt that she was going to faint, and then his mouth left hers and he pushed her backward. As she started to fall helplessly, he grabbed at the front of her dress, tearing it, pulling her toward him again. Within a minute he had contrived to strip her naked except for her pantyhose, and she began to shiver, feeling the air cool on her body.

He *meant* it, then. He actually intended to rape her —he had not merely been trying to frighten her.

Disjointed thoughts, words, phrases tumbled around in Eve's mind. This is something out of a scary novel. David, *save* me! How could I have underestimated this man so, after all the warnings, after the feeling I had about him. This is a nightmare. Wake me up somebody! David? She had said it so often, his name was her talisman.

She moved backward now—warily, fearfully, like a terrified trapped animal.

"Don't—please—this has gone beyond a— *Stop* it, I won't let you—"

He laughed. His eyes, she thought, looked like polished stones, reflecting the light. She had seen cats look at her that way with unreadable feline eyes. She noticed then that whatever drug he had used had enlarged his pupils, so that his eyes looked more violet than blue.

He made no move to come at her this time; he was standing there watching her, with his hands now at his belt—strong, capable-looking fingers moving so quickly and efficiently as he started to undress.

"That's better, Eve Mason," he said softly, "that's much better. You really do have a beautiful body, don't you? Francie kept telling me you were too skinny, but you're not, under your clothes. Be a good girl now, and take off those pantyhose, too, won't you?"

Goaded by his words, and suddenly finding some strength left in her legs, Eve whirled and started to run desperately for the door. She had reached it, was actually turning the handle, when he caught up with her and held her immobilized against his body from behind. He chuckled softly in her ear while his hands moved slowly and insolently down her cringing body, squeezing her breasts, pressing between her legs, making her squirm and begin to cry with shame and fear and anger while she attempted to flail at him with her hands.

He held her—and after a while, the drug, whatever he had had put in her drink, made her so weak and dizzy that he must have felt her weakness and turned her around to face him. Without warning, then, his hand lashed out at her, slapping her backhanded—first one side of her face and then the other.

Eve heard her own scream of pain echo in her ears as she instinctively brought her hands up to her face. While she swayed on her feet, she could feel, with helpless anger, how he tore away her last shred of protection, the thin nylon ripping under his fingers.

He pushed her backward, holding her shoulders, and as she felt the edge of the bed behind her knees, she fell back onto the bed as he meant her to do. The lights blinded her, and above her a mirror reflected her own too-pale body back at her until his body covered it.

Eve started to struggle as soon as she felt his weight on her. Panic-stricken, she began to claw and tear at him with her nails, seeing his eyes at last register some emotion—surprise? Had he really expected her to succumb easily?

"No!" she screamed again. "I won't, damn you, I won't, I won't!" She kept repeating the words through bruised lips, not even caring when he slapped her again, sharply and impatiently.

"Oh, for God's sake! What do you want, foreplay? Want me to go down on you first to get you ready? Hold still, then, you stupid bitch, and I'll give you what you want."

He hit her again, this time stunning her momentarily. She saw in the mirror, through tear-blurred eyes, his sun-bronzed body slide down the length of hers, between her legs—his hurtful hands now holding her thighs apart. She fought against him, felt her body slip on the shiny taffeta spread until she was suddenly poised on the edge of the bed with her legs hanging down on either side of him.

"Oh, n-no!" she wailed with horror, but he didn't seem to hear or care, as his fingers held her open.

"You *are* beautiful. Here, too. You have the ripest, loveliest lips I've ever seen hidden down here, doll, and I've seen plenty. Why hide anything so good?"

He bent his head, and she felt his lips on her, and then his tongue.

She thought suddenly that if only this were David doing it to her—David whom she loved, and not this hateful, self-contained egomaniac, then—but this was Brant Newcomb, not David, and she would never, never let him take her this way, not unless he killed her first, or. . . .

Sobbing, gasping with fear and humiliation and rage, Eve struggled to get away from him, her body twisting and writhing, while he tried to hold her down with his hands. *He* was at a disadvantage now, she felt with a surge of triumph, for he still knelt between her flailing, thrashing legs.

"Damn you, Eve Mason, will you stop playing your stupid games? Lie still, bitch, or I'll have to—"

She was half-sitting up by now, her legs still kicking out wildly at him, but his sudden stillness caught her off balance. His grip on her slackened, then let go, and she fell back momentarily, to sit up again, eyes wide with horror.

The door was open—God, when had they opened it? —and people had crowded in through it, filling the room, grinning at them both as they seemed to freeze in a tableau of fear or frustration.

How many of them were there? She couldn't tell, but quite suddenly they seemed to press in on her, all around her, with their grinning, vacuous faces and their eyes—their eyes were all over her body, crawling over it. She tried to scream again, but only a small, choked sound escaped her dry throat. Instinctively, her hands grabbed for the bedspread, and she attempted to pull it over her exposed body. Was there actually regret in his eyes as he got slowly to his feet and leaned over her?

She heard Jerry Harmon's voice.

"We watched you through the two-way mirror for a while, after you disappeared in here. Whatsa matter, Brant baby, you getting selfish?"

"Yeah, you usually call us in sooner. You're slipping as a host—you used to be better about sharing, didn't he, Mel?"

She didn't want to hear what they were saying—even meeting Brant's cold eyes, locked with hers, seemed to be better than the things they were saying.

"Too bad, Eve. But maybe you prefer it this way."

His voice was soft, meant for her only—his words cruel. He pulled the spread from her suddenly nerveless fingers and moved back, shrugging carelessly, letting those others crowd closer in, their eyes leering, their words beating against her ears.

"Hey, Brant, how come you didn't have her all tamed and quieted down for us?"

"Because she's a fighter, and she's stupid. But maybe it takes more than just one guy to keep her happy."

"Bet that's it, huh, baby? But don't worry, we'll make you happy—very happy!"

A man—his face looked somehow familiar, but she didn't know him—put his hand on her breast and squeezed.

She tried to roll away from him, and someone else grabbed her leg.

"If it's going to be a gang-bang, then I want in on it, too—women's lib and all that!"

A woman's wet mouth grazed Eve's; she turned her head away, but not quickly enough. The woman laughed.

From somewhere above her, sounding far away, Eve heard Brant's voice again.

"Hey, Jerry, get that damn camera rolling, will you? Eve Mason is going to get screwed, and we're going to add a new movie to the collection."

There was more laughter and cheering, and Eve wanted to close her eyes—that was her only escape from the nightmare now, she realized sickly.

Hands reached for her, touching, grabbing, holding. There were too many of them to fight off, but she fought, anyway. The lights blazed into her eyes, and her arms and legs had started to feel like lead weights; but the things they were doing to her, the obscene, ribald comments, were not to be endured. She had to do something to feel herself still alive; keep struggling against them for as long as she could.

The smell of their bodies, the heat of them, seemed to suffocate Eve. She panicked and heard her own cries and moans and useless pleading over the laughter and the obscenities and the hoarse, excited breathing.

Someone held a small silver spoon under her nose, trying to make her snort up the white, powdery substance it contained. She screamed and felt her lips and tongue grow numb as it spilled.

Hands pulled at her legs, dragging them so widely apart that she screamed again with agony. A man knelt on the bed, his fingers incongruously gentle as he held her labia open. His voice sounded slurred, and she suddenly knew him even in the middle of her nightmare—Brant Newcomb!

"I want you all to see what I discovered. Isn't she beautiful? Jer, why don't you zoom in and get a close-up of the sweetest cunt in the world."

"Damn you, Brant Newcomb, damn you, damn you!" she sobbed until some other man, kneeling over her head, pushed his penis into her mouth, gagging her, making her retch.

Their hands and mouth and stiff, thrusting cocks were everywhere on her body—hurting her, invading her, ravaging her, while she shuddered and cringed and made choked, terrified animal noises in her throat.

It was no use, they kept telling her; no use fighting, no use struggling like an insane creature. Why didn't she give in and have a good time like everyone else? Couldn't she see that they were trying to teach her how to have fun?

Eve wondered vaguely, with the part of her mind that was still capable of reasoning, why she didn't yield, give in like they said, let them do whatever it was they wanted to do with her. She had been screwed before, abused before, and maybe if she did stop fighting them, their cruel game might lose some of its savor. But she *couldn't* stop—couldn't stop her biting, kicking, and clawing; her screams of fear and almost witless panic.

She continued to struggle and thrash about, so that they had to hold her down, cursing at her stubbornness. Another man thrust his penis in her mouth, and she bit down on it, hearing his yell of pain and shock, and feeling in her turn the pain of his hand slamming across her breasts.

"Bitch! Goddam bitch!"

Someone laughed.

"So keep your pecker out of her mouth, then. There's other ways."

There were other ways, and they tried them all, while her awareness of what was happening and kept on happening began to come in patches now as her brain tried to detach itself from her bruised and violated body.

But by now she wasn't the only one—she was the center of a monstrous orgy, a tangle of bodies, male and female, copulating around her and across her and over her and everywhere else in the room. Reflected in the mirrors, they looked like a mass of writhing, squirming snakes.

Eve struggled to breathe, to remain human, to proclaim her humanity and her individuality—to survive.

Were they still taking pictures and making their dirty movies? The white, bright lights had changed into flashing kaleidoscope colors that seemed to well and surge and glow around her with herself in their center, being sucked down into a Hell peopled with writhing, joined bodies—ugly, hurting—Dante's Inferno come to life. A nightmare! Worse than a nightmare because she couldn't escape merely by waking up—she was trapped, caught up in it, part of it.

But it couldn't be happening, couldn't be real—you read about this kind of thing, but it didn't happen, not to her, not to Eve Mason, Dave's girl. . . . People didn't really do these things to other people; you read about it, talked about it, watched X-rated movies, but you stayed outside of the nightmare—didn't you? Didn't you?

Hell it was, and the voice of the serpent whispered in her ear again. She had been on the point of escaping, detaching herself completely, and then Brant Newcomb's voice brought reality sharply and painfully back.

"Eve, damn you, will you stop trying to fight it? Even Francie had more sense than you. It's too late, baby, you can't stop it, so why don't you join—join in the fun, Eve. Come on, lie still for me and let me fuck you. Don't you know I've wanted to fuck you from the very first time? Stop fighting me, and I'll make it good for you—god*dam* you, stop fighting!"

Mindless, wordless, she shook her head at him, against his insidious words. Someone, straddling her body, grabbed her ankles and pulled them upward and back while Brant knelt between her spread thighs. She felt herself an offering, a sacrifice to the old pagan gods —wasn't this the way primitive tribes raped captured maidens?

Suddenly, she felt him drive himself deep inside her —deeper than any of the others had gone. She felt him battering up against the opening to her womb, and the pain was so great that she screamed, over and over again, until she fainted—with her screams still echoing in her ears.

CHAPTER
TWENTY

Eve came floating back to consciousness again, and she was still in bed. But a different bed this time, in a different room. *Brant's* bed? Brant's room? Horror washed over her all over again when she saw him there, sitting on the side of the bed, watching her.

There was no one else there now, but she was still defenselessly naked, and she hurt all over when she moved. Her body started to struggle again involuntarily. He put a hand on her shoulder, pushing her down against the pillows, and she wanted to scream again.

"You don't have to go on fighting. They've all gone home, and the party's over." His voice was even, betraying no emotion.

"Oh, dear *God!*" she said aloud in a ragged whisper. She stared at him, seeing his beautiful, corrupt face. Her mind was still freewheeling from the drug he must have given her, and she felt as if she were floating, without sensation. Numb inside and out.

"Hardly apropos," he said dryly, making the unreality sharpen. "Didn't you know I'm the Devil?"

Her subconscious mind believed him somehow, and she could feel herself shrink away, bits of long-ago trivia drifting back into her mind. Didn't they use forked, pointing fingers to ward off the Devil? Or, in later times, a crucifix?

Why don't I wear one any longer? She brought her
hand up to touch her bare neck in a curiously childish,
forlorn gesture.

"I had a friend, a physician, check on you while you
were still out. He said you're going to be okay."

His voice was still even, but his eyes, flicking over
her, had a strange and unrecognizable look in their
depths.

She shrank into herself, mistrusting him, fearing him,
suddenly wishing she could cover her body from his
eyes even now.

"Goddammit, you should have been sensible!" he
said suddenly. "The stuff I had the man put in your
drink earlier on was supposed to turn you on and take
care of all your damn stupid inhibitions, but I guess
he miscalculated. So things got out of hand—I didn't
mean for them to go as far as they did, but we were all
pretty high, and you were supposed to be, too."

She winced at his offhandedly contemptuous tone. A
stammer in her voice, she said, "You—you have to take
by *force*? And what all of you did to me—was it just for
kicks? Is that the only way you can make it with a
woman? Is your appetite so jaded it has to be rape, or
a—a gang-bang?"

He leaned over and slapped her coldly and deliberately. The pain brought tears to her eyes, but it helped
clear her head, too. It gave her some pitiful measure of
satisfaction to know that her words seemed to have gotten to him, and now, suddenly unafraid, she couldn't
stop.

"Did what I just said hit home, Brant Newcomb?
Did it get under your hide, you bastard? And what *is*
behind the mask, anyway, man or—or fag?"

No, she wasn't afraid of him now. What more could
he do to her? She could see the angry flush that came
up under his bronze skin, and was glad she had finally

made him react. Was that what his real problem was,
that he was a closet homosexual, trying to hide his real
tendencies from the world by acting the satyr? Was that
part of the reason that he seemed to hate and despise
women? She said so aloud. "Is that why you're a sadist?
Do you have to put women down?"

He stood up, and for a moment she thought crazily
that he was going to fall upon her and *rend* her—finish
what he and his friends had started.

But his voice, when he spoke, was very controlled,
very quiet.

"I think you're trying to provoke me into fucking you
again, baby, and I really don't want to any longer.
There were too many others just now, and even I can
be fastidious sometimes."

He walked away from the bed to a concealed closet
in one of the paneled walls and came back carrying her
coat.

"I'm sorry, but this is all you have left to wear. I'll
buy you a new dress to make up for the one I ripped off
you." He handed her the coat. "Get up and put it on,
and I'll take you home."

Somehow, she found her voice. "I don't want—" she
began, but his voice cut across hers.

"I don't give a damn what you don't want, Eve. I said
I was taking you home, and I am. Either you come with
me, or I have to figure that you enjoyed what happened
a few hours ago and want more. I can always call some
of my friends back, you know. Or would you prefer
someone different?"

She could not help shivering. The look in his eyes
made her afraid all over again. Hating him, hating her
own weakness, she sat up. Her head starting whirling
dizzily. Remembering something she had read somewhere, she lowered her head to her knees and hoped
the faintness would go away.

"You—I'm not going to let you get away with this, you know," she said unevenly. "I'll go to the police— the DA—someone!"

His voice sounded bored, almost weary.

"Ah, you're full of shit, doll. Is that the worst you can do? Once you're capable of thinking straight, though, I don't think you'll do anything. I bet you've forgotten all the pictures we took. We even made a movie, close-ups and all, and I'm sure you're very, very photogenic, even under those circumstances. Now, how would you feel if a lot of other people got to see some of those pictures? Your family, for instance—your boyfriend, whose spying you were doing last night. And of course all the other beautiful people you work with. The underground press would really have a field day. Is that what you want, luv?"

While he'd been talking, Eve had been thinking of the pictures. Oh, God! How could she have forgotten that part of the horror? She felt sick, remembering the flashes, the lights hot on her body—people taking pictures, laughing while the others opened her, examined her body minutely and intimately, touched and fucked her as if she'd been a thing without feeling, a toy for their amusement. And the worst part had been the way they had looked *inside* her, violating her with their probing eyes and fingers, using her without pity or humanity.

Eve had to force herself to look up at him.

"I hope you drop dead. I'd like to kill you myself. I hope I never have to set eyes on you again!"

He recognized the venom as well as the defeat in her voice, and smiled coldly. But his eyes still held the same measuring look that had puzzled her earlier.

She tried to stand, but she was so dizzy that he had to help her—politely wrapping the coat around her shaking body and even buttoning it up for her while she swayed against him involuntarily. He stood so close to her! If only her hands weren't so nerveless and would do what she wanted them to do; if only she had a weapon—she'd have killed him! She wanted to slap his face with all the force she could muster, to leave deep, bloody tracks in it with her nails, marring its perfection. But her hands felt as if they had weights attached to them, and her mind kept trying to escape from her weak and aching body.

Observing her, noticing the way she shied away from his touch, Brant Newcomb could not help feeling a grudging kind of admiration for her guts and stubbornness as well as, he admitted with surprise, a sudden spurt of desire for her body. But this time for her *willing* body, not the way it had been tonight. Maybe if the gang had not burst in when they had, he might have gotten to her after all—made her his casual possession, like countless other women before her, starting with Syl. Yes, always starting with Syl. His usual goddam nightmare, his one weakness. Fighting with himself, he pressed his fingers into Eve's arm as he started to help her walk outside, and felt her flinch. But she said nothing, would not even look at him. Well, what did he expect? She had just been gang-raped and had fought them all, all the way, he remembered with annoyance. She was a stubborn bitch, but it was only natural that she should hate and mistrust him.

They went down in the elevator to his garage in silence, and he helped her into the car he would use tonight—one of the three he kept there. She flinched away from his touch again, so he deliberately lingered over it, letting his fingers close over her thigh after she was sitting beside him, and hearing her gasp of pain and rage.

Sliding into the seat next to her, he wondered if she'd

really try to do anything about what had happened, and grinned mirthlessly to himself. Like hell she would! Now that he had pictures of her and she knew it, all he had to do was remind her occasionally, and she'd be good and manageable, just like the rest of them.

CHAPTER
TWENTY-ONE

BRANT THE MANIPULATOR! He was good at that. Manipulating people, using them—especially women. Never a woman yet that he hadn't been able to control and to break, even Syl—shit, no more thoughts of Syl! He'd paid a shrink for three years of analysis to be rid of Syl and his memories of her—and what few hang-ups and self-doubts he had left by then. And since Syl, he had discovered so many things! Money talks, he had found. Money talks loudest and laughs last. He could buy anything and anyone he pleased, get away with practically anything he wanted to get away with, with all his damned money. Anything at all . . .

Brant drove carelessly but competently, as he did everything else. The traffic had thinned down considerably by this time in the morning, but the usual fog had wet the pavements, so that he was forced to drive a trifle slower than he usually did.

He lit a cigarette and offered Eve one, but she shook her head, refusing even to look at him as she huddled up against the door on the opposite side in the ridiculous greatcoat she wore. They stopped for a traffic light, and now he studied her profile openly, reaching out suddenly to touch a bruise that showed darkly against her cheekbone.

"You won't be able to work for a while with that. I'll send you a check."

She jerked her head away sharply at his touch, turning to look at him at last, speaking with her voice low and husky and full of the venom and hatred she felt.

"I wouldn't accept anything from you, Brant Newcomb. Not even a million dollars. You can keep your goddam conscience money!"

The light changed, and he put the car in gear as they crawled up a steep hill.

"Baby, I *have* no conscience. You ought to know that. But you—you're still full of fight, aren't you? Well, maybe your boyfriend will take care of whatever excess energy you have left. I presume he's good at that."

No reaction from her this time. Well, he hadn't really expected any. And he was starting to feel tired, too; to get that flat, stale taste in his mouth that always came after a party, after the drinking and the drugs and the women and, yes, the men, too—at the kind of party it had been last night it didn't seem to matter very much after a certain point who did what to whom. Ah, shit, he thought bleakly, suddenly, what *is* everything about? The parties, the orgies, the constant search for new faces, new kicks—it was all getting stale and pointless. Maybe what he needed was to go on a cruise again— go island-hopping in the sloop. But *alone,* this time. Or maybe he'd take Pedro along to keep an eye on the boat, spell him while he slept, and do the cooking. Pedro was a good sailor, and he wasn't the talkative kind.

Yeah, that was it; that was what he needed. To get away someplace. No gang, no liquor, no drugs, and no women. Except maybe for the island women who wouldn't know Brant Newcomb from Popeye the Sailor. Women who'd fuck a man only if they wanted him, the man, and not the aura of money and power and wicked-

ness that clung to him. Women who were free and uninhibited and *honest* and had no hang-ups at all. Damn
his money, anyhow! It hung like an albatross around his
neck sometimes. Like the memory of Syl. His lost inno-
cence, his lost love. Syl. He wondered savagely if her
name would hang suspended in his thoughts forever.

He had begun to drive far too fast, and the car went
suddenly into a skid on a sharp curve. He cursed softly
as he wrestled with the wheel, but Eve, who had been
thrown against him, could see the shine of excitement
in his eyes in the streetlight. She realized that they
might be killed, and it came to her that for the first time
the thought held no terror for her. It didn't matter—
she was past caring—and obviously it didn't matter to
him, either—it was the challenge that excited him, as
if the car were just another object to be mastered and
conquered at his hands.

The car under control again, Brant drove on as
though nothing had happened, but Eve could sense him
looking sideways at her. Well, she wouldn't give him the
satisfaction of a comment, not even a gasp of fear. She
had felt no fear while it was happening—she had felt
nothing but an intolerable tiredness and sadness. She
wished that he would hurry, skid or no skid. She needed
the security of her apartment now—and David. Oh,
God—David! What would he say? What would he do?
She must look a mess, and there would be telltale marks
all over her body. She could feel the alien juices seeping
out of her, and she shuddered uncontrollably.

"Cold?"

His voice prodded at her again, hateful and mocking.
She disliked and feared this man beside her more than
she'd ever thought it possible for her to hate anyone.
Her anger made it impossible not to answer.

"Don't start worrying about me *now*, Brant Newcomb. Worry about yourself, why don't you? About
your—your immortal soul, if you have one left."

She didn't know why she had said that, why she had said anything at all. What part of her subconscious mind had dredged up the old church precepts that she had long ago pushed away as being archaic and unacceptable?

Surprisingly, she sensed a sudden rigidity in him, a tensing of his hands on the wheel before he laughed, his laughter sounding forced.

"My immortal *what?* Doll, I lost my soul, such as it was, to the Devil a long time ago. Maybe I never had one. Anyhow, the priests gave up on me years ago. And as long as I give enough money to the church, they leave me alone. We have a real nice arrangement, you might say! And I believe they even pray for me."

"You—*you're* a Catholic, too?"

She couldn't keep the surprise and the loathing out of her voice, and he chuckled again.

"We have another thing in common now, don't we, luv? Maybe it'll make for a convenient arrangement between us."

"I already told you—I'd rather be dead."

She moved as far away from him as the car would permit, hatred edging her voice.

"You really ought to cut out the melodrama, Eve. You're beginning to sound very, very boring."

His voice turned cold and contemptuous again. His words were meant to goad her, but she was determined to ignore him this time. She could feel his eyes on her until, shrugging, he looked ahead once more, pushing down on the gas pedal almost viciously and causing the car to leap ahead with a jolt that almost snapped her neck. She kept her eyes obstinately closed for the rest of the ride, refusing to acknowledge either fear or his presence beside her.

When he braked to a stop outside her apartment, Eve fumbled for the door handle immediately, but it wouldn't open; he leaned across her with an impatiently muttered "Oh shit!" and unlocked it for her. She cringed away from his arm, and because she did, he could feel the cold anger come up from inside him, and he deliberately held her pinned there, pulling her face around to his while his eyes raked over her body, which shook with fear and disgust.

"No word of thanks? No goodnight kiss? I took you for a well-brought-up girl. Shame on you, Eve Mason!"

"Ohhh—damn you, damn you!" she hissed at him, and he laughed thinly as he brought his mouth down over hers very slowly and deliberately.

Her lips seemed to quiver and vibrate under his long and brutal kiss, and he could feel the rigidity of her body under his arm for just a moment until she suddenly went all soft and lay there passively and limply, refusing to fight back anymore. Why hadn't she done this earlier, in the game room? Kissing her now was suddenly like kissing a doll made of plastic. Her lips were as cold and lifeless as plastic; only her eyes, defiantly open, glared hatred at him.

With an exclamation of disgust, he pushed her away from him, so that she half-fell through the door and he had to grab at her arm to steady her. He saw her wipe the back of her hand across her mouth childishly before she pulled herself free of his grip and was gone, her heels clattering against the damp and empty sidewalk before she disappeared into the doorway. He looked upward then, and there was a light on in one of the upstairs rooms—hers? As he watched, he saw a man's shadow stand silhouetted, peering down. Brant grinned mirthlessly. He slammed the door that she'd left standing open, and gunned his motor loudly, waving mockingly at the man's outline as he roared off, his tires screaming into the silence of the deserted streets.

Well, one childish gesture deserved another! Damn that frigid bitch and her cowardly boyfriend. From all of Francie's accounts, David sounded like an overbearing, selfish hypocrite. A latent Puritan who wanted to screw every cunt in sight but despised the women who let him have them. According to Francie, Eve Mason was crazy for David—she pursued him endlessly and shamelessly, allowing herself to be used and humiliated. Also according to Francie, David would never *marry* Eve, because she was too cheap, too easy, too available. And yet tonight—no, heck, it had been *last* night—the stupid broad had kept fighting. Not just him, but all the others as well. Struggling even when she could see there was no point in it, and that of course was what had provoked and excited them into hurting her as much as they had. Not just the others, but him, too—he had felt what was almost hate for her, a need to crush her, to force her into submitting. He'd really lost his cool, and she wasn't worth it. In fact, she wasn't worth the time wasted in thinking about her, goddam her, anyhow! He'd put her out of his mind just like all the others—the women he'd taken and used and discarded.

Brant drove home through the thinning night, grimacing as he imagined facing the mess in there. Well, the hell with it! Good old Jamison would be there in—he glanced at his watch—about three hours from now, to take care of everything. All *he* had to do now was shut himself up in his bedroom, shower, and then get some sleep.

He let himself into the house, picking his way through the littered rooms, and took his clothes off as he went, dropping them carelessly for Jamison to find. He walked up the sweetly curving staircase that the country's leading architect had designed and into his bedroom. He thought he could smell Eve Mason's perfume on his body and grimaced again. Well, a shower would fix that. He poured himself a drink at the small bar he kept in his room and swallowed it down straight before he stepped under the scalding needles of his shower. Hot first—then a burst of cold, and the warmed towels from the rack. He tossed them into a hamper and walked over to his bed, fiddling impatiently with the dials until he had the music just the way he liked it, coming softly at him from all directions through the concealed speakers—soothing him, holding him in the center of sound. He lit a cigarette and lay back on the pillows, not bothering to pull the covers over himself.

Damn Eve Mason, the stupid bitch! Why did she have to linger in his mind? His mind was, after all, Syl's province. Lovely, golden, corrupt Syl, with her soft hands and wet mouth and gurgling laugh—his "teacher," he used to call her. Syl, who had been his teacher and his love and his mistress—Syl, who also happened to be his aunt. Goddam! He crushed the cigarette out and lit another. By now he had realized that he wasn't going to get any sleep until he had wrestled with his demons, an expression his analyst had used. This was something else the good doctor had taught him. If something was on his mind, he must get it out into the open, examine it, *think* about it, instead of pushing it away into the depths of his subconscious. Once he had thought something out or had made a decision of some kind, he could always relax again. Once he had decided on a certain course of action, he never looked back. It was the only way to survive, to stay in control. He thought about the way he'd had to wrestle with the car earlier, to pull it out of the skid. The challenge had excited him. Any challenge did, even the challenge of wrestling with his own thoughts—and particularly certain memories.

His eyes narrowed against the cigarette smoke, Brant stared up at the raftered ceiling. No mirrors here. No mirrors anywhere in his room. And no one else had shared it with him, ever. The game room was for his women of the moment and his friends' women and their orgies. For playing. This room was his alone, and no one else entered it except Jamison.

He turned restlessly on his pillow, smelling Eve Mason's perfume again, and was tempted with a spurt of anger to fling it away from him. Of course, he'd brought *her* in here. He didn't know why he'd done it— he'd never brought another woman in here (except Syl, and she was in his mind only)—but after the doctor had left, and the last stragglers, she'd looked so pale and *lifeless*—as if she were really dead and not just drugged. It took some people that way, Jack had reassured him, after he'd given her the shot. It was just a sedative; she'd wake up on her own and be just fine. Still, after everyone had gone, he hadn't wanted to stay there in that damned room any longer, and he couldn't very well leave her there by herself, so he'd carried her in here, noticing grimly that bruises were starting to show all over her ivory-tinted body, and feeling the soft silkiness of her hair against his arm—the only thing she had in common with Syl, the texture of her hair.

He turned out all the lights and stared unseeingly into the darkness while he wrestled with his demons.

The money. Always, he had known about the money. It set him apart, forced him to build from within himself, *for* himself. The money belonged, at first, to his grandfather. And then that enormous, fabulous, written-about fortune had been left to him—all of it—carefully skirting his jet-set, indolent parents. Willed to three-year-old Brant Newcomb, II—the senior Brant being his grandfather—a small, bewildered child growing up surrounded by old people and silence. He remembered the silence most of all. For a long time, he hadn't dared to break that silence. If he cried, or even if he laughed, he was quickly picked up and carried away by his nurse, who would whisper to him that his grandfather was old and did not like noise. After a while, he had not been bewildered any longer, and they had not needed to remind him to be quiet.

His parents? They had sufficient money, as much as they needed for the duration of their lifetimes. His gay, flapper mother had dutifully given birth to a son, who was promptly and with secret relief handed over to the forbidding Newcomb in-laws (the old man had been the one who had *really* wanted a child from them, anyway), setting Fay and her darling Dickie free at last to do as they pleased. They visited occasionally—short, strained visits that ended with relief on both sides.

Fay Newcomb thought her son a pale, cold, and reserved little brat who had no real feelings, or warmth. And Richard, her husband, almost *disliked* the boy himself, resenting somehow in his dull, vaguely thoughtless, and pleasure-seeking soul, his son's self-containment and cold withdrawal from any bluff overtures. Well, Richard would think, Father has trained him well. Better than he has been able to do with *me*. And having produced an heir, Richard and Fay were at last free— and in command of all the money they needed for as long as they lived. No more stern lectures and strict allowance invariably overspent; no more painful interviews with a father who could not quite understand, nor hide his disappointment, how any son of his could turn out to be such a cloddish, plebeian individual. And above all, no more staring up at his fragile, golden-haired mother's portrait, which hung on the wall of his father's study to remind him constantly that it was he, Richard Carlson Newcomb, all ten pounds of him, tearing through those frail, thin tissues, who had been the cause of her death.

The boy, Brant, was fortunately considered to be like his grandmother; the boy, Brant, was to get all the family fortune; the will had been drawn up, it was all settled. Brant Newcomb, Sr., while he kept many mistresses, never remarried—they said he had worshiped his young bride, and now his grandson, who looked so much like her, became the reason for his existence.

Fay had one sister, much younger than she—as blond and curvaceous as Fay was brown-haired and fashionably thin. Sylvia was sent to a convent school, her flapper sister held up to her constantly as a bad example, until she ran away often enough to get expelled. After the last expulsion from her third school, and a quickly hushed-up episode concerning a boy who had given her a ride, Sylvia went to live with Fay and was married at seventeen to one of Richard's friends. She divorced him a few years later to marry again, this time a French movie producer who put her on exhibition in some of his movies. Sylvia did well enough with her lush good looks and what little talent she had, but divorced him at length to go to live with an Italian movie star who was regretfully but permanently married to his childhood sweetheart.

Sylvia, blond, voluptuous, and beautiful, was fond of her sister, and because she could not have children of her own (a botched-up abortion had taken care of that), she paid special attention to her nephew and seemed, indeed, to love him more than his own mother did. Sylvia visited the child much more often than his parents ever bothered to do, and would send him small gifts and brightly colored postcards from all over the world. Brant's grandfather did not actually *approve* of Sylvia, but he was shrewd enough to realize that her love for the boy was genuine, and so he let them alone.

Sylvia was the only young and beautiful thing in Brant's existence, the only person he let himself care about. When he was old enough to be sent to a private school and didn't see her for some years, her letters were the only bright spots in his otherwise strictly regimented life. He was studying hard, as his grandfather wanted him to do, and she was back to acting now, and somehow their vacations never seemed to come at the same time. Sylvia was traveling a lot—her letters and cards bore strange and different postmarks every time she wrote. But she *did* write—long letters in her large and sprawling handwriting, describing places she had seen and people she had met. Brant saved every one of them.

Far ahead of his contemporaries because of his private tutors and high IQ, Brant was ready for college before he was fifteen. He studied for his degree with the same concentration and lack of enthusiasm as he had done everything else that his grandfather had planned for him to do. It was something to be done and put out of the way. And then, when Brant was eighteen and almost ready to graduate, his grandfather died.

Richard and Fay didn't fly down for the funeral; they were cruising on some Greek millionaire's yacht and didn't see why they had to leave such charming, interesting people for a funeral. The old man was dead, wasn't he, and his will no mystery. Why be hypocrites? Why pretend? But Sylvia, hearing about it, flew over from Switzerland, where she had been vacationing.

She found Brant, her little nephew, a man already— in appearance, at least. On the surface the same air of coldness that was almost a withdrawal, but with a kind of arrogance added now, and a blazing, Greek god kind of beauty and purity of feature that took her breath away. Brant took after his dead grandmother, as everyone was swift to say, but Sylvia saw, too, with a kind of joy, that he resembled *her* also. They had the same thickly lashed eyes, the same finely chiseled lips. They could be brother and sister, she thought, and was determined that she would not let him shut *her* out, as he did the others.

"Brant— Oh, Brant, I'm so *glad* to see you again!"
She avoided his formally outstretched hand and

kissed him warmly on the lips; her familiar perfume enveloped him and made him a boy again. He held her close, enjoying the strange and unusual feeling of a soft and melting body against his—the unfamiliar closeness to another human being.

"Syl!"

He had always called her that. Starting with "Silly" when he was very young and she was still a giggling but gently affectionate teenager who always had time for him, in spite of the thirteen-year difference in their ages.

"I'm happy to see you, too," he said. And then, diffidently, "Will you stay?"

She was the person he asked to stay on after the funeral, in the big house with all its guest rooms and its staff of impeccably trained servants. Everyone else went back to town, shaking their heads in disapproval and talking in shocked whispers about the lack of manners and feeling displayed by the younger Newcomb. But neither Brant nor Sylvia cared a whit for their opinions.

CHAPTER TWENTY-TWO

SHE STAYED ON. They rode together, talked for hours, and he even taught her to shoot, laughing at the way she winced each time she pulled the trigger of the rifle. He talked to her and confided in her as he had never been able to do with anyone else. He thought afterward that their closeness made what happened later inevitable.

Sylvia had been at the house ten days. She grew restless after a while and wanted to go *out*. But out where? Why, she said, anywhere, it didn't matter. Did he enjoy dancing? Then he could take her to a discotheque. She had heard there was one in town. Did he mind escorting her?

"Wait, wait," she told him mischievously. "I won't let you be embarrassed. I don't look as old as I really am, do I? I know, I'll dress eighteen, and you—you could easily be twenty-one. You look older than you are, do you know that, Brant? But you need to act younger, be younger. Why, sometimes you seem much older and wiser than I!"

During the drive out to town, she snuggled close to him, asked him teasing questions about other girls, just as if she were really his date. *Were* there any girls in his life? He shrugged coldly. Yes. Grandfather had—he grimaced—had him duly initiated. It had been an in-

teresting experience, albeit clinical. And, he added
carefully, he didn't trust women. Or have time for girls.

"Oh, Brant!" Syl said, half-laughing, but upset all the
same because she thought he needed some warmth and
love in his life. She squeezed his arm.

Her hair hung down her back that evening, and she
had threaded a ribbon through it. She looked no older
than eighteen, as she had promised.

Brant enjoyed that evening as he had enjoyed nothing before in his life. The men all looked at her hungrily,
lustfully, for she was as gay, laughing, as a young girl;
but she had eyes only for *him*, her date. There was
nothing in his life as beautiful as Syl that evening—
Syl dancing close to him, her perfumed hair grazing his
cheek; Syl hanging on his every word, ignoring every
other man in the room.

Outside the private club, afterward, he kissed her
unexpectedly and felt her lips part under his, tasting
of the bourbon he'd used to spike their drinks. Suddenly, she'd blinked her eyes and stiffened, pulling
away quickly, pretending she was high.

"Ooh—I don't even know if I can stand straight.
Guess you'll have to carry me home. But oh, Brant,
it was such fun!"

"We'll have to do it again," he said slowly, feeling
the unfamiliar tightening and swelling in his crotch,
trying to slow his breathing—damning himself for being gauche and hating himself for being young.

Abruptly, needing to break the silence, Sylvia began
to talk about having to leave.

"I—I have to go back sometime, Brant. Besides, I
have a movie to complete, and—well, Europe is my
home now, it's where I belong."

She saw the look on his face, and groaning inside
herself, she touched his arm pleadingly.

"Come with me? Oh—but I *mean* it. You need
Europe; you need change, travel, to find out what the

rest of the world is really like. You need—you need to
live, and to love, and, yes—even to be hurt. You need
to learn how to feel. How can I describe it?"

She threw her arms out in a wide, dramatic gesture,
and he began suddenly to laugh, throwing his head
back, feeling the excitement and the strange new and
forbidden tingle that started in his groin and spread
all over his body.

Yes, he decided then. She was right; he needed to
feel. He needed to get away, to see new things, meet
new people—learn about life. And—he was rich, which
helped. For the first time in his life, Brant began to
realize how free and independent the money made him.

"Syl—let's go. Let's go—oh, I don't care! Tonight,
if we want to. Will you let me stay with you?"

In his young, eager selfishness it never occurred to
him that she might have someone else, some man in
her life. But she, with her own kind of selfishness, did
not care, either. She was caught up with the excitement
of the moment, of feeling young, loving him. She caught
his hands.

"Brant—Brant—of *course* you'll stay with me! Come
on, let's hurry! We have to go back and pack and make
reservations, and while we're doing that, I'll tell you all
about it—about life in France and Italy and London
and—oh, it's all going to be so wonderful!"

She stopped, giggled. "Just think, we might even run
into Fay and Richard. Imagine their *faces* if we do!"

At the thought, he laughed, too. She had brought
laughter into his life, and he felt as if he'd only just
learned how to laugh and have fun.

Syl taught him much more; she taught him everything. It was inevitable that it should happen, after all,
and it did. She was too weak and too willful to let
herself fight the lust she had begun to feel for Brant,
mixed up with the real love she had for him; he was
too young and hotblooded to let her stop him. She

taught him slowly and with infinite patience that was rewarded by his retention and practice of everything she could show and teach him about sex. They made love endlessly and tirelessly—he was her young stud, her rich young lover, and she was the envy of all the other women in her set.

Under the warm sun of the French and Italian Riviera, Brant's body tanned to a golden brown as his hair bleached and grew longer. He became indolent, easily bored, and even more arrogant—except when he made love to Sylvia. With her, he was always tender, always seeking, speaking only to her of love, of caring. He grew, also, more sure of himself as a man and as a lover.

Brant had quickly gotten used to the money he had inherited and the power it gave him. He bought and learned to race fast cars and boats; he skiied on snow and in the water and took risks. He gambled in the casinos, and inevitably, too, he discovered other women. But they were all too easy and therefore eventually boring, without challenge. They offered themselves to him, and he took what they offered if he felt like it, but there was really only Syl for him—only Syl he could burrow into, stay in, let himself *care* about. With his youthful, selfish arrogance, he expected her to be all his, waiting for him; his alone, while he, being a man, could take what he wanted and needed of the other women who threw themselves at him.

The nights and days of frantic, endless loving began to take their toll of Sylvia, for Brant was almost insatiable as a lover. Under the harsh and burning sunlight, he began to notice the new, slight lines on her face, an almost imperceptible softness of her thighs and breasts. He became more open and blasé about his other women; and one day Sylvia caught him making love to her new maid and threw a fit of screaming hysterics. She was almost ugly in her rage, and he slammed out of her house sulkily. When he returned repentantly that evening, she had gone out to dinner with the Spaniard, Morales, who was directing her new movie. Burning with an unfamiliar, jealous rage, Brant went to a party thrown by an expatriate Englishman and stayed until the end, becoming involved in his first three-way sex orgy that night.

Filled with remorse afterward and a sick kind of disgust, he went back to the villa. Syl was still with Morales. They lay together, sleeping, in her bed, which had been *their* bed. The covers, trailing onto the floor, exposed her body to the waist; her heavy breasts and tangled hair were half-covered by the man's revoltingly hairy body.

All injured vanity and hurt pride, seething with a mixture of rage and hate and pain, Brant walked out— left her house and took his own apartment in the same city. He would show her! He became a member of the most depraved and decadent set in Rome, going with both women and men according to the circumstances or as the inclination took him. He joined in orgies, experimented with drugs, made the scandal sheets regularly.

Having wanted only to punish Brant, and frantic now because instead of merely getting jealous and returning penitently to her, he had instead seized on her infidelity as an excuse to leave her, Sylvia tried to get him back. She telephoned; she wrote him letters; she made tearful scenes in public. He was coldly adamant.

She came to his apartment one hot noon, pounding on his door and screaming insults until he opened it to her. As soon as she saw him, she began to cry, her voice pitiful, pleading.

"Oh, God—don't you see that I love you? I love you, Brant. Don't hurt me anymore. Stop punishing me!"

"Sorry, but you blew it. You told me I should learn about life, Syl, and I've only just begun to learn. From all kinds of teachers, too. Man, am I learning!"

His voice was cruel, mocking her—her tear-ravaged face, her too-lush body, her lack of pride.

She couldn't speak, and he hammered home the last bolt, the last and most painful insult.

"It's *over*, Syl. Find another gigolo, another stud, huh?"

"Do you honestly believe that's all it was, Brant? Do you?"

She had stopped screaming at him, her voice suddenly quiet, ragged-sounding.

"What was it, then? Was I looking for a mother, you for a son? Well, maybe that was it—maybe that's all it was. I wanted a mother, and you— What *was* it you wanted, Syl? Someone young and untiring to fuck you? Ah, who knows, who cares? Sorry, Syl, but I've still got a lot to learn, and *you* have already taught me everything you know."

He was standing in the doorway of his apartment; he hadn't let her come in, and the door opened wider behind him, the girl of the moment looking out sulkily. Sylvia knew her—she was the young French starlet who'd had the ingenue lead in her last picture.

"*Chérie!* It's cold in bed alone."

Something in Sylvia's face, in her sudden stillness, made him reach his hand out to her almost instinctively. Had he really needed to be so cruel? Why had he felt like lashing out at her?

"Syl . . ."

"It—it's all right, Brant. I'm sorry. It really is okay now, I mean—I think I understand. I won't bother you again, I promise."

She turned, went running down the steps, her heels clattering. Why did she always wear such ridiculously high heels? He started halfheartedly to go after her, but the girl clutched at him from behind, her greedy fingers spread over his crotch. Shrugging, he went back inside with her. She was still new, very young and wild and experienced—he hadn't yet got over craving her body.

Inside, the air conditioning hummed softly as they twisted and turned in bed. The thick, soundproof walls shut them up in a cocoon of their own breathing and broken sounds and words.

Outside, in the sunlight, Sylvia died without a sound under the wheels of a taxi that came careening around a corner just as she reached the street, still running. She died very quickly, and an ambulance shrieked up soon after that and took her broken body away. Brant knew nothing about it until the next day.

Some weeks later, when the nightmares he had started having had become worse and more frightening in spite of all the excesses he had pushed his body into, Brant Newcomb went back "home." He was only twenty. He felt as if he had done everything; there had to be something new to experience, some way to stop thinking.

He joined the Air Force because he enjoyed the challenge of flying, was promptly commissioned an officer, and went into flight training to learn to fly fighters. He volunteered for Vietnam as soon as he could, and spent two years there flying fast jets at the time when the conflict was at its height. Then, still not having succeeded in killing himself in spite of all the chances he took and the extra missions he volunteered for, he came back to the States and resigned his commission—his tour of duty over, a free man again. Free of the monotony that was military life when he was not actually flying, he was determined this time to be freed of his nightmares and his ever-present demons as well. He went into analysis.

"You loved her. Why are you afraid to admit it?"
"Why in hell do you keep insisting upon that? I

thought a psychiatrist isn't supposed to put words in a patient's mouth. No, I didn't love her. Christ, I've never loved anyone! But she was the first—naturally, that made it different."

"But that's not all that made it different, is it? She was your aunt, your mother's sister. You risked the church's excommunication for her. And she was the only woman, the only thing you ever really cared about, wasn't she? Why are you ashamed to admit to me now what you have already admitted under hypnosis? Because she was older than you? Or is it because of some deeply suppressed moral code, perhaps? Because it was incest?"

"J'accuse! That's what you sound like, do you know that? Ah, come on, man! Incest, shit! Syl was only my aunt, for Christ's sake! So at the beginning I suppose I made a kind of mother figure out of her, but later—no, incest never entered into it, I never gave it a thought. She was a woman. Great in the sack, but too damned possessive. And that's all."

"Is it? What about all the years before—before you saw her as a woman. The visits, the cards, the little gifts. You were a small boy then, and you loved her. Wasn't she the only person who really cared about you? And even afterward, wasn't that still so?"

"Goddammit, are you trying to say— Ah, yes, that is what you're saying. That Syl loved me for myself. To everyone else it's the money and the fact that I'm known as a cocksman, a stud."

"Yes, that's right. Is there anything else to you besides that? Do you ever give a woman, or any other person for that matter, any part of your real self? Sylvia was the only one to whom you gave of yourself, wasn't she? I think that with the others you only take...."

"You're smart, you know that? That's why I pay you too damned much money and keep coming back. But

*no—what is the real self? Has it ever occurred to you
that I might not be real at all?"*

"Very dramatic, Brant. But let's go back to Sylvia."

"Oh, damn Sylvia! Damn her, damn her! Goddam her
for dying!"

"Ah!"

Seeing an analyst hadn't cured Brant of Sylvia's ghost,
but he had learned at least to accept what had happened, and above all, to accept himself as he was. No
regrets, no more self-torment for Brant Newcomb.
When something started to bug him, he had learned to
bring it out into the open and think about it objectively.
He had even learned to think about Sylvia without too
much pain, too much guilt. Poor, damned, darling Syl!
Did she know, wherever she was now, that by dying
she'd made him forever hers?

And then, from Sylvia, Brant's thoughts veered unwillingly back to Eve Mason, and the present. She had
hair that felt like Syl's, and something else about her—
perhaps her pathetic, foolish, useless defiance—that
nagged at his mind. She had made him want to put her
down, to defeat her and degrade her, to show the stupid
bitch that after all she wasn't really different from Francie. It continued to irk him that he hadn't succeeded.
And he wasn't used to regretting anything he did, either,
except for Syl. . . .

Brant lay awake thinking a long time before he was
ready to sleep, and then he fell asleep peacefully and
quickly, his mind emptied of thought, decisions made.

CHAPTER
TWENTY-THREE

EVE WALKED INTO THE ROOM very slowly, her feet dragging, and from his place near the window, where he still stood looking out, David swung around to face her.

"For God's sake, do you know it's *five* in the morning? Who was the guy who brought you home? You were supposed to find *Francie*—that's why I've been sitting up here the whole goddam night while you partied. Eve—" As she moved slowly forward into the light, he really saw her at last, and she heard his indrawn breath. "God, you look terrible! Will you tell me what the hell *happened?*"

She was suddenly too tired to stand, almost too tired to talk. Why didn't he just take her in his arms and exorcise all the evil spirits, instead of acting as if she were on the witness stand? Why didn't he?

She went to him, stumbling, half-running, and pressed her body against his.

"David—oh, David, please! Just hold me. Just hold me, please!"

She waited for his arms to go around her, but instead, something in the rigidity of his body communicated itself to her, and very slowly she raised her head to meet his eyes.

"David?"

He could feel her body trembling against his, and

tried to keep his voice level. What was the matter with her? What had she done this time?

"Eve, I have to know what happened. What are you trying to hide? Let's start with Francie, my sister. Was she there? And who in hell was the guy in the Mercedes?"

She moved away from him. He hadn't put his arms about her. She felt better, stronger, standing alone. She turned her face away from him so she couldn't see his cold, accusing eyes, and clung with both hands to the back of a chair for support.

"Eve!" He said again, more impatiently this time.

"All right, David. I'm trying to—to put things together so I don't sound too incoherent. Francie was there, but she wouldn't listen to me, although I tried to— She went away in the end, with a man they called Derek. They—he told me he's a psychiatrist. I tried to stop them, but he—wouldn't let me. He—"

"You're not making sense, Eve! He—who's *he*? The man in the car?"

"Yes! Oh, God, I *told* you he was dangerous, I told you! And then I forgot to remember— Brant Newcomb. Your client. He sent Francie to New Mexico with Derek. I don't think she wanted to go in the end, but he gave them money and sent her away. You know what? He auctioned her off. He really did. That's the kind of man he is; only he's worse!"

"This is—your story sounds impossible, Eve! Are you sure you were sober?"

"Sober? Yes, I was sober! Until he put something in the drink he gave me that was supposed to make me stoned out of my head like everyone else, only it didn't. No—don't interrupt me now, David. I have to go on talking, or I could never tell you—" Her voice dropped to a kind of breath-torn whisper, but she turned her head and looked at him now, and he saw the pupils of her eyes. Yes, she *had* taken something. David opened his mouth to say something to her and closed it again.

"Well, you want to know, huh? You're sure you want to know what he did to me, David? He took me into his game room—that's what he calls it—it has mirrors and lights everywhere and an enormous bed—and he—he was like an animal. He was high on something, too, I guess. He tore my clothes off, and he hurt me when I fought him, and then—then everyone else joined in. *I* was the party, David. There was nothing I could do to stop them, although I struggled and fought. They did everything they wanted to do with me, and they took pictures, and he said if I tried to *do* anything about it, he'd—*no!* I don't really want to talk about it; I don't want to think about that girl in the mirrors being me, *me!*"

She was gulping in deep breaths of air as if talking had exhausted her. David's voice shook, too, but she couldn't tell whether it was from shock or anger.

"My God, everything you've told me sounds like part of some crazy trip—some coke nightmare. How can you expect me to believe any of it? I've heard some stories about Newcomb, but dammit, the man isn't a *maniac*. Why should he want to rape you when there are a thousand other women he can *buy* with all his fucking money? And Francie—what about Francie? What *really* happened, Eve?"

"I don't *know*—I told you that, didn't I? And I'm not trying to explain his motives, I'm just telling you what did happen, damn you! It *happened*—I just wish I *had* dreamed it!"

She shrieked the words at him, and he stepped backward. Had the drug she had obviously taken maddened her? He'd never seen her like this before.

"I'm sorry Eve." He tried to keep his voice controlled and reasonable. He was hardly in the mood for an hysterical scene after an all-night vigil, and she seemed determined to make one. "I just find it difficult to be-

lieve that a man like Brant Newcomb, as filthy rich as
he is, and a good-looking bastard into the bargain—
why he'd want to rape you. Why you in particular?
And you, why would you—" He stopped, wondering if
he was going too far, especially in the state she was in.

Eve had begun to giggle hysterically, one hand up to
her mouth.

"Why didn't you finish saying it, David? Why would
I resist? Oh, but that's funny! But I did try to fight them,
you know, and mostly because of *you*, because I thought
I was your girl, I thought you—but you really believe
deep down that I'm some kind of a tramp, don't you?
You think I'm easy, that I'd do it with just anyone—
as *you* would. And you know what? I should have given
in—maybe they wouldn't have kept on hurting me,
then. Don't you see how *funny* it is? He offered me
money the first time we met; he said I could name my
price. And just a little while ago, he said he was going
to send me a check. Does that make me a whore, David?
You'd like to think of me that way, wouldn't you? It'd
salve your conscience, I guess. Wait—you still don't
believe, do you? I'll show you what they did to me.
Take a good look, David darling. It might even turn
you on. Look here—*look* at me, damn you!"

She began tearing at the buttons of her coat, clawing
them loose so that they popped free and rolled all over
the room. Then she tore the coat off herself and he saw
the bruises that covered her body—that once-beautiful
body he knew too damned well. He stared, horrified—
and fascinated in spite of himself.

"Dear God, what—but Eve—it couldn't have happened. It doesn't make *sense*, dammit, that Newcomb
should have raped you and then invited everyone else
at the party to join in. No, it's crazy!"

"But it happened. It did! It did!" She laughed again,
foolishly. "Look at your face; you should see yourself
watching me. Do you like what you see? Would you like

to fuck me, too? One more wouldn't make much difference, would it, and right now I'm too beat to fight."

Her laughter turned suddenly into sobs, and she slid
to the floor unexpectedly, crouching, hiding away from
his eyes behind the hanging curtain of her hair—kneeling there in a caricatured attitude of grief and peni-
tance.

Something in the way she knelt there sobbing got
through to him, and he took a step toward her.

"Eve, I'm just trying to make sense of all this. Quite
apart from Francie, and whatever you say happened to
her, why did you let Newcomb bring you back here
after what he'd done?"

"Stop talking like a lawyer, damn you, David! Don't
you understand? I was *afraid!* Don't you see that? He's
a—a very frightening man, so cold, so completely evil—
what else could I do?"

"He kissed you goodnight, and you let him. Don't
bother to deny it, because I *saw* through the window,
dammit! I was watching, waiting for you. . . ."

"I couldn't stop him, David. He's so damned strong,
and I'm so tired. And I came in here looking for refuge,
looking for *something* from you, and you *judge* me instead. You don't *want* to believe me, do you? You used
me, and now that I've failed, you'd like an excuse to be
rid of me. Because deep down you really think I'm cheap
—you always did think that. I was good enough to
screw but not good enough to marry."

"And that's all *you* ever wanted, wasn't it? Marriage,
a guy to show off to your friends, a meal ticket—"

"That's not fair; that wasn't it at all, and you know it!
You always twist my words around and try to make
them into something else; you'd like to keep me crawling to you, apologizing, explaining—"

"Goddammit, I deserve *some* rational explanation,
don't you think? You went to this party to find Francie,
and you come back at five in the morning with some

wild tale about being gang-raped—how can I tell what to believe? I know all about the other men you've had, "the new morality," you called it—what's okay for a man should be okay for a woman, too, and what's wrong with an occasional screw on the side, anyhow? Then, suddenly, I'm supposed to believe that you've changed your viewpoint, that you tried to fight off God knows how many guys just because you're my girl. Well, how do you account for continuing to see Peter while you were still supposed to be my girl? Christ, Eve—"

"Shut up, shut up! I can't listen to any more. I can't— I don't want to believe this is you, and this is how you really think about me and that in spite of it I let you *use* me. And because I did, you think I'd let all those people use me, too—it wasn't all guys, there were women, too, and oh, I can see your face change again! You really think I'm shit, don't you? And I am—God, yes, I'm shit and even less than that, I'm *nothing* because that's what you made me into and I let you—"

"You're not even coherent any longer, Eve. Perhaps I'd better leave now and talk to you again tomorrow, later—"

"Oh, no, you won't, David. There'll be no later, no tomorrow. I never want to talk to you or listen to you again. Get out, just get out quickly, will you please?"

"You're hysterical, you don't know—"

"Oh, yes, I do know! At last, David, at last I know where I really stand with you, and I should have seen it a long time ago, only I— Goddam you, get out! Get out of here, or I'll start to scream and I won't be able to stop!"

She looked up at him with her face ravaged and contorted and suddenly ugly now, with a big purple bruise showing darkly against her cheekbone.

She saw the way he hesitated, and read the irresolution in his eyes, and she hated him for it and for his pettiness and weakness, and most of all she hated her own weakness for him. He didn't really believe she *meant* it this time; he was still waiting for her to take the words back, crawl to him for understanding. The finality of it, the futility of her pleading for his sympathy and pity hit her like a sudden blow, and she started to whimper with pain and grief.

"You—you self-righteous bastard! What are you waiting for? What am I supposed to do? Would you like me to grovel at your feet, David? To tell you I did what I didn't do?"

There was a note of rising hysteria in her voice that both frightened and unnerved him, and he moved swiftly, grabbing his overcoat from off the couch, skirting her huddled figure.

At the door he turned.

"I'm sorry I asked you to go to the damned party, and I'm sorry if you feel I've let you down, Eve. Perhaps tomorrow—"

"Get *out,* damn you!" She screamed it at him, and he left quickly, the door slamming behind him.

And after David—silence. Only her own tearing sobs that threatened to rip her chest apart. She lay flat on the floor, fists pounding at the rug while she cried and cried until she was drained of emotion. After some time, she managed to pull herself onto her feet, shaking and sick with reaction.

Nothing mattered now in the face of David's rejection. Nothing that had happened to her counted against David's betrayal. She had disgusted him, and disgusted herself even more. God, he had even managed to forget his own sister in his need to accuse her and show how little he thought of her. If he had been any kind of a man, it would have been Brant Newcomb he'd have gone after, no matter what the consequences.

Eve closed her eyes and opened them again with a

shudder, seeing once more the blank eyes and obscene, grinning faces as they had looked down at her body earlier. And David's face just a little while ago—so closed against her.

She walked slowly into the bathroom, catching a glimpse of herself in the full-length mirror as she passed it.

It was like seeing someone else—just a vacant face, a body that had been stripped of its humanity along with the clothes they'd torn off her.

She stepped under the shower and let the water soak her. Even her hair, her eyes, were drenched and streaming. Automatically she reached for the shampoo and began to wash her hair carefully. Thank God for reflex action. It was better to be all reflexes than to feel— to do everything like a robot, without a mind, without thoughts that could pursue and tear at her like furies. And she even thought casually that it would be easy to die this way, but far too much trouble right now.

I'm too tired; it's too late. Too late to undo anything or do it over again. I should have a tape recorder, so I could talk myself into sleep. Peter, you should be here now; here I am, a guinea pig.

Toweling herself dry, Eve watched herself in the mirror, seeing her body emerge mistily as the steam began to edge backward. The bruises looked as if they had been painted on, clumsily and carelessly—finger-paints! It was weird to be able to look at your own body this way and to feel as if you didn't belong to it. She wanted to laugh, but laughter would not come. There were not even sobs left in her now—nothing!

Eve dropped the towel and walked into her bedroom, lay back on the bed. Without any real curiosity, she wondered what would happen now. Suddenly, the tiredness welled up in her, enveloping her like a shroud. She closed her eyes and let it take her without a struggle.

CHAPTER
TWENTY-FOUR

THE TELEPHONE WENT OFF in her ear, ringing insistently, forcing Eve up out of a deep and frightening dream. She thought it was the alarm on her clock at first; she reached out for it with an arm that felt like lead, knocking it over. The ringing went on, and suddenly habit made her think, "David?" She felt the familiar, the unwanted quickening of excitement making her catch her breath.

Still half-asleep, Eve cradled the green trimline against her face, lying on her side.

A voice said warmly and softly in her ear, "How *are* you, Eve baby? Did you have a nice sleep and get all rested? Because I have some new friends coming in from out of town—you haven't met *them* yet, but they think they'd like to meet you. Why don't I pick you up around eight? And this time you won't play hard to get, will you, sweetheart?"

She was cold—suddenly so icy cold that she felt the telephone had frozen to her ear. She swallowed, but her throat was dry and no words emerged.

"Eve? You wouldn't try to hang up on old Jer, would you, sweetheart? Listen, I've just been telling Brant that I know you're really a very sensible girl; and you photograph so *well*, too. I just feel bad that you didn't have any fun last night—tonight will be different, I promise. And there'll be quite a bit of money in it for you if you cooperate."

She found her voice at last, but there was no emotion left in it. It was cold, like the rest of her—cold and dead-sounding.

"Is your friend Brant listening on the extension? I hope he is, because I want him to hear this, too. You see, I don't give a damn what you two do with those pictures, and I'm sure Brant can find better uses for his money. Buy yourselves some other girls to play your sick games with. And just remember, blackmail is a felony and so is rape—I'm sure your damn pictures will show I wasn't willing. *Don't* bother calling again, will you? I'm late for an appointment with my attorney."

She put the telephone down, holding it away from her as if it could sting, and found that she was shaking so hard she had to lie there for a while, pressing her hands against her forehead as if to push her thoughts inside—keep them from tumbling out to overwhelm her.

Last night—God, it was already late afternoon! She had actually slept, managing to blank out horror and shock from her mind, maybe because she'd thought that nothing worse could happen to her than had already happened. But this was worse. Had they been testing her? Or did Brant Newcomb really think she'd be willing to play the whore for him and his friends? And there had been David, *thinking* her one. Not believing her. If it had been *David* who had called . . .

The telephone began to ring spitefully again, and with a mindless, vicious motion, Eve yanked the cord out of the wall jack. Let them all go whistle up the wind. David, too; she couldn't care any longer; even if there was a hurt place where love had been before, he'd taken that from her, too. Right now the only feeling left in her was a cold, deadly hate for Brant Newcomb. She wanted to *get* him, to show the world what he was, he and his friends with the famous names—sick, perverted animals, all of them! The hell with the pictures, she'd—she'd do a news story, an exposé. He couldn't stop her. And if it was too hot for television coverage, she'd sell the story to the *Record*.

"Eve baby, you can't do it. You'd have to be crazy to try, because all you'd end up doing would be to destroy yourself, don't you see that?"

Marti had been horrified, sympathetic, full of fury. But Marti was also pragmatic, pointing out to Eve just how *impossible* it would be to try to "get" Brant Newcomb.

"But you don't understand!" Eve said wildly. "If—if everyone he hurts or brings down the way he did me says the same thing—don't you see? It's like women who don't report rape because they're scared of the scandal. So some bastard gets away with it, to try again. Marti, I can't let *him* get away with it! He hurt *you*, remember? And there was Francie—what he did with Francie, who isn't even eighteen yet—"

"Think David will like his kid sister's name plastered all over the newspapers? Or yours, and his connection with you? Christ, Eve, nobody knows better than I what a bastard Brant Newcomb is—I warned you about him, remember? And if you tried to get your story heard out in the open, he'd find a way to stop you. It would be the word of everyone else there, against yours. He'd accuse *you* of trying to blackmail *him*. Shit—I don't mean to scare you, Eve, but he might do even worse than that; and no, I'm not being melodramatic, either. Brant possesses neither scruples or conscience—haven't you found that out for yourself?"

"But—"

Marti's voice softened; she put her hand on Eve's shaking shoulder.

"Look, honey, I *know* what you're feeling. Think I didn't feel the same way? And I'll tell you what—I feel madder at that prick David for sending you there than I—"

They both heard the buzzer at the door and stiffened.

"*I'll* get it," Marti said brusquely. "You just sit there and think over what I've been saying, will you?"

Eve got up and fixed herself a drink while Marti went to the door. She couldn't stop her hands from shaking, and she poured Scotch all over the top of the bar. Marti was wrong, she knew. And then, not daring to look around, she thought sickly, Not David, please! I couldn't face him again, not so soon. . . .

It wasn't David, though. It was a messenger, a young man in a brown uniform.

"Personal, for a Miss Eve Mason."

Marti's voice: "Just a minute."

She came back to Eve, holding a long white envelope. Thick paper. Linen finish. Not stopping to think, Eve tore it open. A check fluttered out onto the rug. There was a note with it, and she read it disbelievingly while Marti was saying, "If you'll sign for it, I can— Eve?"

Sorry you couldn't make it this evening. The check is to take care of last night. Maybe another time?

There was no signature on the note, but she recognized the name on the check.

"Wait," Eve said, and from somewhere inside herself, hate and fury hardened her voice. She tore the note and the check, over and over, until the paper shredded in her hands, and then handed the untidy scraps to the gaping man.

"Give him this—the man who sent you. And there's no message."

A dramatic, satisfying gesture, but where would it get

her? Where would anything she had planned to do and still wanted to do get her in the end? Even Marti wouldn't understand. Marti kept arguing with her, pointing out consequences with ruthless logic. And giving her advice she didn't want to hear.

"Go back to work. Tell them you were in an automobile accident and banged up your face. Why don't you call your shrink friend and ask him to prescribe a tranquilizer for you? Eve, you've got to try to put what happened out of your mind."

Eve felt as if her head were bursting. Hate and frustration joggled against despair while she kept saying doggedly, "But I must—don't you see that I must do *something?*" until Marti used the last, unanswerable argument.

"All right. You want to do something about it? Call David. He's an attorney, isn't he? And God knows he owes you some free advice, after all he—well, *call* him! See what he has to say."

Eve looked up at Marti, standing over her, and began to cry helplessly, hopelessly.

"Oh, God," she said, hearing the defeat in her own voice. "Oh, *God!* What am I going to do?"

But in the end it was all decided for her. Her future, and her chance to break with the past.

Just a week later, Eve found herself on a plane bound for New York, her mind still reeling. Even when they were halfway across the continent, she kept staring sightlessly at the same page she'd turned to in *Mainliner* magazine, listening to piped-in music through her headset while she tried to reconstruct how it had happened. The sheer, pure luck of it—the chance she had dreamed about and waited for without quite realizing it. She hadn't really had time to think too much during the past few hectic days, spent in packing and last-minute arrangements. Perhaps because she hadn't *wanted* to think.

Now—God, if she could only relax! Be calm, remember Peter's last bit of free advice, handed out when he'd seen her off at the airport.

"You're a lucky girl, Eve. Just try to look *forward* from now on, luv. And—you'll put me on your show, won't you, when I get that book of mine published?"

Marti had helped her pack, but she'd had to fly down to LA "to talk to a man about a movie, darling." Did that mean that Marti was finally over Stella?

Stella, who'd been responsible for her first meeting David— Forget David! He was a part of the past, too. She'd left her telephone unplugged all of last week, and he hadn't come over. So that was that. She was better off remembering that other telephone call to the studio, which had everyone wildly excited for her. But at first, when Ernest Meckel had called her into his office, she'd wondered sickly if he'd *heard* something, if he were going to fire her.

"Sit down, babe." His face had been red with suppressed excitement. "You'll need to be sitting down when you hear what I just heard."

She'd almost fainted. It couldn't be true. It was a cruel joke, a hoax.

But Ernie was saying, "I have the official letter right here, signed by the president, no less. You know that since Babs Barrie left the 'Going On' show they've been looking around for a replacement, huh? Someone they'll groom to be the next Barbara Walters? Well, sweetheart, someone caught *our* show and thought you'd do just great! Of course we'll be damn sorry to lose you, but—"

A telephone call from one of the vice-presidents of the network had confirmed it, though. They wanted her for "Going On This Morning," and they wanted her right away. Could she leave within the week?

That was why Eve hadn't had time to think, and why she was traveling—first class, no less—to New York.

She put her seat back, leaned her head against the headrest, and closed her eyes, refusing the drink that the flight attendant offered her. Two more hours, and they'd be landing at Kennedy Airport. There'd be a limousine to meet her and take her to her suite at the Plaza Hotel. A cocktail party two hours later, where she'd meet everybody.

And for the first time, Eve began to feel that it was true, it was all really happening and not some fantasy she'd dreamed up. New York, new life—here I come!

CHAPTER
TWENTY-FIVE

BY THE END OF THE WEEK, Eve felt weak from a combination of exhaustion and excitement. She'd had to have vitamin B$_{12}$ shots to keep her going.

She'd had experience, sure; but San Francisco, the tiny, bare studio at KNXT hadn't really prepared her for New York and its racing pace. From the moment she'd walked into the big gray building on her first morning, it was as if she'd been chained to a treadmill and couldn't get off. Photographs, interviews, publicity —and learning in between; meeting people and encountering their curious, measuring eyes. Learning to get up at 2:00 A.M. every morning to be rushed to the studio. Just observing everything that went on at first, getting the feel of it. Then a couple of days of actually sitting in on the show itself, making ad lib conversation with Randall Thomas, whom she was still a little bit in awe of. Her evenings were equally busy. A few hours' sleep with the sun still shining outside the windows of her hotel suite, and more parties to go to—she had to meet everyone and be charming to everyone. Being a person wasn't enough. They were going to turn her into a Personality.

Eve called Marti—or had Marti called her? She couldn't remember.

"How's everything going? You're a big celebrity already, you know that? The *Record* gave you a great write-up. And KNXT is doing reruns of some of your earlier shows, even the 'Our Girl on Location' interviews you used to do. Are you coming back to pick up your stuff or staying on?"

"I don't know!" Absently, Eve had started to massage her temples to ward off a headache she felt coming on. "My God, I haven't even had time to *ask*, you know? I'm—at least I haven't had time to think, which is good." She heard Marti's patient sigh and hurried on, "What happened with the picture deal in LA? Did you—"

"I told them I'd think about it—very seriously." Marti's voice sounded cautious, and Eve wondered if Stella had anything to do with her hesitation. Poor Marti!

Marti was saying, "Shit, I really think I'm going to do it in the end, why not? And if you're going to be moving out— Anyhow, I have a month or so in which to make up my mind while they're raising the bread for the production. I'll let you know—you might give us some publicity!"

"Did—were there—" Damn her own weakness!

"No calls, baby. He might have tried, but I just unplugged your telephone. And by now he knows the big news, I'll bet."

After she had hung up, Eve could feel her hands shaking. Oh, God, would she ever be completely over David? She was crazy-stupid to think about him at all, after the things he'd said—his rejection of her when she'd needed him most. She could never go back to him again.

She stood in front of the mirror and started putting on her makeup. She had to hurry. The limo would be waiting downstairs for her in exactly fifteen minutes. Her face stared back at her. She practiced smiling, and turned the smile into a grimace of self-disgust. She was turning into a commodity, that was what. Plastic doll image of the successful woman, smiling, intelligent, witty, never at a loss for words. They liked the way she wrote her copy; they liked the way she could ad-lib easily. She had *made* it—why wasn't she happy?

"That's a good question." Randall Thomas looked at her rather owlishly over his famous hornrims. They had gone to see *Chorus Line*, had had dinner at the Four Seasons with the rest of the crowd. Eve had been surprised when Randall suggested they might have a drink at the Oak Bar before she went up to bed—just the two of them. He'd been *nice* to her all these days, of course, but rather aloof, weighing. Now, after three drinks, he seemed relaxed and friendly, asking her questions about herself. She felt she'd like to have him as a friend.

He put his cigarette out, still watching her, and shrugged. "I suppose we all ask ourselves that. We all work our asses off to get what we want and where we want to be, and then suddenly—no more goals to strive for? It's an empty feeling in the beginning, but then you learn, as *you* will learn, my dear Eve, that you have to keep fighting and striving to stay on top. You have to keep on being good, hoping you're better than the competition, and praying like hell that the Nielsens keep you where you are. Scared?"

Eve sipped her drink. "I don't know. Maybe it's partly that—I really haven't had *time* to think about it yet. I want to be good, I don't want to fail, and still—sometimes I feel like two different people. The outside me and the inside me. Will I have time for a personal life?" You really screwed *that* life up good, didn't you? her mind laughed back at her.

Randall laughed shortly. "Sure, when you're not being a public person! But you ought to know by now that doesn't leave too much time for yourself. It's part of the package. You going to accept the job?"

His sudden question took her by surprise. Of course she was. She had to, to prove— And then he answered his own question.

"Of course you are. You'd be stupid not to, and you're not a stupid woman. You're going to be great. And you're going to have plenty of offers to fill up the times when you're not busy working." He lifted his glass to her. "You're a beautiful woman, and you'll have every guy in town chasing after you, especially since you're not taken yet. You're not, are you?"

Eve was booked on the noon flight back to San Francisco the next day, which was Saturday. They'd given her two weeks to make up her mind, although she, along with everyone else, took it as a foregone conclusion that she'd be joining the "Going On" show by the beginning of the following month. Just a matter of going over her contracts with her agent and an attorney.

This was her last night in New York for a while, and she'd really begun to *like* Randall. So why not? Why lie in that big bed alone again with her old dreams and new nightmares?

Randall as a lover was unexpected. Very different from the polite, friendly man she'd found so easy to talk to. He was—he was almost businesslike, she thought with vague surprise, after he'd first surprised her by carrying her to bed soon after he'd locked the door behind them.

"I lift weights at the gym," he explained to her almost proudly. "Only way to keep in shape, with all that sitting around." But after that, he didn't talk much.

He didn't try to undress her but started quickly to take his clothes off, obviously expecting her to do the same. She was slower than he, and he stood and watched her as if fascinated by her body.

She thought, Thank God all the bruises have gone; I wonder what he'd have thought— And then she lay back on the bed and watched him come toward her.

To her surprise he started to go down on her very efficiently and expertly. Eve made protesting murmurs at first, but her protests were only halfhearted and he ignored them, concentrating on what he was doing. She began to breathe faster, to move her hips involuntarily, and tried to stifle tiny whimpers with the back of her hand.

"Do you like that?" His tongue stabbed at her clitoris. "Tell me what else you like," he asked her politely.

"I—I don't know—don't stop now. Do whatever you want."

"Did you come yet?"

"Not—not yet . . ."

His mouth attacked her again, his tongue digging deeply into her, his fingers pressing down, down until she climaxed shudderingly and satisfyingly. And then he climbed on top of her and screwed her as efficiently as he had gone down on her a few moments before.

"You're so beautiful, so natural in the way you let go," he whispered to her. "You're quite a woman, Eve."

He put one hand under her, and she felt his finger pressing up, probing into her— She cried out, jerking up against him.

"Do you like that, then?"

"No—yes—I'm not sure!"

She hadn't had this happen to her before; against her will, she heard herself cry out again, felt her excitement rising to meet his.

Suddenly he withdrew himself, pulling and lifting her body so that she lay with her own thighs pressed against her breasts, her legs over his heavily muscled shoulders. And now that he had her helpless, he began to fuck her in the ass, and there was nothing she could do about it except drum her legs ineffectually against his back.

After the initial shock of his entrance and the pain, however, she suddenly found the new sensation was wildly pleasurable, especially when he put two fingers into her vagina at the same time.

He kept watching her while she moaned and thrashed about, waiting for her orgasm; and when it came, he

pumped himself into her at last, moving very fast and
hard, then leaning on her so heavily that her doubled-up
legs hurt her breasts and she cried out with pain. With
a grunt of apology he pulled himself out of her, hurting
her again—leaving her sore and throbbing but *satisfied*
all the same.

Randall left at seven in the morning, considerately
waking her up with the warning that she mustn't miss
her flight. He kissed her, patting her face, and told her
again that she was really a wonderful woman, she
mustn't ever change, and he looked forward to seeing
her again as soon as she got back.

Eve soaked in the bathtub afterward, wondering how
it had happened. My God, she thought crazily, my
mother watches him every morning—I wonder how
she'd react if she knew. . . . Eve started to giggle. After
all, she *had* enjoyed it.

CHAPTER
TWENTY-SIX

EVE BARELY MADE IT to Kennedy in time for her flight.
The traffic was murder all the way—there was a four-
car pileup that slowed them down even worse. She
supposed she was fortunate that the man at the ticket
counter recognized her (all the recent publicity paying
off when she needed it most!) and rushed her through,
with a conspiratorial smile. They were boarding when
she reached the gate, breathless from running.

She'd made it with five minutes to spare. Eve glanced
at her watch, fastened her seatbelt, and leaned back
with a sigh. She turned down the flight attendant's offer
of champagne, closing her eyes. Suddenly, all the tiredness of the past week seemed to catch up with her, and
she was unutterably weary, needing only to sleep all the
way back to San Francisco. Five hours. She hadn't been
able to reach Marti before she'd left, so she'd sent a
telegram. But if Marti wasn't at the airport, she'd get a
taxi—she thought wryly that it was a come-down after
the limousine treatment she'd become used to without
even thinking about it. Back to reality for a couple of
weeks, and she needed it. Cinderella Girl—she forgot
which columnist had called her that.

Don't think—relax. She tried the Yoga breathing,
keeping her eyes closed, but her mind kept clicking like
a computer, planning ahead, measuring out her time.

She had to go back home, spend some time with Mom and the kids. Explain how suddenly everything had happened. That she'd still be at the other end of a telephone if they needed her. Before then she'd have to pack, arrange for some of her stuff to be shipped—why didn't it seem *real* yet? Was she ready for such a drastic change in her life, or would it be a change after all? Would there be someone else to replace David? Randall . . . Somehow the night she'd spent with him didn't seem quite real, either.

Eve wondered vaguely why they hadn't taken off yet. This particular flight seemed a popular one—even first class was full, except for the seat next to hers. She had a window. 3A. Good. Her thoughts became hazy and disjointed as she forced herself to relax. She heard someone else behind her ask querulously the same question she'd been thinking.

"We're late taking off, aren't we? Hope there's not going to be a delay at the other end—I have an important meeting to get to."

"We'll be arriving right on schedule, sir. Traffic's been delayed by the fog this morning. We have to wait our turn."

Eve didn't really care. God, I'm tired! she thought. Maybe Peter would give her a vitamin shot when she got back; the one she'd had three days ago had really helped. In her half-asleep, half-awake state, the title of an old song popped into her mind. "Is That All There Is?" Crazy, not knowing what she really wanted—not even now, when everything had been offered to her on a platter.

She was hardly aware of the slight stir as a late passenger arrived. Soft voices of the flight attendants, hovering. Someone settled in beside her; she heard the click of the seatbelt and couldn't be bothered to open her eyes. She heard the heavy door thud, and soon after the sound of the engines screaming to a crescendo as the

big DC-10 started to move. At last! That ought to keep
the fussy guy behind her happy. . . .

"Would you care for a drink? Sir? Miss?"

"Scotch, please. On the rocks, for me. With soda for
Miss Mason, if I remember right."

Eve had to force herself awake, coming out of a
nebulous nightmare in which she heard Brant Newcomb's mocking voice. "Have a drink, doll. And after
that, we're going to talk, aren't we?"

All she had to do to escape from a bad dream was to
wake up—and then she did.

"Hi, Eve."

She couldn't speak. She felt literally frozen, caught on
fast film, all motion stilled. She felt the faint hum and
vibration of the jet engines, heard the buzz of conversation around her. Normal. Think normal; then she'd wake
up all over again. . . .

"Oh, *no!* Not you!"

Sunlight coming in through the small window caught
in his bright-gold hair, reflected off the blue glaze of his
eyes. She made an involuntary movement of escape and
was trapped by her seatbelt.

"Did you enjoy New York?" The smiling flight attendant set their drinks on the armrest between them,
and he smiled at her.

"Thanks."

"This can't be happening," Eve said aloud. "I won't
sit here beside you."

"There isn't another seat available, I'm afraid," he
pointed out politely. "And since you've managed to be
sensible so far, I wouldn't spoil it all by making a scene,
Eve. It wouldn't be good for your image."

She sucked in her breath, trying to keep herself from
shaking. Brant Newcomb. But even he, Devil or not,
couldn't do anything to her *here*. She mustn't let him
see her unreasoning fear. Be cool, Eve.

"What are you doing here? I don't want to talk to you."

He shrugged, although his eyes, bright blue like a glacial mountain lake, seemed to pin her back in her seat.

"That's okay. But I wanted to talk to you."

"I don't—"

"You'll listen, though." He cut her off as though she hadn't spoken. "I made sure of that. So why don't you settle back like a good girl?"

She shuddered, remembering.

Stop fighting it, Eve. Give in and enjoy....

God, he was a madman. Fury struggled with primitive terror. What did he want with her this time? What had he meant by "I made sure of that"?

In spite of herself, Eve's voice dropped to a sharp whisper.

"I don't know what you want with me *this* time, Brant Newcomb! And I don't care! I don't give a damn about your threats, either—I told your friend Jerry."

"Shit, I know what you told Jerry. And when you sent my check back, I got your message loud and clear, doll. That's not what I wanted to talk to you about. No bribes, no threats. And by the way, in case you were worrying, I burned all that film. Negatives, prints, everything. Goddammit, will you sit still? You almost spilled your drink."

"I—you—" She was stuttering and couldn't help it. Her eyes blazed into his. "Whatever you're up to this time, I'm not buying, do you hear?"

He went on as if he hadn't heard her, speaking quietly and concisely, as if he were reading from a list. "If you're still concerned about Francie, she's okay. As I told you that night, Derek, in spite of the way he looks and dresses sometimes, is a psychiatrist. He specializes in disturbed adolescents. And Francie's a lot better off

now than she was before—or would have been, let
loose."

"Why are you telling me all this? Why bother to
explain anything to me?"

"Hell, I don't really know. Except that I thought I
ought to get everything cleared up before I asked you
to marry me."

She hadn't heard right, of course. Either that or she
really was going crazy. *He* was, obviously. Or else he
was playing one of his sick games with her, hoping to—
hoping to *what?*

She was silent, staring at him, and he smiled mirthlessly.

"Look, Eve, I haven't ever proposed to a woman
before. I guess it's one of the few things I haven't experienced. But I mean it for real."

"You can't!" She couldn't take her eyes off his face,
feeling the blood drain from hers. "You can't think—"

Why didn't she wake up? Why didn't the flight attendant come back? Brant Newcomb—*Brant Newcomb*
was asking her—no, he was telling her he wanted to
marry her, and it was all some kind of a joke, a game. . . .

He picked up his glass and drained it, still watching
her. She saw him all over again as she had seen him
first—a too-handsome, coldly arrogant stranger. A
dangerous stranger. She didn't want to remember the
last time she had seen him.

"I suppose you want reasons," he was saying formally.
"And I have a couple I can put into words, I guess.
You're the only woman I've ever known who kept on
fighting and wouldn't let herself be bought off afterward. And then—there's the way Francie said you were
with Lisa."

"*Lisa?* But how—I don't understand." She was mouth-
ing words, any words. So much for ad libs.

"Francie didn't like you—you knew that, didn't you?
But she did have a grudging kind of admiration for the

way you drew her little sister out of her shell. She admitted you'd probably make a good mother, even if she didn't want you for *hers*."

"You—you seem to know a lot about me, but that's still no reason—"

"Will you just listen to me for a few moments longer, Eve? You're right, I do know a lot about you because I made it my business to find out. You're a bloody Puritan in some ways, and yet you like to fuck, but only when you're ready and when *you* want it—and that night you wouldn't give in, would you, you stubborn bitch? You made us take it, and even I had a rotten taste in my mouth afterward, when the goddam drug wore off. Shit, I don't know why, Eve. Maybe you've made me curious and I want to find out more about you. Or maybe it's just because I'm suddenly so sick and tired of the whole phony, sick routine—the endless, pointless rat race—going through the motions, one predictable move after another, and for what? Hell, maybe I want to be saved—my immortal soul, remember?"

His laugh was wry and short and not really laughter at all, and through all he'd said she could do nothing but sit there helplessly, no longer knowing what to say and feeling how damned *unreal* this all was. And without her realizing it, her eyes had dropped to his hands, one still holding the empty glass—the glinting gold hairs on the backs of them, the same strong, capable-looking hands that had hurt her and corrupted her body. How could she trust him now or believe anything he said?

"I—I don't really believe this is happening," she stammered at last, stumbling over the words. "I mean— I keep looking for the *real* explanation—for some kind of trickery. What *is* it, Brant? Do you need a front, is that it?"

"Damn you, no! That's too facile, Eve. You wouldn't

know it, but when I say something, I usually mean it.
I haven't really thought about marriage before, and I
never thought I'd want to try it, either. But suddenly—
it's the one trip I've never been on, Eve. And it's not
just that. I'm sick of the life I lead, my so-called friends
and hangers-on, and the searching, always searching
for new kicks, and the boredom afterward when they're
not new anymore. Having everything you want is really
having nothing, baby. Stick around the swinging scene
and you'll find out, too, and be just like everyone else.
They'll grind you down and screw you to death, every
way there is, and in the end you won't be anything, not
even yourself."

"*You've* been there, I haven't. . . ." The words seemed
to escape her.

"Not yet. Do you want to? You can take that job in
New York and find out. Have your affair with Randall
Thomas, play it to a finish, and move on to someone
else. Play the celebrity circuit, fuck on the side, and
shit—you'll stop fighting, won't you? You'll go to a lot
of parties like mine and pretend you're enjoying them.
It's your choice, baby. What I'm asking you to think
about is the whole, old-fashioned bit, Eve. Marriage,
kids, no other women for me and no other men for you.
And if you're still afraid that I'm going to try to destroy
you, I'll put half my money in your name the day we
marry—Christ, you can have all of it if you'll have my
children. *Fuck* the money, anyhow!"

"I—I still don't seem to understand what you're saying, Brant!" Eve squeezed her hands together in her lap,
wondering why she was talking to him at all.

"Don't you? What I'm saying is, what can we lose?
Everything's a gamble, but if we can start out with no
illusions, being honest with each other—hell, who
knows?"

For the first time he touched her, putting his hands
over hers to still their nervous, twisting motion.

"Eve, no swinging parties, no 'old friends,' no drugs.
I promise you that. They gave you two weeks, didn't
they? Stay with me. Find out. I won't try to coerce you,
and I won't hurt you. You can walk out anytime you
want to."

"You—my God, you're crazy! You're the rudest, most
impossible, most arrogant man I've ever—"

Incredibly, he smiled at her with laugh crinkles
showing around his eyes, and his hands squeezed hers.

"That's a feeling, and better than indifference, I guess.
Maybe I can persuade you to change your mind. And
if not, you're free to chicken out anytime you feel like
it."

"*Chicken* out! My God, you leave me speechless,
you—"

"So stay speechless, my sweet. Finish your drink. Go
back to sleep if you want to. Just think about it. I have
a car waiting at the airport, and when we land, I'm
going to take your arm and lead you off the plane. I'll
drop you off wherever you decide to go—your choice."

He released her hand, smiling almost mockingly at
her before he leaned back in the seat. And that was
when, for the first time, Eve realized that he really
meant it—all the crazy, incredible things he'd said to
her, making her listen against her will.

What was even more incredible, and positively in-
furiating, was that right afterward Brant had the added
effrontery to plug in his headset, adjusting the earphones
with careful concentration, while she sat there literally
dumbstruck and seething inside; and *then* he pretended
he was trying to sleep while she was still searching for
words that were scathing enough.

Eve had to fight the impulse to snatch the headset
away and slap him as hard as she could, or to get up
and demand that her seat be changed. She glared at him
—his bronze-and-gold Greek god profile, his tanned,

well-kept hands. And wanted to scream from sheer
frustration. How dare he? Just because he'd stunned
her into listening to his ridiculous, unbelievable proposition, he had no damned right at all to assume that
she'd let him lead her off the plane or even consider
for a moment—

She noticed suddenly she was being stared at—
enviously—by two women across the aisle from her.
They looked away quickly, whispering to each other,
and Eve's hands clenched themselves on her lap. Damn
Brant Newcomb, anyhow! How had he known she was
going to be on this flight? How had he arranged to
have the seat next to hers? And what had he meant by
that crack about Randall Thomas?

CHAPTER
TWENTY-SEVEN

AFTERWARD Eve couldn't remember how it happened that she *did* let Brant lead her off that plane. She had sat there looking out of the window, still seething. And then when the cabin was darkened and they started showing the movie, she must have let herself fall asleep. The next thing she knew, Brant was shaking her awake.

"Come on, we've landed. You looked like you needed the sleep, so I told Marcia here not to wake you up for lunch. If you're hungry, I'll buy you dinner on the way back."

The prettiest of the flight attendants stood there smiling. She had Eve's carry-on baggage, and Brant took it from her with a casual "Thanks, honey."

He'd taken advantage of her drowsiness. Before Eve had time to come back to awareness, he already had her arm and was leading her outside, down the carpeted corridor, and through it to the crowded gate area where everyone was greeting everyone else. Eve would have pulled away from him then—if she hadn't seen David.

David? She couldn't help the way her heart lurched, and she would have stumbled on her too-high heels if Brant hadn't tightened his hold on her arm. She was watching David's hurtingly familiar face, seeing the expression of shock chased away, to be replaced by a

tight smile. She thought, Oh, God, no—now he'll think
—he'll be sure I—

She heard Brant say, "Hi, Zimmer. You Eve's wel-
come-home committee?" And he moved her forward
inexorably so that she noticed for the first time the girl
who was standing too close to David. Short, dark-
haired, rather pretty. She was looking awed, and her
hand rested on David's arm.

"Well, I heard from Stella Gervin—my secretary—
that Marti Meredith had to leave for Los Angeles, and
since Wanda here has been wanting to meet Eve, we
thought—"

Wanda turned out to be Mr. Bernstein's niece, fresh
from Smith College. And David had actually brought
her along with him—to prove that he and Eve were
just *friends?*

Eve forgot what else was said—she knew that she
managed to smile and give quite a creditable imitation
of coolness. She was extra nice to Wanda, and she even
managed to force herself to take David's hand. Head up,
Eve! And let him see you don't give a damn. Let him
think anything he pleases. . . .

She heard her own voice, the voice of a poised, self-
possessed stranger, saying:

"David, it was really nice of you to drive out here to
meet me! And I'm sorry I hadn't the time to call Marti
back and tell her of the change in my plans. But when
I ran into Brant and he offered to give me a ride
back. . . ."

More polite murmurs. They all walked down toward
the baggage claim area together, and all the time Eve
knew that he was furious. She could feel him vibrate
with rage, even while he asked the obvious questions
about New York and her new job and Wanda giggled
at something Brant said. She was a somnambulist. Eve

went on feeling that way, even when she was sitting beside Brant in his car—a white Mercedes SL450 this time—top down, her hair blowing in the wind.

Let the wind blow her thoughts away, too. Brant was silent and she was silent until they had taken the on-ramp and were on the freeway, headed toward the city. Eve wondered crazily if he had known that David was going to be there—whether he had arranged that, too. But at this point, she felt she didn't care. She felt numb. She might have been sitting between David and Wanda, still trying to smile, keeping it light. Damn you, David! How could you do this to me? Why come at all? Why with another girl? It had been obvious that Wanda had a crush on David—had they been to bed together yet? She tried to excuse him in her mind the next instant, despising herself for it. Maybe he'd been uncertain of her reactions. Maybe he'd thought that if he came alone, she'd turn away from him and refuse to accept his offer of a ride. He'd have called her after he'd dropped Wanda off—she *knew* he would have! And then . . .

God, how could I be *thinking* this way? Prideless, spineless, crawling . . . Yes, she'd been all of those things with David. She'd let him turn her into a masochist, anxious for crumbs; and he'd shown her exactly how he felt about her the last time they'd been together. . . .

"Would you like to stop off somewhere and get something to eat, Eve?"

Brant's expression was as impersonal as his voice, and Eve caught herself wondering what he was thinking, what was really behind his improbable, impossible suggestion earlier.

"Eve, I want to marry you." And later, "It's your choice. Eve." She had to have dreamed it, of course. Not Brant Newcomb. And what was she doing sitting beside him in his car, trapped into closeness with the one man of all men that she feared and hated most? *She* was the crazy one!

"I'm not really hungry, thank you."

"Polite girl, aren't you?"

She flashed him a quick, angry look, meeting his measuring blue eyes for an instant. "Is there something wrong with that?"

"I like it." And then, without giving her a chance to reestablish her defenses, he said evenly, "Why don't you come back to the house with me and have a drink?"

Her reaction was instinctive. "Oh, no! If you think I—"

"For Christ's sake, Eve. I mean everything I said to you earlier. And this isn't part of some elaborate plot to kidnap you. If that was all I wanted, I could have it done by experts. There's no one else at the house; I promise you that. And you can leave anytime you want to."

She thought again, My God, he *means* it! What am I going to say?

Eve put her hand up to brush flying strands of hair out of her eyes, teeth worrying her lower lip. She had to resist the desire to laugh hysterically at the sheer irony of it all.

"Well?" he said impatiently.

Damn, he was an impatient, far too arrogant man!

"You're insane!"

He laughed shortly. "I've been called far worse than that! Is that all you have to say?"

"No. I mean I—I really don't *understand*. Me—you—David at the airport with that girl—how—"

"If there's anything you're still curious about, we could talk about it over that drink I offered you. Hell, Eve, at least we're not starting off with any illusions about each other, are we? And maybe we both need to exorcise old ghosts."

She saw his hands clench whitely over the steering wheel—that was the first and only indication she'd had so far of any tension in him. It was the first *human* thing. . . . And when he spoke of ghosts, why did David's name, David's face flash across her mind?

Brant, still maneuvering the Mercedes with amazing skill, turned his head to glance at her with one eyebrow slightly raised. Eve felt her pent-in breath expelled with her sigh.

"All right, I—a drink sounds fine. But that's *all* I'm committing myself to for the moment."

Why had she added "For the moment?" What did she have to lose, anyhow? Feeling suddenly tired, Eve leaned her head back, closing her eyes, letting her hair blow free and wild.

Eve, you're such a wild bitch in bed! David again. David, who had also named her a tramp, a whore; using her just as if she had in fact been all those things. And she'd let him. She'd felt this way before, after David had walked out on her that first time. Reckless, uncaring, wanting to spite him. She had a feeling that he'd call her apartment later on that night. Checking up—just to make sure. Of what—her? His hold over her?

Eve opened her eyes, watching Brant's profile almost furtively. What was *he* after? She didn't quite trust him, but some part of her mind that was wiser, older, pragmatic, told her that at least this complex, surprising man beside her *did* want her for some strange reason of his own, that he really didn't need to play games or tricks on her and wouldn't bother if all he wanted was a female body to use or party with.

The leather upholstery was soft to lean against. Eve looked toward Brant again, measuring, and caught him looking at her. For a moment, like strangers first encountering each other, they stared—then looked away.

They had reached the city now. When they stopped

for a light, Eve noticed people watching them. Two young women crossing the street slowed down to stare. A woman in a car alongside, fur jacket open indolently at the throat, looked at Brant hungrily, openly. Well, he was that kind of man, and if she had not been warned about him, had not found out about him, she, too, might look at him that way. Hadn't she stared, too, the very first time she had seen him? Until she had become afraid. . . .

But she wasn't afraid any longer—was she? The car stopped abruptly, and Eve found herself looking upward at the closed, private face of the tall row house again, seeing it in the sunlight this time. A shiver of fear shot through her. Oh, God, what am I letting myself in for *this* time? How far down will my need to shrive myself of David's memory take me?

It was too late for regrets; Brant had already opened the door on her side and was helping her out, his fingers closing around her cold hand, warming it.

"No tricks, Eve. I won't hurt you again—I give you my word."

He said it quietly, and it was the nearest he would come to an apology of any kind. She accepted it silently, but a small sigh escaped her and her knees felt weak as she walked inside the house with him, the sunlight suddenly shut out.

Being back in there felt strange. It was so dark, so quiet, with no crowd of people and no party noises. The huge living room looked empty—clean and tidy, too, smelling faintly of lemon wax; bowls of hothouse flowers arranged on tables. She wondered who cleaned for him and where they hid.

He released her hand and walked behind the bar. "Still drink Scotch, Eve?" Catching her tiny hesitation without seeming to, he produced a sealed bottle of Chivas Regal, opened it, and poured amber liquid into two glasses, dropping in ice cubes. "Nothing in there but Scotch and ice cubes. Pick either glass."

Suddenly Eve was able to manage a wry smile. She reached for a glass, holding it with both hands. "You must be a mind-reader."

"Hardly that. I try to read faces, and yours is pretty transparent."

"Oh." It was ridiculous; she could think of nothing to say. She tasted the drink, and it was strong and cold, just what she needed.

Brant was watching her, leaning his elbows on the bar, leaving a distance between them deliberately—to give her a sense of security? Thank God for the drink—that first sip had helped relax her; the second swallow she took now made her feel stronger, braver.

Silence stretched between them. From somewhere behind her, a clock chimed softly. Time. Too little of it left, with so many things she had to do. And if not for David showing up when he did, she wouldn't be here with Brant—he with nothing to say, she with nothing to say.

"Now what?" She hadn't meant her thought to slip out into words, but she got a reaction from him. He grinned at her suddenly, his teeth white and even against the bronze of his skin. She thought again, illogically, that no man had a *right* to look like Brant did.

"I was thinking the same thing myself," he drawled, those very blue eyes of his keeping hers trapped somehow. "Do we spend the next hour or two playing question-and-answer games, or will you come upstairs with me?"

Catching her instinctive movement of recoil, he said impatiently, "Dammit, Eve! I'm trying to talk you into marrying me. And I wasn't talking about a Platonic relationship, either. I want to make love to you—and listen, there's no need to shy away like that. I said make love, not screw. If we can't make it in the sack, we're never going to make it, so what the hell difference will it make? It's going to happen if we marry; it's something we're both going to have to accept and *enjoy*. I don't expect *that* from you yet, but at least you can find out for yourself if you can stand me or not. If you can't— if my touch turns you off—I'll take you back home, and I promise I won't bother you again. As it is, you can still back out at any stage of the game. I won't try to rape you, Eve. And you're the only woman I've ever taken into my bedroom. I do my playing in the—other room."

She thought he added the last deliberately, bringing the memory of what had happened the last time she'd been in his house out into the open between them— another specter from the past that needed exorcising?

Afterward, Eve didn't know why she hadn't turned to run or why she stood there while he came from behind the bar and took her hand in his. Afterward was already too late, because she had let him take her with him, and they were climbing a beautifully curving staircase, passing through rooms she didn't remember seeing before.

The door to his room stood closed, somehow forbidding—a massive and aged-looking carved door that seemed embedded in the rough-textured wall. There was no knob or conventional handle on it—Brant pressed a button somewhere in the carving, and it swung open like the entrance to some robber baron's cave or secret passage. Catching her look, he smiled.

"Relax. There *is* a handle on the inside. Turn it, and the door will open right away. No magic to it, just electronics."

Inside the room, Eve was surprised all over again at its starkness. She hadn't been in a condition to notice very much the last time she'd been inside here, but now she looked around curiously and saw sparse, austere-looking antique Spanish furniture, heavy and dark. The lack of anything that was in any way fussy or elaborate. It was a *functional* room; there was nothing in it to show what kind of person he was.

It was also an enormous room by any standards, but when he pressed the switch on the wall that made the drapes move apart, Eve caught her breath. There was an effect of a whole wall opening suddenly to let in a new dimension of height and breadth. There was the sky and the rooftops and treetops and even, somewhere in the distance, the blue curve of the bay.

Eve couldn't help being entranced. "Oh—but it's beautiful!" she said, being completely natural for the first time. Brant turned the music on, and she turned, surprised again.

"I love that, too. Handel?"

" 'Water Music.' It seemed to fit."

"You surprise me. I didn't expect—"

"You didn't expect I'd like Handel? Who knows, Eve Mason, I could surprise you some more if you'll let me. Want another drink?"

She shook her head, turning back to the window wall and the amazing view; standing there still undecided, poised for flight, maybe—not yet knowing what she would do in the end, how she would react to whatever *he* might do next. Nervously, with the toe of her shoe, she tested the softly opulent pile of the carpeting. Persian, all dark reds and night-blues—somber colors that matched the rest of the room. She had noticed that there was a fireplace in here, too, in the wall to the side of the bed. And no mirrors. No mirrors anywhere at all, not even over the large triple dresser.

Eve felt, rather than saw, him come up behind her, and fought down the impulse to shiver. She didn't want to turn around—but she did, making herself do it, her chin tilted defiantly. Her thoughts echoed her words earlier. Now what?

promise. And there'll be quite a bit of money in it for

CHAPTER
TWENTY-EIGHT

BRANT COULD TELL, from her determined stance at the window and her almost studied avoidance of his eyes, that she was still afraid—probably already regretting having come up here with him. Impatience rose in him, the urge to tear down her defenses in order to penetrate to whatever lay beneath that defiant surface manner of hers. She was wearing a brown-and-beige silk dress that suited her coloring—high-necked and long-sleeved. And suddenly, something in the set of her shoulders under the thin silk reminded him of Francie, of all people. Perhaps because Francie had sometimes shown the same defiant attitude. But in Francie you knew it was scheming and calculated with an eye to *effect*, while with Eve it was real—maybe more defensive than defiant after all, as if she were telling him hands off, she wouldn't let him hurt her or have her.

He walked up to her, standing behind her, and after a moment, when he could hear the catch of her breath, she turned quickly to face him. He caught her shoulders and looked down into her face, unsmiling. Her eyes mirrored fear, and something else, too—a kind of despair, maybe, or hopelessness. And suddenly he felt a stab of contempt for David Zimmer, the man she was regretting. Her lost lover, who was probably the main reason she was here now, with him.

235

They stared silently at each other, adversaries about to do battle. And Brant began to wonder at himself. What had made him go after her and offer her marriage, anyhow? What was he doing here with this particular woman? Lust was such a casual thing. It had always been so for him. You saw; you wanted; you took. And after that—it was finished. Hurt feelings could always be paid off. What was the difference with Eve?

Suddenly, not desiring to think any further, needing for a change not cerebral but physical reactions instead, Brant bent his head and kissed her half-open mouth, cutting off whatever it was she had wanted to say—at first harshly, feeling her tense up, and then, recalling himself, very gently and almost exploratively.

Her body, so rigid and unyielding at first, began very gradually to relax against his. Now she was giving her mouth to him, at least, and he became conscious of her high, rounded breasts pressed against him; aware of her firm, smooth thighs lying against his, slightly parted as she stood braced against him. And between those thighs —he *knew* what lay between them, had looked, had touched, had tasted. He'd meant that much, at least, when he'd told her that night how beautiful she was down there. And then, soon afterward, the others had come bursting in and he'd called for a camera, for them all to see the prize that for a moment had been his alone by right of capture.

He brought his mind back to the present. Well, this time, at least, there were just the two of them, and he wouldn't think dark thoughts. He could smell her hair again, faintly perfumed, and he suddenly put his hands in it, feeling again its particularly soft and silky quality. It was a new experience for him to be consciously and carefully gentle, to take the time to kiss and hold a woman he wanted to fuck. Normally, he wouldn't have wasted time on preliminaries—the women he'd had, had known what they were there for, so why bother? But now, remembering the time he had promised her, conscious of the newness of this particular experience, he stood there and did nothing but kiss her, his hands still in her hair, until he felt her begin to kiss him back—her body leaning into his, instead of away.

"All right, let's do this properly," he said in her ear a little later.

He carried her over to the big bed that waited, and she lay there with her face averted and her eyes closed while he undressed her, still trying to be gentle with her.

Eve's body was the color of old ivory, its feel just as smooth, almost polished. His lips grazed her breasts, finding a path between them, tracing their outline and their peaks until he could feel her sudden trembling. He touched them, letting his fingers resume the exploration he had begun, while his mouth moved lower, finding the indentation of her navel, traveling lower and feeling her body move, responding in spite of herself. But when he would have kissed her between her legs, she shuddered and closed them together, pleading with him breathlessly.

"No . . . no, not that . . . not yet . . ."

So she remembered, too? Understanding her reasons and wanting her response again, he let his mouth move upward to her breasts, feeling the hardness of her nipples, her quickened breathing.

Not wanting to wait any longer, impatient now, he covered her body with his, nudging her thighs apart with his knees.

He tried to make himself gentle, but it was not possible for either of them to forget the last time and the way it had been when he'd raped her bruised, unwilling body, although this time her hands were not held over her head but rested complaisantly on his shoulders.

Eve had turned her head away from him, her face profiled against the pillow, teeth caught in her lower lip. She was doing this to forget David, to put him out of her mind, but her mind was betraying her, bringing back the memory of the last time David had made love to her—the way her body had arched willingly, eagerly up to meet his while she had clung to him fiercely, never wanting to let go. She knew with a feeling of despair that she couldn't respond to Brant the way he wanted her to respond, the way *she* wanted to respond. His body was too insistent, forcing movement from her, a purely physical reaction that she couldn't feel with her mind.

Why had she suddenly begun to hold back? Brant had had enough women in his life to recognize, in spite of the automatic movements of her body that matched themselves to the rhythm of his, that she wasn't going to make it. Not for a long, long time yet, and he felt suddenly savage and selfish, wondering what was going on behind those closed eyes of hers. Well, he wasn't going to wait for her—goddam all that garbage about self-control, about hanging fire, holding back until the woman was ready to come. Hadn't Syl always told him, "Just *come*, darling, come for me when you feel it, as soon as you feel ready—that's what counts, the *feeling*."

He'd always done just that, not giving a damn if the woman under him, or over him, or beside him had an orgasm or not. He used to think, contemptuously, that a woman was either hot and ready for it or she wasn't, and if she wasn't, then it was too bad for her. The few times he had waited, taking his time, were because *he* wanted to, because it was better that way, holding back until his climax was a hundred times more powerful, more achingly complete. It was always for himself, though, that he came; the only woman whose feelings and reactions he'd cared about had been Syl. . . .

Now, with Eve, he could tell that she wasn't ready and wouldn't be ready soon enough for him; and he was already impatient for the *next* time, wanting to be finished so he could *talk* to her, try to break through the damn wall she had put between them. Putting his hand under her taut buttocks, he lifted her body up higher, grinding her pelvis against his until he had forced a muffled cry of protest from her.

Eve felt him swell inside her, start to throb—spasm after spasm. She opened her eyes then, wanting perversely to watch his face. It was funny, with men, how different they all were at this particular moment. Most of them would grunt, or groan out loud, or shout something to her. David was like that; there were always words mixed up with his climax, like "Oh, my *God*, Eve!" or "Baby, oh you wild bitch you, you're so damned good!" But Brant didn't make a sound—his body tensed and he breathed a little faster and his eyes blinked shut for an instant and that was *it*. Just as if it had been nothing, as if that whole minor explosion of passion inside her had been nothing but a single hot spurt of semen, expended without emotion or any feeling that could ruffle or contort his guarded, handsome face.

He rolled off her, reaching for a cigarette, and they lay side by side in silence, their thighs touching.

The speakers she couldn't see were playing something by Bach, and without asking her, Brant handed Eve a lighted cigarette, lit one for himself. She saw his profile etched against the lighter's flare for an instant before he clicked it shut, and could not help thinking again how beautiful he was, his features surely too perfect, too handsome to be real. Hadn't she wondered if he was gay the first time she saw him? She was still not quite certain; he could be a closet queen or a bisexual— so many men were these days, and were not afraid to admit it, either. There was a certain purity of line and plane in his features and indeed his whole body that was almost too perfect—he should have been a movie star or a male model, Eve thought almost resentfully. It was like seeing an old Greek statue come to life, and the artists of that period had been kinder and more flattering to their young gods and satyrs than they had been to females, goddesses or otherwise! Why was she engaged in this monstrous, impossible experiment with Brant Newcomb, of all people? For that matter, why was *he* stepping so far out of character? She had sensed his patience with her earlier, and it amazed her. He had to have a *reason* for wanting to marry her, for pursuing her, that he hadn't told her about.

"You didn't make it, did you?"

His voice was dry and oddly withdrawn, and Eve wondered with a little shock of surprise if he could actually be human enough to *mind*. Well, he had asked her for honesty and she could be honest with him—she didn't care if she hurt his ego, it didn't matter—but could anyone actually do that?

"No, I didn't. But why should it matter? I—I suppose it could be a sort of cumulative effect. New York was exhausting, *you* were surprising, and then—seeing David—you *did* know about David, didn't you?"

She waited for him to say something cutting and hurtful to her, but instead he only laughed shortly, patting her shoulder.

"Was there anyone in town who knew *you* that didn't?" His voice was mocking, but gently mocking. "Are you still in love with him, Eve?"

She said too quickly, "No! It's just—something I can't explain, even to myself. It wouldn't have worked with us—I know that now. I let him use me, and I suppose he despised *me* for that—only I didn't want to see it, I kept hoping desperately that he— Why am I telling you all this?"

She felt the movement of his shoulder against hers as he shrugged.

"Maybe because I asked, and you needed to bring it out into the open. You see how easy it is to be honest when you're not all hung up on a person and can be objective?"

She put the cigarette out, wondering how they could both be lying there naked together after sex, calmly discussing David.

She said slowly, "I—I suppose I see what you're saying. But I don't know if I'm the kind of person who can be objective about anything—even this, my being here with you. What *am* I doing here with you, Brant?"

"You're here because I brought you, because I caught you in a weak moment when you were confused and unhappy and you wanted to show David that you didn't care. And because I took you by surprise when I asked you to marry me, isn't that it?"

He kept his voice flat and expressionless, but she had the impression that he was challenging her in some way. She looked at him, but his eyes were unreadable.

"Maybe you're right, but I'm still confused. Tell me again, Brant. Why did you ask me to marry you?"

"Because I *want* to, dammit! I'm not going to try to feed you a line of bull by saying I've fallen madly in love with you, but I do want you. Even now. There's something about you, Eve, some quality in you I haven't come across in any of the other women I've met. I can't define what it is, but it keeps bugging me—*you* keep bugging me, and I'm not used to that. I think I need you, I think you'll be honest with me and that— Shit, I talk too much sometimes. What about you, Eve? You were brought up an old-fashioned Catholic girl. Why haven't you been married before?"

His words stung her somehow, and she retorted without thinking.

"Because I never thought about marrying! I wanted to be free to find myself, *do* something, learn about life instead of reading about it. Marriage always sounded like a trap until I met David, and then I—"

"Did you really think he would marry you?"

"Why not? He made me feel right at the beginning he—he didn't want me to go with anyone else. He called me every day, took me everywhere he went! If that stupid house party hadn't happened and that bitch Gloria Reardon hadn't pulled what she did, he might have—"

"You going to console yourself with might-haves, Eve? Shit, doll, he was using you, you said so yourself, and I've used enough women in my life to know how easy it is. Did he tell you he loved you? That you were the greatest lay he'd ever had? Talk's cheap, baby. What else did David Zimmer do for you besides screw you when he felt like it and keep you dangling with half-promises? Yeah, Francie used to talk a lot about her big brother and the way he operated with women."

"Brant, don't!"

She felt attacked and would have squirmed away if his hands hadn't pinned her shoulders down. His bright blue eyes were hard.

"Tell me something, Eve. That night, the night of my party when you went running back to him for comfort, when you told him what had happened, what did he do for you? Take you in his arms, apologize for sending you here to do his dirty work for him, tell you to file a complaint—or did he accuse you of being a willing participant in that little orgy you were a part of? You don't have to answer that—I can see the answer in your eyes! Why don't you admit the truth to yourself? You're hooked on the way the bastard screwed you, the way he manipulated you and kept you dangling, never quite certain—isn't that it? Me, I'm the expert on kicks, baby —all kinds of kicks, like the party scene, and that poor little bitch Francie with her SM hang-up, and anything else new or different. Is that the route you want to go? Were you going to wait around and hope that David would come back to you? Would you have gone with him and that new chick he's been seeing if I hadn't been there at the airport, telling yourself that he was only trying to make you jealous, that maybe he'd call you afterward?"

His voice sounded harsh and almost evil, and Eve could feel herself flinch from every word he'd flung at her, every *truth* she hadn't wanted to hear.

"Brant, please!"

"Please what, Eve? Please leave you alone, or please don't say anything more that you don't want to hear, or please fuck you again so you can close your eyes and pretend it's him?"

She shut her eyes against the studied cruelty of his words and reached out blindly, touching his thigh.

"Please, try to understand that I'm afraid! I don't know what to believe in any longer—everything's been happening so fast. In New York, I felt like I was dreaming all the time because I'd got to where I'd always thought I wanted to be, and that scared me, too, and I wanted to put David out of my mind, but I didn't want that to be the reason for— Oh, God, I don't even know what I'm *saying!*"

She was crying, and she heard his sigh before he pulled her up close against him and held her with his face against her hair until, amazingly, she began to derive a kind of comfort from the warmth of his body and the feel of his arms holding her.

He let her cry until her sobs had subsided into ragged breathing, and then, almost inevitably, he made love to her again. This time he was very slow and very tender. Touching her and kissing her, but not going inside her yet, not for a very long time.

He was infinitely patient this time, waiting until she had forgotten everything but the way he made her body feel and react—forgetting who he was, and forgetting even David—forgetting herself in feeling that turned to wanting—wanting him inside her, squirming under his hands, gasping at the sensations his tongue and teeth on her nipples evoked. She was moving, opening, wanting, needing—until at last he was *there*, in deep, and she locked her legs behind his back, holding him there, coming up to meet every thrust of his body into hers.

Eve's head fell back, and she felt his mouth come crushing down on hers, and now there was only *this*, only feeling and the release she needed him to give her —now, now, now! She held him with her nails digging into his flesh, she made stifled female noises in the back of her throat, and then at last she was aware of the heat pulsing through her body, centering in her loins—the uncontrollable arching and thrashing of herself under him before the final floating back to reality, not even knowing if *he* had come or not, not really caring now, but feeling the indescribable peace inside her after the fire and the fierceness.

No words—there was no need for any words between them this time, nothing to say. But it was as if, in some strange way, what had just happened between them had sealed the bargain between them and Eve felt herself bound to him already—possessed and taken, afraid and yet not afraid.

He had moved so that their bodies still lay alongside each other with their legs still intertwined, and his quickened breathing was warm against her temple. There was almost—she could almost feel—and then he withdrew from her, rolling away to the side of the bed, and the ephemeral almost-thought went away and she wondered if he would always draw away afterward, and if, in time, it would begin to matter to her that he did.

CHAPTER
TWENTY-NINE

SHE MUST HAVE FALLEN ASLEEP. When Eve woke up, it was dark except for the lights of the city outside the windows—spread out all the way to the water. There were a few moments when she didn't remember where she was, and then it came back to her, along with the soft music—Mozart, this time—that continued to play.

With a smothered exclamation, Eve sat bolt upright. She had no idea what time it was, and she was alone in shadowed, half-lit darkness with only a fire to keep her company. The feeling of unreality she had fought back earlier returned, bringing with it a sense of panic. She was torn between the desire to leap out of bed and escape—or to slide back under the covers and go to sleep again.

Light shone across the bed as Brant came out of the bathroom. "Hi. Have a good sleep?"

She thought resentfully that he must have eyes like a cat. He touched a wall switch that brought dimmed lights on, and Eve saw her two cases sitting by the dresser. He was taking too much for granted, he—

He seemed to read her mind again. "You might want to make some telephone calls. Go ahead. There's no extension on the phone by the bed. What would you like for dinner? Jamison's downstairs, and he's an excellent chef."

He came to her at last, and sat on the bed beside her.
He was nude, fresh from the shower, his hair still damp.
She was still drowsy, her mind struggling to get used to
everything she was suddenly faced with. He put his
hand on her neck, under her hair, and kissed her lightly.
"Eve—you'll stay?"

In the end, she did stay. She thought, Why not? And
she was still tired—too tired and confused to protest or
argue.

Eve tried calling Marti, but there was no answer. And
if Marti wasn't back yet, she didn't want to be alone in
the apartment, jumpy in case the phone should ring. She
thought about calling her mother and decided not to.
And she thought about calling David's number and
hanging up if he answered—but what would be the
point of that? David was part of the past, and she wasn't
certain yet what the future would be. Time enough to
think tomorrow.

Eve unpacked one case and hung her clothes in
Brant's closet, noticing that it was less than half-full of
clothes—those were mostly casual. He didn't have many
personal possessions for a man of his wealth.

She used his big bathroom, soaking in the sunken
blue-tiled bathtub—the first one she'd taken a real bath
in. He offered, politely, to soap her back for her, and she
refused just as politely but was surprised all the same
when he didn't insist but went away, closing the door
behind him.

Later, they had dinner on a covered terrace upstairs
with a view almost as magnificent as that from the bedroom. Through the glass roof, Eve could see the stars
and a silvered crescent moon. There was soft music
even here, and the table was set with linen and silver
and a heavy branched candelabrum—with crystal
glasses for wine. Jamison turned out to be a thin, gray-

haired man with a prematurely seamed face—as excellent and unobtrusive a waiter as he was a chef. He didn't turn a hair when Brant offhandedly introduced Eve as the young lady he was going to marry; merely inclined his head politely as he offered his congratulations, accepting with equal politeness Eve's praise of his seafood crêpes.

When he had cleared the table and left them alone with their wine, Eve said, half in anger, half in exasperation, "Are you *always* so—so precipitate? There's a job waiting for me in New York—a whole new career. What makes you think I'm ready to marry and throw it all away?"

She noticed that he leaned forward to stub out his cigarette before he answered her. "Aren't you the one who's associating marriage with giving up your career, Eve? You see, you *are* an old-fashioned woman after all."

"And you're hedging!"

"All right, so I'm hedging. What is it you want me to tell you?"

A thought—really a suspicion—had been growing inside her ever since she had looked up to see him beside her on the plane.

Now she said slowly, "The job—it was all very sudden. I'd read that Joan Nelson was supposed to replace Babs Barrie on the show. And there was the way everyone seemed to be walking on eggshells around me in the beginning. Even Randall seemed to be—well, weighing me. You didn't—Oh, no! You couldn't have—"

His face was shadowed, and she couldn't read its expression.

"My grandfather believed in diversified investments, Eve. And afterward, I— Shit, for a while it was almost fun, a kind of challenge. I put money into the wildest schemes, the most unlikely to pay off—and damned if they usually didn't. Bill Fontaine is a friend of mine, in any case."

"Bill Fontaine!"

Fontaine was an almost legendary figure—head of the network, a man known personally by very few people who worked for him, but feared by everyone.

Brant shrugged. "Eve, if you hadn't been good and they hadn't thought you'd do, the job wouldn't have been offered to you. And that's on the level."

"You were in New York when I was—you *arranged* to be on that flight, didn't you? In the seat next to mine. Oh, God, maybe you own the damned airline, too!"

"Just some shares." How could he be so cool, so nonchalant?

Eve slammed her glass down on the table, spilling some wine. He lifted an eyebrow and refilled the glass for her, reducing her to a state of impotent fury.

"And I suppose you had me followed all the time I was in New York? That's why you mentioned Randall, why you implied—" Against her will, remembering the night with Randall, Eve felt her face flaming. She could almost have wept with frustration and embarrassment.

"I didn't have to have you followed, Eve. You were being kept damn busy, weren't you? And as for Randall Thomas, everyone knows he likes to make the new girls in town—through the back door, isn't that right?"

She stared at him, and he looked back at her. Eve felt the heat in her face spread right through her body.

She said stiffly, having to force the words out, "Knowing what you know, I'm just surprised that you still want to—to—"

He reached across the table, stilling the convulsive movement of her fingers as they played with the stem of her wineglass.

"That particular wine's better downed than spilled,

Eve. Hell, what makes you think I'm likely to condemn
you for anything you've done? I'm not a David Zimmer.
Shit, I've never tried to hide what I've done or what I
am—and the only thing I haven't been is a hypocrite."

She felt compelled to fling back at him, "That's because you've never *had* to conform. To live by other
people's rules. You've always been—"

He released her hand, leaning back in the chair. "Set
apart by the money I inherited? I guess you're right
there. Sure, it's given me freedom—or license, if you
will—to do as I damn well please. My grandfather tried
to teach me to look at it as a responsibility. But I was
too young to understand when he died, and I had other
teachers—" He broke off abruptly, draining his glass,
filling it again with the last of the wine. "Well, Eve? Do
you want to run away, or will you stay?"

She stayed. She was tired, she'd had too much wine to
drink, and he had, in some subtle, indefinable way, chal-
lenged her.

They went back to bed—and the bed was big enough
for them both to lie in it without touching. Strange that
the man she was in bed with, knowing they would spend
the night together, wake up in the morning together,
wasn't David. Randall—or the others she'd let fuck her
mindlessly, thoughtlessly—didn't count. All the lights
below made a kind of glow that washed in through the
enormous window wall. She liked the music; it was
soothing, mind-emptying.

Later that night, he made love to her again, and then
they both slept—she heavily and dreamlessly, and he
lightly and restlessly.

Getting used to having a woman, the same woman,
around all of the time, and particularly having her sleep
beside him in his bed, would take getting used to. The
first since Syl—if he didn't count the women in Vietnam
who'd had no homes to go to. He wasn't used to it yet,
but he felt somehow that it wouldn't be too hard to

adjust to having Eve around. She was quiet, she walked and moved gracefully, and yet, dressed or undressed, she was one of the sexiest women he'd ever known. They were still strangers to each other—almost adversaries—and there would be a lot of changes in his way of life. But he'd already thought about that, hadn't he?

Brant moved onto his side, instinctively tugging the sheet up over Eve's sleeping body before he did. That instinct—was it a sign? He couldn't help but wonder how it would be to have someone else to consider besides himself. What would it be like, living with a woman, taking her with him when he felt like traveling? But he'd made up his mind. Deliberately, he stilled his thoughts, closing his eyes and emptying his mind until sleep overtook him again.

Brant had called his attorney the previous evening while Eve lay sleeping, and he arrived early in the morning with a briefcase full of papers. It was only 10:00 A.M., but Brant had already been awake for a couple of hours before then. Already showered and shaved, he was eating breakfast in the sunny dining room when Jamison announced that Mr. Dorman had arrived.

Wilson Dorman was an old man. He had known Brant's grandfather and had helped draw up his will. While it was impossible for one man to handle all of his complex affairs, Dorman was the only one Brant trusted with the really personal matters. Now the white-haired Dorman, who had known about Syl and his client's lifestyle and excesses, sat across from Brant at the polished mahogany table, refusing his offer of breakfast. Like Jamison, Wilson Dorman had long since trained himself not to show any emotion. This morning, however, he was, if not exactly rattled, slightly discomposed and patently cautious, wondering if perhaps his instructions of the previous afternoon had not been brought about by some drug-induced moment of weakness.

Brant gave him a cup of coffee and went upstairs to wake Eve. She came down about a half hour later with smudges under her eyes, but otherwise quiet and composed. She was wearing beige corduroy pants and a rust-colored silk shirt, with a gold Tiffany heart on a thin chain around her neck to match her earrings. She looked younger, not as polished and sophisticated as she had appeared on the early news show Dorman had occasionally watched. He noticed that she seemed not quite wideawake and almost confused as she tried to read through the papers he kept handing her across the table.

"You're going to be an extremely rich young woman," he commented once. Was there a slight undertone of disapproval in his voice? Perhaps he was wondering if she was a—a golddigger—or did anyone use that expression now? Eve looked almost desperately across at Brant, who rescued her from having to say something in reply.

"She knows that, Wilson. And she'll probably do a better job of managing the damn money than I ever could—or cared to do. This is a sudden decision for us both," he offered in explanation. "I guess we can go through all these papers again after we're married and things have settled down. For now, why don't we skip reading through the fine print and just sign whatever has to be signed right away? Just read out aloud all the really important clauses—whatever Eve really ought to know about—and that should take care of the preliminaries, shouldn't it?" He glanced at Eve. "Is that okay with you, Eve?"

"It—that's fine. Thank you."

She tried to concentrate while Dorman told her dryly and at considerable length what he thought she ought to be aware of. Nothing really sank in. She watched Brant signing papers, his hair reflecting the sunlight that slanted in through the open windows. And then, her hands shaking, she signed, too, not really understanding anything that was happening except that once these papers had been notarized she would be suddenly *rich*, not belonging wholly to herself anymore.

Dorman left at last, and it was almost noon by then; there was nothing left to talk about or do. They were still in the dining room downstairs, and Brant had opened the doors that led out onto another terrace. A light breeze blew in, carrying with it the faint sea smell of the bay.

Eve moved around the room nervously, studying abstract paintings and the carefully arranged bowls of flowers. Upstairs, half-dressed, she had seemed desirable and somehow even vulnerable, but now that she was dressed again, Brant thought she seemed to have become withdrawn and almost impersonal—even slightly afraid of him again. Watching her, Brant wondered once more, as he had done so many times during the night that was past, at the speed and finality of his decision to marry her—and why he had chosen her, of all the women he had known. Sure, the reasons he had given her before were all valid, still were—but were they the only reasons? And was he making a mistake in choosing for his wife a woman who had admitted she wanted another man—or was that the whole point of it, that she represented a challenge he wasn't used to facing?

Tired of introspection, he asked her abruptly if she'd like to go sailing, and she accepted quickly, sounding almost relieved.

CHAPTER THIRTY

EVE LOVED BEING out on the bay—the movement and salt-sea smell of the water, the gulls' shrieking cries, and the wind blowing in her face, blowing back her hair. Because it was choppy that day and she wasn't used to sailing, Brant had decided to take out his cabin cruiser instead—there would be plenty of deck space for sunbathing, and he told her, critically, that she needed some sun.

Eve changed into her new, brief bikini in the forward cabin and came out to join him on deck after they'd gone out several miles. The water was not too choppy out here; there was a slight swell and an occasional white-capped wave to rock them.

She watched with interest as Brant locked the wheel and maneuvered the sea anchor overboard. Seeing him concentrate on what he was doing, being natural and unguarded, she caught herself thinking that she could almost like him at moments like these because he wasn't watching *her* and she didn't need to hide. And then the thought: Hide? Hide from what? Was she still afraid of him? She realized suddenly that here she was, completely alone with Brant, not among people or even in a house surrounded by other houses, but miles out at sea. He could drown her if he wanted to (the ultimate kick?), and who would know it wasn't an accident?

Why had she agreed so eagerly to come out here with
him?

Eve lay down carefully on the polished, sun-warmed
deck and closed her eyes. If he wanted her overboard,
he would have to pick her up and throw her over the
rail, struggling. She wondered if the smiling girl who'd
sold her the bikini in that little boutique in Sausalito
would remember her. She'd certainly noticed Brant—
there were few women who didn't.

ANCHORWOMAN DIES IN BOATING ACCIDENT, the head-
line might read. Or perhaps: BILLIONAIRE PLAYBOY
SUSPECT IN DROWNING. If *she* were reporting it, how
would she write her copy? David would read the news
—and be sorry!

An unwilling smile curved Eve's lips as other, more
dramatic news headlines sprang into her mind.

"That's a woman-witchy smile if I ever saw one,"
Brant's voice commented from somewhere above her.
She felt the coolness of his shadow fall across her thighs
and refused to answer, squeezing her eyes tightly shut,
forcing herself to lie still. Would he want to? Did he
want to?

"Okay, don't let's talk, then."

She heard him move softly away from her. Silence
then, except for the suddenly loud noise of the water
lapping against the sides of the boat, a seagull's occasional cry, and the slight creaking of the timbers. Where
was he now? she wondered. Was he watching her still?
She had to open her eyes just a fraction to look.

He was sitting across from her, leaning against the
rail, a hat pulled low over his forehead. Barefoot and
bare-chested, just the same pair of abbreviated white
shorts he'd been wearing in the picture on Francie's
bulletin board. And he *was* watching her, after all, but
she couldn't read what was in his eyes—could anyone?

He didn't say anything, just continued to look at her,

and she closed her eyes again quickly. What was he thinking? In spite of the hot sun on her body, Eve couldn't suppress a small shiver. Damn him! And damn her own stupid gullibility, too, for being here—for believing anything he'd told her. She must have been mad to agree to have anything to do with him in the first place, but being let down by David always made her do crazy, spiteful things. Was this one of them? But Brant wasn't the kind of man you could play games with. Brant Newcomb was *dangerous*, a cold, deadly man she shouldn't trust—hadn't she had enough occasion to find out just how dangerous it would be to underestimate him?

What was he planning right now? Eve wondered, and thought she didn't want to know. Forcing her body to remain limp and relaxed-looking, she twisted around to lie on her stomach, feeling the comforting warmth of the deck beneath her. She felt safer now, turned away from him, her face hidden in the curve of her arm. He hadn't moved at all. What was he waiting for?

Brant, too, was wondering. What was she thinking, wrapped in silence? What was *she* waiting for? And why had he brought her out here? She was still all nerves, too wary of him to relax—he could sense that. But she had appeared eager to come out in the boat with him. Did she feel safer out here in the open, under the sky? He couldn't help wondering why she had agreed to go through with the whole crazy idea he'd outlined to her. Marriage—the conventional bit. Oldest trap of all. What had been her *real* reason? He knew what he was looking for, but did she? Security—the money, maybe. Perhaps his offer had even provided a kind of escape for her. It was a gamble they were taking, but then any relationship between two people was an almighty gamble. What was the difference between taking a chance on marriage or racing a fast car or a speedboat—even racing an airplane and doing crazy stunts with it they said shouldn't be done? Either you made it or you didn't. Hell, maybe it would work out for them in the end. He had the feeling that if she actually went through with it, she'd make a gallant try, at least. And so would he—you always tried, especially when you had reached the stage where you had nothing left to lose and just maybe everything to gain. Lay Syl's ghost—could he ever do that? Wasn't that it?

Brant closed his eyes and lifted his face to the sun, stretching. Suddenly needing to sleep. He dropped flat onto the deck, put the hat over his face, and ignored her faint stirring. She wasn't going anywhere, after all. She'd still be there when he woke up.

The sun grew hotter, and Eve stirred, rolling her body over so that it was partly in the shade of the cabin. Thank God she tanned, not burned. She squinted through half-closed eyes, and he was asleep—or pretending to be. But thank God for that, too. She wished that she, too, could fall asleep as easily.

She lay still for a few moments longer, trying to make her mind a blank—a trick learned from Peter. It didn't work. The boat moved under her almost sensuously, and the sun had made her feel hot and sticky. She needed a drink—something long and cool. Eve rose cautiously and tiptoed into the cabin. Yes, there was a small refrigerator here, stocked with cans and bottles. She poured orange juice into a glass and added lots of ice.

"Fix me one, too, would you, please?"

His voice called to her politely from outside, and she jumped, juice sloshing over her bare toes. Damn him! Did he have to sleep as lightly as a cat? She poured juice into a second glass, dropped in ice cubes, not bothering to ask him what he wanted to drink.

Bracing herself against the slight rocking movement

of the boat, Eve went outside with the glasses. Brant was still lying exactly as she had left him—flat on his back, the hat covering his face.

Forgetting her earlier fear and mistrust, her mind registering only annoyance now, Eve walked over to him and stood there, waiting for him to acknowledge her presence. When there was no reaction, she dropped to her knees on the deck beside him, holding both glasses carefully away from her body.

The boat rolled slightly, and the ice clinked in the glasses; little drops of liquid splashed downward and lay glittering against his skin.

He moved at last, stretching out a hand that found her ankle and slid upward.

"Don't—you'll get me off balance, dammit!"

Her body jerked, and more juice splashed onto him, making him grimace.

"Good grief, woman, you're clumsy!"

He sat up abruptly, taking a glass from her dripping fingers and squinting his eyes at her. They knelt close to each other, eyes measuring, wary. Her teeth worried her lower lip for an instant, and then, recovering, she sipped her drink nervously, still watching him—catching him start to smile.

"You know this won't do. We're as awkward as strange animals around each other."

He put his glass down and very deftly and quickly untied the top of her bikini before she could either protest or resist him.

"Brant, no!" she objected, but her tone was soft and unconvincing. He bent his head, and she felt his tongue, cold from the ice, on her nipples, making them swell. Her hands caught his shoulders; he felt her body quiver and pushed her gently backward.

"Suppose someone—another boat comes by?"

"Suppose they do? I'll cover you with my body; we'll fuck the traditional way."

His hands eased her brief, side-laced panties downward. His tongue traced the outline of her navel and traveled lower, then lower still, and she heard her own sigh of defeat and desire.

"Don't," she started to say.

"Yes, I must."

Eve stopped trying to fight the sensuality of her own body and gave herself up to his hands and lips and tongue, her mouth tasting him in turn—the slightly salty sea-sweat taste—tasting herself on his mouth at last when he eased himself very slowly and very gently inside her, going deeper and deeper inside her.

Eve closed her eyes against the sun and let herself go to feeling, being man-ridden and man-fucked, filled and then emptied, only to be filled again. She went suddenly wild under him as her desire rose and grew almost unbearable; no sooner was it sated than it seemed to rise again. And now what was happening between them was a contest, a battle of wills and staying power that went on and on with neither of them wanting to be the first to give in.

They began to experiment, moving easily from one position to another as if they were already used to each other. Their skins became wet and slippery with sweat, the heat of the sun being absorbed and then given off by their bodies. They lost identity and became male and female, fucking and being fucked, taking turns.

When it was finally over and they were spent, the sun had moved. The shadows seemed longer and darker, and the breeze had returned to rock the boat and chill their bodies. Eve felt as if every ounce of strength and will had been drained out of her. She lay flat on the deck, exhausted and literally unable to move, even after Brant had got to his feet and left her.

He came back with a warmly damp towel and began to sponge her body slowly, touching her gently between her breasts and legs, down her belly and up her arms.

It suddenly seemed so incongruous that this man, this tender stranger, was the same Brant Newcomb who had welcomed her to his party with icy, impersonal eyes only a month before.

"Here, you look as if you could use another drink. I've brought you a beer."

He had to lift her and prop her up against the side of the cabin so she could drink, holding the bottle with both hands. He leaned back beside her, nothing but a towel covering his nudity, and tossed both halves of her bikini between her legs, laughing shortly.

"I could fuck you all over again, just from looking at you now."

"But I don't think I could take it."

"I'd make you."

She looked at him almost fearfully.

"I know you could. But—"

"But I won't. I'll try to learn to take you only when you're ready. I'm not used to that, but I'll try."

She touched him lightly, leaving her hand on his bare, warm thigh.

"I'll try, too. But you'll have to be—I mean, be *kind*, won't you, please? Or at least, be patient with me. I don't like being hurt, Brant. Nor do I like inflicting pain."

"Yes, I know that. I won't hurt you—I've already promised you that."

She closed her eyes, leaning her head back against his shoulder for the first time, and the boat rocked gently beneath them.

CHAPTER
THIRTY-ONE

STELLA WAS GOING to marry George Coxe. She told David first—they had been off-and-on lovers for some time now, and she had grown used to confiding in him. But this afternoon he seemed preoccupied, and his only reaction was to congratulate her somewhat absent-mindedly.

Stella supposed he had things on his mind—she had really felt for him when he'd told her bitterly that his teenaged sister had eloped and run off somewhere with a guy she hardly knew. Poor David, she had thought. But what could you do with kids these days? As she'd told David, if Frances was almost eighteen, then she was certainly old enough to know what she was doing —or at least to take care of herself.

"I certainly hope so!" he'd said, and she'd sensed all the pent-up frustration he was trying to hide. David was really sweet and kind, and he deserved better—he really shouldn't blame himself, and she'd told him so.

Maybe because they'd become so much closer after that, she'd hoped for more of a reaction to her news about George. But Stella was pragmatic enough to shrug it off and think to herself: Why? Just because David had been the only man she'd actually *made* it with didn't mean that either of them was emotionally involved. David had his own problems, poor baby. That bitch

Eve . . . Even Marti had been closemouthed as to what
had *really* happened, and David wasn't the talking kind;
still, from what he'd *implied*. . . . She wondered what
was really going on between David and Mr. Bernstein's
niece. The girl had a crush on him, that was obvious;
and Gloria was mad, which gave Stella a secret pleasure,
because *that* was something Gloria couldn't do a damn
thing about!

Stella glanced toward the telephone. One of the lines
was busy—David had kept it tied up for most of the
day.

She couldn't help wondering if David had *done* anything after she'd told him that Eve was expected back
from New York and Marti wouldn't be at the airport to
meet her. He'd taken the afternoon off yesterday, but
she hadn't seen anything different in his manner when
he'd come in this morning, except for his preoccupation.

Marti . . . Stella couldn't help sighing. Marti didn't
know yet, although she'd made it a point to be honest
with Marti, right from the time she'd begun dating
George. She *wanted* Marti—maybe she always would
—but marrying George was the best, most practical
thing for her. He was rich, and *she'd* be rich—free at
last. No more nine-to-five job. Money really made you
free; whoever said money couldn't buy everything had
to be kidding.

There was another line that she could call out on if
she really needed to. . . . Stella reached for the phone
and then pulled her hand back, frowning. No, she was
crazy. Let Marti call *her*. She knew that Marti should be
back from LA, from that mysterious trip she wouldn't
say too much about. Something to do with a job in the
movies—maybe it was supposed to make her jealous.
And in a way she was; only—why couldn't Marti *understand?* They could still see each other, still share and
enjoy the fire that always erupted between them. But

not in public—Marti's preference for women was too well known, and Stella regretted that they'd ever been seen out together. But if she could make Marti see why she had to marry George, make her see that it didn't really have to change anything for them . . .

The large diamond on Stella's finger winked and glimmered under the lights as she reached for the telephone. Why shouldn't she call Marti? Just to explain, of course. She owed her that much.

Marti answered the phone on the first ring, but her voice stayed flat, almost indifferent, even when she knew it was Stella.

"Los Angeles? Oh, it was okay. I met lots of people, and a few old friends." Did Marti's voice take on a strange inflection when she said 'old friends'?

"Marti, didn't you miss me at all?"

"Sure I did, baby. But I was busy, very busy most of the time. In fact . . ." Marti paused, evidently wondering if she should tell Stella something, and then went ahead. "In fact, Stel, I might get a small apartment in LA— stay there some of the time. I was offered this part that sounded really interesting, and"—there was that little pause again—"very challenging."

"Marti!" Recovering herself, Stella said quickly, "But that's wonderful. I'm very happy for you." So Marti was trying to play hard to get?

Her voice soft, Stella said, "I've got some news, too. I'm going to be married." She wished she could see Marti's face when she said that. How would she react?

"George, I suppose. I'm glad for you, Stel, if that's really what you want."

God, how could Marti sound so polite, so indifferent, when only a few weeks ago she had actually *cried*. . . .

"I'm glad you're not upset, Marti. I knew you'd understand. But we can still see each other sometimes, can't we?"

How difficult it was to let go when you'd shared something good with somebody. Marti had really loved her. *Had?*

"No reason I should be upset, Stel. You've told me often enough that this life wasn't really for you. It's just as well."

"Just as well what?" Was that really her voice, sounding so sharp?

"Just as well for us both, baby. Don't worry, I'll be around here sometimes, and we can get together if you still want to."

"Marti, of course I'll want to. Don't you?"

"Sure." But Marti's voice didn't sound convincing.

After she'd hung up, Marti stayed by the phone, staring at it. Well, so much for Stella. Lovely, wanton, selfish Stella. No more love; no more heartbreak. Let someone else do the falling in love with *her* for a change.

I'm stronger than Eve, Marti thought. Stronger than Stel, too, because I know when it's time to let go, even if I feel like it's going to tear my guts out.

She knew by now how it felt to hurt, to agonize, and she wasn't going to let it happen again. Not in LA, Celluloid City; the atmosphere there just wasn't right for love, anyhow. *Lust* counted; that was what everyone was paying for down there, one way or another.

Marti thought about the movie she'd made, and smiled. You sure as hell didn't need to be an actress to star in one of those! And her partner in some of the scenes—she had been really delicious. So damned experienced for a kid that young; so damned *good*. There was lots more where that came from—why should she mourn for Stella?

Suddenly the phone started to ring again, and she picked it up, making a wry face when she recognized the voice.

"No, David, I don't know where she is. I haven't

heard from Eve since I've been back—maybe she
changed her mind and stayed on in New York. . . . Oh!
Well, Stella had no damn business telling you when Eve
was due to arrive, and you—you men can be such
bastards sometimes!" Marti's voice was vicious, and
David flinched from the venom in it.

Goddam lesbian bitch! he thought furiously, wondering why in hell he felt driven to call and keep calling,
again and again. Eve hadn't been home last night—she
was probably partying it up with Brant Newcomb and
his friends.

"I'm sure she's enjoying herself—you needn't bother
to tell her I called." Filled with rage and frustration,
David slammed down the phone. He shouldn't have
bothered. He'd only gone out to the airport out of a
sense of obligation, and he'd been careful to take Wanda
with him. Thank God she, at least, wasn't Eve's kind.
She was still naive, still idealistic. And he was pretty
sure she was a virgin. He hadn't been able to teach Eve
anything; she'd done it all before she'd met him. He'd
accused her of being a bisexual once, and she'd denied
it, although later he'd dragged a reluctant admission
from her that she *had* tried it once—yes, with Marti,
dammit! He hadn't told her that he'd already known
because Stella had told him. Her confession, and the
details he'd wrung out of her, had excited him so
damned much at that point that he'd stopped his ques-
tioning and started to fuck her. But he'd hoarded her
admission as a kind of weapon to use against her if he
had to. He'd always felt, with Eve, that he needed to
have a weapon, something to use in order to keep her
from clinging too close—from smothering him with her
love.

Love, hell! He should have treated her as he had
treated Gloria. The Four F's—find 'em, fool 'em, fuck
'em, forget 'em! Eve didn't deserve any more. Not that
he had ever considered *marrying* her. When he married,

it would be someone like Wanda. But he'd like to fuck Eve one more time at least, to prove to her, and to himself, that she was a cheap, too-easy lay—nothing more.

Eve—damn her! He wondered what, exactly, she was doing right now.

She was helping Brant moor his boat at the dock, her hair pulled back decorously now and held in place by a scarf. There was an unaccustomed soreness between her thighs that made her feel strangely shy and yet strangely proud, too. She couldn't believe that the woman on the boat had been *her*, letting go completely.

Such an unusual feeling, to have a guy of her own suddenly—to be engaged to be married, and *not* to David. She wondered if she'd ever get used to the idea, or to the fact that she was going to be Brant's wife, of all things.

Later, in the car, she asked him if he would take her back to her apartment.

He looked at her quizzically.

"Tired of me already? I thought you might be resigned to being my kept woman for a few days."

She managed to laugh, shaking her head.

"It's not *that*. But Brant, I really should go back just long enough to check with Marti if she's back, and pick up the rest of my clothes, and— God, I'm suddenly beginning to realize how damn many things I have to do, like call New York and—"

He touched her hand.

"Okay, okay. We're on our way."

David would have become impatient with her or grumbled—he hated having his plans delayed or interfered with. Brant was just as polite and reasonable as he'd been all day. Would he ever lose his temper with her, or were all his rages held inside and as carefully controlled as his other emotions?

When Eve started to let herself into the apartment, Marti came out of her room at once, heaving an exaggerated sigh of relief.

"Well, for God's sake! I was beginning to think you'd developed amnesia! *He's* been calling all afternoon, driving me nuts! I . . ." Marti's voice trailed away almost ludicrously when she saw whom Eve had brought back with her.

"Oh, my God!" she burst out spontaneously. "Not *you!*"

"Hi, Marti. I'm afraid it is." Brant's voice was cool and slightly mocking, as usual.

"Marti," Eve stammered, "I—well, we—" She couldn't seem to get the words out in the face of Marti's obvious shock.

"Why don't you get whatever clothes and stuff you need and attend to your telephone calls, sweetheart, and I'll explain to Marti."

Telephone calls! Eve glanced sharply at Brant. Did he mind that David had called her? Had there been a touch of sarcasm in his voice?

But he had turned away from her already. He and Marti were eyeing each other coolly, like adversaries. Weakly, Eve decided to let Brant take over; he was good at that.

"*Explain!*" Marti was saying furiously. "Explain what? Eve's not going anywhere with you, Brant Newcomb. I won't let her. You forget, I know exactly what kind of a bastard you are!"

Eve retreated, closing the door of her room on their voices. For a moment, she leaned against it, closing her eyes. David had called. David—wanting what of her?

Automatically, even as she was thinking this, Eve had started to walk toward the telephone. But she stopped, stood looking at it for a moment, and then turned away. She *knew* what David wanted. His willing and accommodating mistress—giving in, expecting nothing, mak-

ing no demands. This time, he wasn't going to get her
back. This time, Eve Mason wouldn't be available, and
he could think what he pleased. I can be stubborn, too,
Eve thought. I can be practical and cool (learning from
Brant?), even if I feel it's going to kill me inside, in that
secret part of me that still wants David.

Hastily, almost frantically, Eve began to snatch
things out of her closet, rummage through drawers,
dumping everything out on the bed. She wanted to tear
down the mirror that reflected her every movement back
at her. Not wanting to think about David and the times
he'd shared this room, this bed with her.

God—if he called *now!* What would she do? Or say
to him? Where in the past she had always prayed
silently for David's call, now she found herself hoping
fervently that he would not—not until she was safely
gone.

Presently, Marti came in to help her pack, sorting out
things she could send for later. Marti's magnolia-
skinned face was paler than usual, and she wore a
stunned, disbelieving look.

"I can't believe it!" Marti exploded, the minute she
walked in. "Eve, are you sure you know what you're
doing? I keep thinking that this is *Brant,* and he has
to be playing some kind of cruel game. I— Oh, Eve
baby, I'm just fond of you, you know that. I just don't
want to see you cut to pieces by a—a barracuda!"

Eve shrugged helplessly.

"It's too late, Marti. I've committed myself, and we're
going to be married in a few days. I even signed all
kinds of papers this morning, and—it's as good as done,
I suppose. Don't look that way, I can hardly believe it
myself."

"You're making a mistake, Eve. I warned you about
him, remember? But it's your life. Damn, I guess I feel
almost protective—you don't need any more hurt. First
David, and now—" Marti glanced toward the door.

"And what about David? What am I supposed to tell him if he calls again—or are *you* going to do that?"

"I don't want to talk about David! Oh, Marti, I'm sorry, I didn't mean to snap, but—something happened with us and—and it's over. David did it—I guess he opened my eyes for the last time."

"So you're marrying Brant to get even?"

"I don't know! I don't really know why I'm marrying Brant, except that he wants me to, and I—maybe I'm finally ready for marriage!"

"Huh!" Marti said sourly. She started folding Eve's clothes neatly in little piles on the bed, and she didn't say much more after that, although her disapproval was palpable.

In the end, Eve took just two cases with her. She left Marti a check for her share of the rent for the next two months, and the keys to the apartment. Somehow, that seemed to make everything so *final;* she felt as if she had put herself in Brant's custody, and the feeling made her quiet and withdrawn. She had the sudden impression of being on a roller-coaster that was out of control and racing toward destruction. Would he end up destroying her?

CHAPTER
THIRTY-TWO

AT THE TOWN HOUSE, like a bad omen, Jerry Harmon was waiting, leaning up against the weathered brick exterior, his eyes watching them both. Somehow, just seeing him standing there made Eve sickly afraid—unreasoningly so, because, after all, it had been *Brant* and not Jerry who had started it all that night. Brant who . . .

She felt quite suddenly as if she couldn't get out of the car, didn't want to, but Brant's firm, strong fingers grasped both her hands, pulling her upward and onto her feet, moving her forward. Jerry ignored her, and she felt a kind of relief at that.

"Hey, Brant! I've been trying to get in touch all day, man—figured that if you'd gone sailing, you wouldn't be out *too* late." His glance flicked over Eve at last, and she wanted to cringe under it.

"Partying all alone, huh? Well, how's about joining the crowd tonight at my place? Got some new faces coming in from the southland, man, and they all love to ball. I came all the way up here just so I'd be sure to catch you."

Brant kept smiling his cold, polite smile, but he was shaking his head, and Eve felt relief flood through her. For a few horrible seconds, she had been afraid that he'd want to go and would force her to go along with him.

"Sorry, Jer. No more playing for me for a while, and I guess you might just as well pass the word around that I'm leaving town again tomorrow. Eve and I are getting married."

He'd said it easily, conversationally, but Eve could see Jerry's eyes bug, his mouth open and then close, as if he were having difficulty finding words.

Finally he said slowly, "Man, you have got to be kidding! This is all a big put-on. Go on, tell me that and I'll laugh. Because, Brant baby, it's not your *bag*, man. I mean, you're cool, sweetheart. Just a little crazy, maybe, like the rest of us, but not that crazy. Come on, now, tell old Jer you were fooling—the sun got to you, maybe. . . ."

Inexplicably, Eve found that she, too, was watching Brant, waiting for his laugh, waiting for him to shrug and tell Jerry that he wasn't serious at all, it was a put-on.

But instead, here he was telling Jerry something quite different.

"Sorry, Jer, but I *am* serious—finally. Maybe everything just got to be a drag—you know? Anyhow, why don't I just let you think up some story wild enough to tell the gang. I'm going to be too damned busy to make any announcements myself."

Jerry stood there shaking his head for a long time after they had gone in the house—Eve still silent, and Brant explaining casually that they had a lot of packing to do.

"You're eloping?"

"Guess you could call it that. We haven't decided *where* yet, or when, exactly. Just soon. We're leaving in the morning, so be a sweetheart and keep everybody away, huh?"

Jerry had agreed, his expression still stunned, but now he found himself wondering if Brant weren't, after all, playing some monstrous kind of trick. On the girl, on him, on them all. Brant could be a kind of weirdo sometimes—he was as difficult as hell to figure out at all times.

But to marry Eve Mason, of all people? Everyone knew she was crazy about that lawyer guy, Francie's brother. And then there had been all the publicity about her going to New York to take Babs Barrie's place on the biggie morning show—what about that? Hell, he thought, only a week or so ago, Brant had invited everyone at his party to screw the broad—had even helped. To think that he, Jerry, had actually thought he knew Brant Newcomb better than most people did! That was a laugh because did you ever really get to know anyone as rich as Brant, or as self-contained as he was, even if you'd been stationed at the same base in 'Nam?

Brant Newcomb was a loner even when he was the center of a crowd, the laugh of the party. There'd always been women in his life, of course, and even an occasional man if it was an orgy scene with everyone doing it to everyone else. But Brant, unlike most guys, had never had a special friend (unless you could call *him* one, and Brant had sure as hell shown him different, hadn't he?) nor kept a mistress. Not even when he lived in Europe, where it added a certain cachet to a rich man's reputation as a lover to keep a well-known movie star or an opera singer.

Brant, with his looks and his millions, could have had his pick of the women; instead he would use them— fuck them and forget them. He genuinely didn't give a damn about ayone. Some jealous women, their vanity hurt when he'd picked them up and dropped them just as quickly, had even tried to start rumors that Brant was a closet queen, but nobody really believed that because Brant balled too many women—some of them too

publicly—and took too much enjoyment in the doing of
it. He was as horny and ready as often as an eighteen-
year-old.

So what in hell did Brant think he had found in Eve
Mason? She was beautiful, but beauty was cheap and
easy to come by these days. She was a product of middle-class suburbia, nothing special, and had had the
usual quota of men on the way up. What had Brant
discovered that was so special—there had to be *something*, only Jerry hadn't figured it out yet. Oh, well,
they said a leopard couldn't change its spots, and Brant
couldn't change overnight. He was human, too, like
everyone else, and he'd be back in circulation after a
while, with or without his bride.

Jerry had been walking back to where he'd parked
his car, deep in thought. Brant's sudden announcement
had shaken him more than he wanted to admit, even
to himself. After all, they'd been buddies since Vietnam,
and Brant hadn't even asked him in the house this time,
the cold bastard!

Suddenly, as a thought struck him, Jerry's footsteps
quickened. Hell, why hadn't he thought of it before?
He had the juiciest piece of gossip in the city right now
—he knew something no one else knew. City, hell! This
piece of gossip was *news*—international, wire-service
type. It was a goddam scoop, and if there was money to
be made, Jerry baby was going to make it. Maybe his
old pal Brant would let him take some pictures at the
wedding? All he had to do now was get on the phone to
Evalyn Adams in Los Angeles, and she'd jump at the
chance to be the first to run the story—she always paid
well, too. Bread. He could use some. Parties were expensive.

Eve thought that the thing that frightened her most
about Brant was his cruelty. It wasn't a conscious, *considered* cruelty most of the time, perhaps, but it was all

the more frightening because it seemed instinctive and thoughtless. After seeing Jerry Harmon, the fear that had returned to haunt her hadn't gone away yet, and since they'd been back, she felt they were farther apart than ever.

There was nothing for her to do here—everything was being taken care of, even her final packing. If she needed anything else, all she had to do was ring for Jamison and tell him, and he'd see to it. She wondered nervously what Jamison thought of all this, his employer's latest whim—did he think at all, or was he merely a robot? Was that what you had to be to survive around the man who was going to be her husband?

She'd paced around the rooms on the first floor of the house until Brant, looking up from the telephone, had offered her a tranquilizer. She'd refused, and he'd shrugged and gone back to his telephone calls. Now Eve wondered whom he was calling—he'd been on the phone for what seemed like hours, making one call after another.

"I have to take care of a few things before we leave tomorrow," he'd said. Well, of course she wasn't his wife yet and she didn't have the right to ask questions, but would she ever feel secure enough with him to do so?

At last, Eve came upstairs to lie on the big bed and flick the switches that would bring her music again. Bach—cool, measured, soothing sounds. But they couldn't stop her thoughts. She wondered if she should have taken the tranquilizer—it might have helped, after all.

Oh, God. What's going to happen to me in the end? Do I really *want* this? I'll have the money, of course, but he'll have *me*. I'm afraid of him. And everything's moving so damned *fast!* When he's making love to me, he's all there and it's good, and for a little while then I'm not afraid. But the rest of the time, he's too controlled, too carefully remote. I can't read him; I can't understand him.

She had closed her eyes, but his voice cut sharply through her thoughts.

"Eve, don't go to sleep yet—we have to call your mother, remember?"

She remembered. And wondered all over again what she was going to say. Her mother would be shocked, of course. She was old-fashioned enough to jump to the conclusion that Eve was pregnant. But Mom wouldn't ask that question. Poor Mom!

"Brant, can I cop out and have *you* talk to her first? She's going to think—"

"That you're pregnant. Well, baby, maybe we ought to get you that way in a hurry."

"Brant!"

"You sounded just like a wife when you said that. Better watch it."

He sat on the bed beside her and smiled at her, and she realized suddenly that he very seldom smiled at all.

"I wonder if I'll ever understand you?" The words slipped out quite accidentally; she had only meant to think them.

He raised his eyebrows at her, his face composed again.

"That's hard for me to say. Sometimes I don't even understand myself, but that could be because I gave up wondering a long time ago. The only thing I learned from three years of analysis was to accept myself as I am."

His hand touched her unconsciously clenched fist, which lay between them.

"Relax, Eve. You're going to have to learn to stop being so scared and tense around me."

"Brant—"

"Yes, I know. You have reason to be."

"It's not just that." She sat upright, so that she faced

him. "It's just that I have this feeling that being cruel is an instinctive thing with you—that you don't really care about people unless—unless they're necessary to you, for whatever purpose you have in mind."

After she'd said it, she wondered nervously if she'd gone too far, but he merely looked thoughtful, as if he were considering her impulsive speech.

"I suppose you're right," he said at last. "Ever since— well, ever since I was young, I've known that there was no one but me to watch out for me. And I figured that everyone else could learn the same thing for themselves. If you play a game, you'd better know the rules. I learned that, too. So if I'm cruel, or someone gets hurt, I never gave it a second thought. Guess I've never really thought of other people as *people,* if you know what I mean. Just convenient adjuncts to the way of life I'd chosen."

"You mean the kicks circuit? But why that? You could have become a—a *monk* and thought about it all in some monastery or ashram, or—or done anything else you wanted to that the world has to offer!"

He laughed suddenly, a short, mirthless sound.

"A monk! Yes, funnily enough, I did think about that once, but it seemed too much of a drag, living by rules— all that crap about obedience and chastity, with no real reasons *why.* And at the time I didn't want to be alone too much. I had my reasons. But you want to know why the life I lead now, don't you? The theory behind it— sensualism, hedonism as the pure flame, consume the body with excesses rather than fasting in order to set the mind free. Something like the old ascetic monks believed in, the desert-livers, the hermits who insisted on seeking their own path to salvation—only my way offers much more scope. I've turned on with pot and coke and acid and speed—you name it, I've tried it at least once. Sometimes drugs help intensify the feeling of *feeling,* you know? But then after a while nothing's

new, and sometimes the walls close in on you and
you're alone and so damned scared because you're not
in control any longer. Having a crowd around helps,
but only at first. After a while . . ."

His eyes had looked blank and opaque while he'd
been talking, but suddenly, for one fleeting moment,
they looked directly into hers, and Eve thought she
could actually see *in* them. Something that was almost
pity made her reach out to him and touch him.

"Don't—I didn't mean to pry, I just want to *understand*, you see."

"Understanding takes time, baby. Lots of time and
learning to care, which is something I'm not used to.
You'll have to help me. I'm a moody bastard sometimes,
and I'm going to have to learn to give instead of taking
all the time. But dammit—"

"Be careful," she said shakily, "you're letting too much
of yourself show. And I might—I might end up liking
you, you know—would that bore you?"

He put both his hands on her shoulders, his eyes
searching her face.

"Maybe that's what I need—to have to work at per-
suading someone to like me. And maybe you interest me
enough to dig deeper under your soft-seeming sex-kit-
ten surface, just to see what I'll discover."

She half-expected him to push her backward onto the
bed, but instead he kissed her chastely on the forehead.

"Okay, enough soul-searching. Why don't we call
your mother right now, before Jamison announces dinner."

Eve found herself agreeing meekly. Brant kept surprising her, damn him, often enough to make her curious. Perhaps that was what he had meant about wanting
to dig deeper.

CHAPTER
THIRTY-THREE

BRANT SURPRISED EVE all over again when he seemed to genuinely like her mother. She had expected that after the initial shock her mother would like *him*—or at least like the idea that her daughter was finally getting married—and how many women could boast of having a millionaire son-in-law?

Her mother, as usual, fussed first and then hugged and kissed. The younger children stared from a safe distance to begin with and then slowly came closer, to tag at Brant's heels.

"Hey, are you really going to marry Eve? She told us she was never going to get married."

And shyly, from her little sister, Pat:

"Wow! You're gorgeous. Wish *I'd* seen you first!"

She hadn't quite remembered how enveloping, how smothering and personal her family could be, and she expected Brant to withdraw behind his polite smile. Instead, he seemed to become really human for the first time, kissing her mother back and telling her he could see where Eve had got her looks, promising her brother, Steve, that he'd play ball with him, even whispering to Pat that he wished he'd seen *her* first, too.

It had been Brant's idea that they be married from her home—her real home—and helplessly, more than ever unable to fathom him, Eve let herself be taken over and swept forward by what was happening.

She didn't ask *how*, but Brant had arranged for their blood tests and their immediate results, and he had arranged for a special license. The wedding was to be held the next day, in church, and the neighbors and family friends had been told already, with explanations proferred as to the unexpected swiftness of the whole affair.

Eve listened to her mother make some of the last-minute telephone calls.

"Well, Minnie, you know how young people are these days; they keep saying they don't want *fuss*. They were going to elope, you see, but Eve's young man wanted a church wedding in the end. What did you say? Oh, but their reservations had already been made months ahead for their honeymoon, and there was no way they could cancel them and make new ones unless they wanted to wait another month, and of course they didn't want to do *that*."

White lies! Why did there always have to be explanations for other people? Eve was suddenly tired, tired—when she went up to bed that first night, her face ached from smiling. Still, once she was lying there, gazing up at the familiar low ceiling, she found she could not sleep immediately. She moved and twisted uneasily for what seemed like hours, listening to the voices that still floated up from the living room. Was she the only one in the house who wanted to sleep? Try closing your eyes and letting your body go limp, Eve. Try *not* thinking about David.

It was morning—Eve realized, surprised, that she had actually slept. She lay there, inert, hoping she'd go back to sleep, but the thoughts of last night still clung to the fringes of her mind. Strange thoughts to be having on her wedding day. Wedding to a stranger. But at least with this particular stranger there would be no need for pretense between them. No love, but no lies, either.

Oh—*David!* The thought came unbidden and unwanted, a habit-thought from the days when the thinking of his name was like a litany she repeated in her mind constantly. David—David—David!

She saw her own face reflected in the mirror over her dresser. So pale without any makeup. Scared-looking.

It would never have worked out with David. He'd have drained her dry—of hate, of love, of initiative, of self-respect. She'd made a kind of vampire of him by putting herself so much in his power. By her own weakness and unadmitted masochism she'd almost forced him to more and worse acts of cruelty and indifference.

Eve lay back again, looking at the beamed ceiling of her childhood, thinking of all those nights when she was young and lay there thinking, I want—ohh, I *want* —yet not ever really being able to define in thoughts or words what she wanted. The ceiling became a mirror, and she saw her own writhing body—hers and yet not hers, as it had seemed that night with all the hands crawling over it, touching, hurting, holding her down while Brant's gold head with the hair curling behind his ears went down on her body, down between her spread thighs—*No!* Not today. She wouldn't, couldn't think of that, either.

Her eyes were restless, roaming—through the window now, and there were soft tracings of cloud, almost cloud-shadows, in the sky beyond the apple-tree branches. She'd wear white—her wedding dress had cost a small fortune—and her Uncle Joseph would give her away.

Give her away—to Brant. Into a stranger's keeping. No, she mustn't think that way. All people were strangers to each other. She and Brant—they had at least seen each other at their worst and best.

Eve closed her eyes. God, let it be all right! It popped

into her mind, the silly little ritual phrase from her childhood. Her favorite prayer-thought. When she hadn't wanted it to rain on her birthday; when she'd wanted the lead in the class play; and for Mom not to find out about the lipstick she'd filched from Andrea.

She was suddenly aware of voices outside the window —laughter. This was ridiculous! Some stupid, pointless, pagan custom that dictated she shouldn't see his face until this afternoon, when they were to be married. And there *he* was, playing ball, of all things, with the kids (with Pattie following him around adoringly, no doubt), while *she* was cloistered in her room.

Her thoughts of him grew softer, turned deeper. There was, she had to admit, a natural spontaneity about the way he'd made friends with the kids. He was more at ease, less remote with children, and she had noticed that right away.

No wonder he expects me to be a brood cow! But after all, that thought, too, was not as impossible, as unbearable as it had been ten years ago, say—or even less than that. Lisa had helped her rediscover her love for children, and she would miss Lisa, poor neglected baby. Lisa's love, at least, had been real and freely given, while David's attention had been conditional— on loan, at best.

Her mother, knocking diffidently at the door, brought her thoughts back to the present. Oh, God, surely Mom wouldn't give her the old, traditional facts-of-life talk? No, certainly not after their first private conversation yesterday.

Her mother came to sit on the bed beside her, carrying a cup of coffee—another ritual from her childhood, only then it had been chocolate. Eve sat up, sipping, postponing conversation.

"Eve darling—are you *sure?*" So her mother had, after all, sensed her uneasiness. It was strange that after so many years her mother could still see through her facade.

She squeezed her mother's shoulders.

"As sure as anyone is when they get married, Mom. I'm—just nervous. Are *you* sure you can take all the publicity? Brant's photographer friend will be there, you know, and people from newspapers and magazines and maybe even television." She made a wry face, not able to help herself. "They'll be asking questions and taking pictures—"

"If you can stand it, then I can, dear. I—just wanted to make sure in my own mind that you do love him and—that it's not just the money, you know. Or thinking that since your father is gone *you* have to be responsible—" Her mother flushed red, and Eve realized suddenly that it had been a hard thing for her to say. They had been strangers for too long; her mother had not said too much after she'd left home, but Eve knew now that it must have hurt and confused her to have one of her daughters turn her back on all the values they'd tried to teach her.

Oh, *Mom!* she thought suddenly, wretchedly aware that she'd even, at one time, been ashamed of her large, Catholic, middle-class family. Looking into worried brown eyes, Eve took a deep breath and lied convincingly.

"Of course I love him, Mom. Don't *you*, already? Oh, come on, admit it! You're happy I brought home a nice, suitable young man, after all—aren't you?"

"Darling, yes! Yes, you did, and I can't begin to tell you how happy I am, even if it *is* a trifle *sudden*. I just wanted to be sure, and now I am. I do like him, Eve. He's such a nice, polite young man, and I'd never have dreamed he was so rich if you hadn't told me."

Eve remembered, suddenly, Brant saying furiously, "*Fuck* the money!" and wondered if she'd ever get used to being rich.

CHAPTER
THIRTY-FOUR

To COME GROPING out of the dark of weeds and water into sunlight; to lie panting and exhausted on a warm stone; half-dream, half-subconscious impression. Something from the universal unconscious that Jung had written about, Eve supposed. It was something like that old dream of hers, to feel herself cut away so completely and finally from the life she had made for herself—and from David, whom she'd felt to be her life source.

And suddenly, here she was—married to someone else, and by a priest, no less; her wedding to Brant Newcomb the biggest event in her hometown for years, with the small church filled to overflowing and flashbulbs going off continuously and Brant wrathful because Jerry had brought so many people down with him. Thank goodness it was all over finally.

Eve had felt like a marionette—as if she were modeling her own wedding gown. She and Brant, both beautiful, like models in a fashion show, making the right gestures, smiling the correct smiles—everything make-believe until Father Kilkenny was facing them both, reading the marriage service, and she and Brant were suddenly isolated up there, being pronounced man and wife. She losing her name and her separate identity,

walking back down the aisle as Mrs. Brant Newcomb—
rich Mrs. Brant Newcomb.

Eve remembered her father, filled with rage when
she'd broken the news that she was going away to Berkeley, first step toward making a career for herself.

"Political science—demonstrations—what is it you're
looking for, Eve?" he had ranted. "You'll not find it there
in a city wearing fancy clothes—or taking them off,
God knows—for a bunch of pigs. . . ."

That was before one of his sudden rages, quick to rise
and quick to pass, had turned into the last fit of fury—
the one that killed him. How would her father have reacted to Brant, or her too-sudden marriage to him?

Eve lay beside her new husband and watched him as
he slept. He slept so damned calmly, without struggles
or grimaces or the clutching, groping, *human* movements that most people made in their sleep sometimes
—as David used to. She had felt for David at those
times a great and crushing weight of love and protec-
tiveness—she'd felt he needed her, just as Lisa (who
was David in miniature) needed her. What was she doing here, lying next to a handsome golden stranger who
slept so peacefully, sated by their lovemaking?

She turned very carefully and lay as far away from
him as she could, looking out through the window at
the gnarled tree branches that swayed and creaked in a
light breeze. She wanted, quite unexpectedly, to cry,
and to shake with the fury and release of great, tearing
sobs, as she had done on so many nights when she had
lain alone and waited to hear from David. But tonight
she didn't dare. Not because of what Brant might do,
but because of some deep-rooted vein of superstition
and stubbornness that dwelt inside her mind somewhere, telling her sternly that David was past and done
with by her own choice, and Brant was her husband.

Eve shifted uneasily, longing for sleep, and heard the
changed rhythm of Brant's light breathing. Damn her

small bed with its slight sag in the middle. They had decided to spend their wedding night here to put off all the reporters—calling the airport to cancel their plane reservations and make new ones for tomorrow.

She could feel his warmth along the length of her body. Sighing softly, Eve let herself slide closer to him and felt his arm come over her body as he turned sideways, his breath tickling the back of her neck. Maybe, she thought, maybe in some ways she and Brant were alike—each looking for refuge in the other. He could be kind—she had discovered that. Perhaps it was only surprising because he had always appeared so selfish and so callous. But perhaps he had become that way as a form of self-protection—be the attacker, the one who inflicted pain, in order not to become a victim.

He began to make love to her again, and as if he had sensed her mood, still half-asleep, his lovemaking this time was very slow and very tender, whereas earlier that night he had taken her almost savagely, forcing a climax from her.

In the morning, facing her mother, Eve felt herself blush warmly and wondered why she blushed.

Everyone seemed quiet and subdued, even the kids. They had breakfast and, soon after, her uncle drove them to the airport:

"Mrs. Newcomb," they called her. Even the pert young flight attendant looking with envy at the rings on her hand—looking with unconcealed desire at her husband. She could almost feel everyone think: Lucky, lucky woman. But was she? Would she think so a year from now? The marvelous job, the career she might have had—would she regret them?

Eve pulled her thoughts back to the present. They had been offered the morning newspaper—there were pictures of their wedding on the front page. As a model she had played the bride so often that she had done

well—she was smiling, happy-looking. David would see
the papers; would he believe that she was happy?
Secretly she wondered, Does he regret me now? Too
late—they were leaving the country and wouldn't be
back to California for at least six months, Brant had said.
They were flying to an island in the Indian Ocean, more
than halfway across the world. Not too many tourists,
beautiful beaches, friendly people, and warm sun. Sri
Lanka, formerly known as Ceylon, had sounded almost
too beautiful and unspoiled to be true when Brant had
described it. If she liked it, they would build a house
there, make a parmanent home there. And, please God,
the thought of David would fade away and she
wouldn't have stupid, dangerous thoughts about seeing
him again, taking him back on her own terms this
time. . . .

David heard about the wedding from Marti, before he
caught the news flash on television or read the newspapers with their smiling, captioned pictures. Marti, he
thought resentfully, seemed to take malicious pleasure
in being the first to inform him.

It was a hell of a jolt to call again, asking about Eve,
because, dammit, he had actually been *worried* about
her. He hadn't been taken in by her attempt at smiling
nonchalance when he'd turned up at the airport with
Wanda because he *knew* Eve too well. And then to be
told by that snotty lesbian bitch that Eve was getting
married—to Brant Newcomb? He shouldn't have
wasted his concern, his feelings of guilt that perhaps
he'd been too hard on her that night when she'd got
herself into a situation she hadn't been able to control.

David was stunned at first—disbelieving—and then
filled with blind rage. At her, and at himself for not
having seen what a lying fake she was.

He couldn't resist telling Gloria exactly what he
thought about Eve. Gloria had started coming up to his

apartment occasionally, whenever he was home and she happened to be in the mood. At least Gloria was honest enough in her way. She didn't keep telling him she loved him—both of them understood very clearly what it was they wanted from each other, and that was the sum total of their relationship.

"She was nothing but a lying cunt from the beginning," he raged to Gloria. "I recognized it, of course, but she kept trying to get her claws in me, trying to pin me down. Christ, she kept telling me that she'd changed since she met me from the cheap, easy lay she was when I first knew her. She even pretended she cared about my younger sisters and brother. And then, after all she told me that bastard Newcomb had made her do at his party, all the other guys he had screw her after *him*, she goes and marries him! I don't get his motives, but where Eve's concerned—I suppose she thought it was the one way of getting all the fucking she needs to keep her happy."

"But David darling, why the fuss? You weren't planning on marrying her yourself, were you? I know you two had this *thing* going for a while, but it didn't really mean that much, did it? I mean, you couldn't stay away from *me* even when you still had *her*, now, could you? Do come back to bed and don't start becoming a *bore*. I hate men who start talking about other women when they're with me. And darling, I *do* like the way you do it to me, as if you hated me. That's what makes it so exciting!"

Gloria was lying nude on his bed. She moved her body suggestively at him and then turned onto her stomach. Over her shoulder, ignoring his glowering look, she said, "Oh, and while you're up, be a pet and fix me a drink, won't you? Something long and strong, with lots of ice. . . ."

Hating Gloria almost as much as he hated Eve at this moment, and despising himself also for not being able to resist the temptation of Gloria's body, David flung himself over her, pinning her down.

"You bitch—it's not a drink that you need right now, is it? Tell me what you need."

"God, I love it when you get *fierce!* This way, David, fuck me this way. Take out all of your frustrations on me, baby. Your little Eve is going to come crawling back to you for more of *this*, with all the lovely loot she's going to collect from her rich husband, and—ooh!"

He rammed himself up her squirming ass, ignoring the way she moaned and cried out under his relentless battering—her protests that he was hurting her, he was a savage *brute.* He knew damned well she was enjoying every minute of it, her struggles meant to egg him on. But then, most women were goddam masochists, anyway. They enjoyed being hurt; they begged for it. Like Eve, crying to him, trying to hold onto him, and smothering him with her so-called *love.* He thrust his hand in Gloria's wet cunt and heard her scream against the pillows as she came.

Well, at least he was sure that Gloria would keep coming back, just as long as he treated her this way, like a bitch. Spitefully and deliberately, he started to think about Eve, about having her in bed with him again, treating her the same way, making her beg for more, and the thought made him start the tightening spiral of his own climax. She'd come back to him, all right! And what a pleasure it would be to cuckold Brant Newcomb. He'd be having his revenge on Eve, too, at the same time. He'd make her crawl for it, by God. And in the meantime the world was full of women waiting to be taken and used.

Eve could wait her turn, labeled "unfinished business."

CHAPTER
THIRTY-FIVE

EVE AND BRANT threw their first big party when their house was finished at last. She had had a gold-and-silver sari made into a dress, and on this occasion, at least, she let Brant buy her jewels—emeralds set in antique gold. She sparkled with them, hardly able to recognize herself in the mirror.

A photographer from *Town And Country*, here to do a story on them, was delighted with her. Here, at last, was a rich man's wife who knew how to pose for the camera, and whose earlier training kept her from complaining.

Eve was very beautiful tonight. The photographer had arrived two days ago and was used to seeing her in cotton sundresses and the shorts she wore to go sailing. He expressed his admiration quite spontaneously when he told her she looked exceptionally lovely. Even Brant said so.

"Have you missed all this, Eve?" he'd asked her abruptly. "The parties, the people, getting all dressed up..."

"Not really. And you?"

Sometimes they still talked like polite strangers, even in bed. Polite, restrained. No quarrels, few arguments. He was always so reasonable, damn him, and always

291

polite. Was he holding back anything? Did *he* miss the parties he used to give and go to?

Eve looked into Brant's face, and it told her nothing, except that he desired her. *He* told her that.

"You make me want to make love to you."

He made love to her well. His words sent a tickle of lust down her spine.

"Why don't you, then?"

The ocean waves washed and thundered on the beach outside and withdrew with sighing whispers of regret. Except for the photographer, who was busy taking pictures of the house from outside, and the servants, who were busy in the kitchen, the house itself was empty of the guests who were expected to arrive at any moment now.

He began to laugh, softly.

"You're a woman after my heart. Always ready. No fuss."

"Why should I fuss? Do you want me to play coy?"

"Hell, no!"

He held her long skirt up and slipped off her panties, kissing her perfumed crotch.

Then he took her standing up, one hand on the small of her back. In the full-length mirror on the opposite wall, she watched him go inside her.

There was a slight roundness to her belly and he caressed it.

"Do you mind?"

"You mean, being pregnant? No. It feels strange, but good, too. To know there's a child in there, growing, waiting."

They were close then, for a few moments of shared passion.

But during the party, Eve felt a difference in Brant. She remembered him, suddenly, as she had first known him. The Brant of the party circuit—aloof, bored, looking for kicks. She felt afraid, but wouldn't let it show.

She watched him across the room with the tall, black-haired girl who acted as if she didn't want to let him go. She was the prime minister's daughter, educated in England, and she was beautiful and very graceful in her red-and-gold sari with rubies in her ears and around her neck. They made a striking pair as they stood together under the lights, Brant's gold head bent down to her dark one.

The man from *Town and Country* took a picture, shrugging apologetically at Eve. She smiled at him, her smile brilliant and forced. Then the baby stirred in her womb, and her fear went away. When Brant came to her, she smiled at him quite naturally.

"That should have made a good picture."

"Sure. They'll all wonder, won't they? Do you, Eve?"

"About her?" Her face became thoughtful. "Not unless I should. Should I?"

"No, baby. I think I'm going to hang onto you."

He did something that surprised her then—bent to kiss her lips, tilting her face up with his fingers under her chin. The photographer got that picture, too, and they put it on the cover the following month, which was when David saw it.

Already there seemed to be a faintly curved, tawny-tinted roundness to her, where before she had been all defiant hollows and pallor. It was as if, without him to crave for and worry over, she ate more and slept better. And the story mentioned that she was "expecting."

Not able to stop himself from looking through all the pictures, reading every word of the article that accompanied them, David felt the familiar yearning tauten his loins to bursting pitch. He reviled her silently— tramp, bitch, whore! Selling herself to a depraved, decadent rake like Brant Newcomb for his money. God knew what excesses she'd been pushed to already— pushed, hell! She probably enjoyed the life. He'd always found her uninhibited in bed—she'd probably done everything there was by now. Did Newcomb, or even Eve herself, know whose child she was carrying? Damn her, considering the kind of life she must be leading, she had no right to look so happy and contented—at least she appeared to be in the pictures.

His affair with Gloria had began to taper off, and he was relieved. She was too much of a bitch for any man to take in large doses, and she was selfish and demanding as well. He was beginning to avoid Gloria now—seeing much more of Wanda, Saul Bernstein's niece. Wanda had come to work as his secretary since Stella had left to marry that old fart, George Coxe. And since Bernstein was a partner in the firm, Gloria couldn't get Wanda fired. Wanda was pretty, young, and a genuine innocent in spite of the years at college. David was glad he'd discovered her before the wolves-about-town had had a chance. And he happened to know she was a virgin—real, gold-plated cherry.

Who needed Eve? Had she still been around, it would have been all over between them by now. He couldn't take her constant jealousy or the way other men looked her over appraisingly. Not to mention the guys he had to meet socially on occasion who had screwed her, like Peter Petrie. Wanda was different. He wouldn't have to wonder about other men with Wanda, nor other women, either. Maybe with Wanda, marriage might not be an impossibility. After, of course, she'd let him make love to her. And she would—he had been very careful, very restrained, but he could tell that she was close to giving in.

Just as David flung the magazine away from him with an exclamation of disgust, the telephone rang.

"David? It's me, Wanda. Darling, I wanted to tell you I'm still at the hairdresser's. Will you be very mad at me if I'm a little late?"

He had to swallow before he answered her. A good

thing she wasn't here right now, in his apartment, or he would have been tempted to rape her, just to get rid of his hard-on.

"Of course it's okay, honey. Just don't be too late. You know your uncle hates late arrivals at his dinner parties."

"I *know!*" He heard Wanda giggle. "Uncle Solly can be such a bear sometimes, but he's really very sweet. David?" There was a pause.

"Hmm?"

"David, I—I *do* love you, you know!" She giggled nervously again, and he wished she wouldn't do that, it made her seem too girlish. "God, I'm so *brave*, aren't I? Blurting it out over the telephone because I'm afraid to say it when I'm with you. But David—I didn't want you to think I—that I say that to everyone, or that I've ever said it before. I haven't. I just want you to know that I feel—well, that I trust you, David. Completely."

She was telling him, he knew, that she would go to bed with him. He felt his erection throb, and shifted uncomfortably.

"Wanda, I hope you'll always trust me. I'd never hurt you, honey."

"I know." She sighed softly. "Oh, David, I wish we didn't have to go to dinner after all!"

"I'm beginning to wish the same thing. Think we could figure out some excuse to leave early? What time will your aunt expect you home?"

"Oh, she won't worry if I'm with *you*. We could say we're going dancing afterward, couldn't we?" Her voice sounded excited, tense at the same time.

So she loved him, he thought, after he'd hung up. Damn, but it was so easy to get a woman to say that. All you had to be was good in the sack, hump them like you meant it, and be tender in between. With the exception of bitches like Eve and Gloria . . . His eyes

narrowed. Well, Gloria would get a shock this evening
when he showed up with Wanda, making the fact that
they were a twosome official.

Let Gloria work on Howard for a change; maybe he'd
get it up for long enough to give it to her tonight. Because tonight it would be Wanda he'd bring back here.
Tonight would be Wanda's night.

CHAPTER THIRTY-SIX

EVERYTHING HAD BEEN WONDERFUL since the baby. Eve supposed that her real feeling was contentment. Having Jeff, who was beautiful and healthy, and learning to be friends with her husband. Enjoying their lovemaking more and more; sleeping together afterward; knowing by now exactly how to turn each other on.

They'd had no more parties since the last one when she was only a few months' pregnant. It didn't matter; she preferred—just *living*. They had traveled all over the island by now, and they could travel anyplace in the world if and when they felt like it—just knowing that made Eve even more content to be where she was. There were so many things to do and to learn. The climate was perfect, and the ocean warm, even at night, which was her favorite time to go swimming. When it grew unbearably hot and humid along the coast, they moved to their other house in the hill country—a former tea-planter's "bungalow" in a town whose name she still had difficulty pronouncing. Nuwara Eliya. There was a golf course there, and she was learning to golf. It came to her with a sense of surprise that she actually hadn't had time to be bored. . . .

Marti had sent Eve a newspaper clipping announcing David's engagement, and though it had given her a kind of pang to read of it, even the thought of David seemed unreal now. She had *loved* him. Well, hadn't she? Or was it a conditioned reflex—was there any such thing? I'm absorbing too much of Brant's philosophy, she told herself. Maybe *I'm* withdrawing from the real world, too. She'd torn up the clipping, telling herself that she was much more interested in what Marti herself was doing. *Acting*—in the so-called soft-core porn movies—and making a name for herself. She'd written that she was going to France next, and she sounded happy. Or was "content" the operative word for Marti, too? Skimming the surface of life, not going in too deep. It was better to be content than to be caught between the two extremes of being happy and unhappy.

And then Brant, of all people (he told her he never got ill), caught malaria. His own carelessness, he told her, before the fever started climbing. He hadn't taken the pills before he'd gone on that trip to the jungle to track down a rogue elephant—an animal gone berserk, outlawed by the herd, and on a killing spree. Brant had gone on a three-day trip with two of his Sri Lanka friends, a colonel in the Army and a doctor.

It was the same doctor that Eve called, trying to fight down her feeling of panic when she realized he lived sixty miles away; and in *this* country, with the roads as bad as they were, it could take him hours to get here.

She was almost afraid to take Brant's temperature— he was so hot his skin seemed to burn her when she touched him. His sun-bleached hair looked dull and lifeless, and his face was flushed, even under his deep tan.

He didn't seem to recognize her by then, and she saw him helpless for the first time, his body heaving and turning restlessly under the thin cotton sheet. His eyes stared at nothingness, and he muttered hoarsely to her in languages she couldn't understand. She thought he spoke Italian most of the time, but she couldn't be certain. She heard him speak about people she'd never met, and then, as she leaned over him, trying to keep him covered and hold an icepack on his forehead at the same time, he repeated a name he hadn't mentioned before.

"Syl," he said, and kept repeating the same name on and on, sometimes with love words and sometimes with epithets.

"Syl . . . Sylvia *cara* . . . Syl darling . . ."

Eve had never heard him mention anyone called Sylvia before—she couldn't remember meeting anyone by that name. Who in hell was she? What had she been to Brant, whoever she was?

Eve leaned over him, holding his hands when he tried to brush the icepack aside, and they were curiously hot and dry. With one part of her mind she found herself wondering almost objectively whether he was going to die before Dr. Wickremesinghe arrived, before she could ask him about the mysterious Syl. Whoever she was. It was strange, the feeling she got when he mentioned that name. And kept repeating it. There was a note in his voice when he said it that she had never heard before, not for *her*. He sounded amused, sometimes; angry, tender, and finally pleading. Brant, her husband, the self-contained stranger she had married —*pleading?*

He had slipped back into English at last.

"Syl . . . Syl, don't—don't do it, don't go! Oh, damn you, Syl! Don't leave me!"

Eve had never heard him sound so despairing before, either—that almost desperate tone in his voice before he lapsed again into Italian.

Eve leaned over him, and the heat of his body made her start to perspire.

"Brant?" she called urgently, but he didn't hear her. He was somewhere in the past with another woman, with—Sylvia. There was an old song, wasn't there?

Shakespeare. "Who is Sylvia, what is she. . . ." What had she been to him?

Oh, God, never mind. Let the doctor hurry—what was he doing, why were the roads so narrow and so badly kept up? And why, why was it Sylvia he called for in his delirium and not *her*?

In the end, it was over a month later before she felt ready to ask him about Sylvia.

The doctor had arrived, after what seemed like an eternity of waiting, and he'd said, smiling cheerfully, that she mustn't worry, her husband had an unusually strong constitution. He'd pull through; there'd be a private nurse to look after him, and Mrs. Newcomb must remember to take *her* pills and make sure there was mosquito netting around all the beds.

Chauvinist! Eve thought unfairly, because the good doctor had implied that now he and the nurse were here, she should go back to looking after the child.

But even with the drugs Dr. Wickremesinghe used to treat him, it took Brant all of three weeks to get back to feeling good again. And in the meantime, Eve had time to rationalize, telling herself that she couldn't fling questions at him while he was still recovering. And later on, her rationalization gave way to a sort of stubbornness. After all, she had no right to question him—he'd never questioned *her* about anyone in her past. She'd married him with her eyes open—hadn't *he* been the one to say that they would be starting off with no illusions?

She had almost decided to let the whole matter drop, to allow their lives to move along smoothly and calmly as usual, but then there was a day when it had been hotter than usual. The kind of muggy heat she couldn't escape, and it made her restless and bitchy.

She took the boat out alone early in the morning. *Her* boat; her surprise birthday present from Brant three

months before. But today it was too hot even for sailing
—hardly any breeze, and the sun was like a burning
brand, reflecting off the polished surface of the sea. So
she turned back, and when she came walking sullenly
into their cool, book-lined study, she felt herself hate
him—lying so comfortably there on the divan listening
to Bach, his face as cool and unruffled as the surface of
the ocean had been.

Eve threw her big straw hat at him, and at least he
had the grace to look slightly surprised.

"You look as though you could use a drink. Want me
to fix you one?"

Polite, innocuous words, but why did he always have
to be so polite, so *bland*, as if there were no strong feelings at all under the surface he chose to show her? The
only *real* emotion she had ever heard in his voice had
been for another woman. She felt cheated; why was she
supposed to be content with a shadow while the real
man stayed hidden?

"I don't want a goddam drink; I want to talk."

She walked across the room and sat at the foot of the
divan, staring at him.

He turned the music off and looked back at her.

"All right, Eve. You want to talk. About what?"

"About Syl, that's who. Sylvia. The woman whose
name you kept calling when you were delirious with
the malaria."

She was close enough to him to feel his whole body
grow taut. His eyes narrowed.

"Who?"

"Don't pretend, Brant! You couldn't seem to stop
saying her name. You called it over and over. Syl. I
want to know who she is, dammit!"

"Cut it out, Eve." The sudden coldness of his voice
sounded a warning, but at this moment she didn't care,
and she went on recklessly.

"No! No, I won't cut it out, Brant. I want to *know*."

She knew she sounded like a fishwife, but she didn't give a damn. At least it showed that *she* was human.

His mouth looked white and taut with anger.

"All right. She was my aunt. And my first lover. I loved her—and I ended up killing her. Is that enough for you?"

Eve felt suddenly calm, and oddly empty inside. She heard her voice persist.

"Tell me about her. About you, as you were then. How was it you were actually able to feel *love*, Brant?"

"No! Goddammit, that's enough. I won't be *probed*, Eve. Not even by you. Syl was a part of my life a very long time ago—let her be! Just as I let David be."

"Ah, you actually said his name. Why haven't you asked me about him, about how I feel about him, or *if* I feel about him? Or is it that you don't give a damn—about *me*, that is."

"Shut up, Eve! What makes you such a bitch today?"

"*You* do. Every now and then, strangely enough, I get this urge to *know* you. To understand what's under the surface. You married me, Brant. Why? You never did tell me the real reasons, did you?"

He stood up and walked away from her.

"No more questions, Eve. I'm not in the mood. Maybe I'm not ready to bare my soul to you yet. So leave me alone, will you, please?"

"Oh, God! Do you always have to be so—so controlled? So damned *polite*? Do you have to make me feel I have to be the same way?"

Hating herself and him, both, Eve felt the uncontrollable tears erupt. They gushed from her eyes, and she was shaken by sobs that made speaking impossible.

He came back to her (unwillingly, she thought—and hated him more) and caught her shoulders.

"Dammit, what am I supposed to do now? I'm not used to tears from you. I don't mean to force you into any kind of behavior pattern, Eve. If that's what I've done, then I'm sorry. But sometimes I find that I'm human, too, you see. Stop it, now."

She couldn't stop. At last, words came from her again, gasping and ragged.

"I want to—I have to be *alone*. I have to think—I must *know*—"

She knew she was doing everything wrong. She should be more rational; she should not say anything, because he would never understand.

There was a kind of baffled rage in his eyes now, and she was afraid of him again, for the first time since their marriage.

"I don't understand you, Eve. I think you're asking me for something, or trying to push me into something. What is it? Do you want to be fucked?"

He hadn't used that word to her for ages. Something in the way he said it now, so offhandedly, so contemptuously, cut into her like a whiplash.

She raked at him with her nails almost instinctively, leaving red streaks down the side of his face.

She heard him suck in his breath with shock and pain, and then he shoved her backward off the divan, forcing her down onto the floor with her arms twisted behind her. When she was lying on her side, moaning with rage and hurt and fear, she felt his free hand rip away her thin cotton shorts—felt him press against her and enter her without warning.

The weight of his body pressing against hers and the cruelty of his grip on her wrists turned her over onto her belly, and she screamed out loud as he went into her roughly and deeply. She found she couldn't move— the breath hissed out of her lungs every time he thrust himself even deeper inside her unprepared, resisting vagina.

"Don't—don't—don't!" she cried out to him, hating him. But it was too late for him to stop now or for her

to stop him, and she knew it and finally lay there with
her face pressed against the rough matting that covered
the floor, accepting his violation of her because she had
to, and screaming again only when he pulled out of her
and brutally and unexpectedly forced himself into her
the other way—the way that Randall Thomas had used
her. The pain of his intrusion was excruciating, and she
kept screaming until he put his fingers up her vagina at
the same time, and suddenly the pain became pleasure,
and she stopped trying to pull her wrists from his grasp
and cried out instead with excitement and shame that
she could obtain such perverse ecstasy from the way
he was using her.

He released her wrists and tangled his fingers in her
hair, twisting her face around, almost snapping her
neck. His mouth burned her earlobes and her cheeks
and the corners of her mouth. Finally she lost all consciousness of anything but their bodies—what he was
doing to her—what she was feeling—the sensations
erupting inside her.

This was being punished and possessed and taken.
. . . She made wordless sounds of protest and need and
lust, and it went on and on for what seemed forever
until suddenly it was over and they were lying together,
exhausted and shaken and spent. She suddenly started
to cry again, helplessly and quietly.

Eve felt him pull away from her and move off. The
smell of cigarette smoke drifted to her, stinging her
nostrils. After a few moments, she felt his arms lift her
and carry her to bed.

"I'm sorry, Eve," he said quietly into her silence. "I
promised I'd never hurt you, and I did. You laughed at
my control, and I lost it. Which proves. . . . I think—
I think it would be best if I went away for a while.
Until we can sort things out. Maybe I need to get back
to the people I used to know so I'll find out once and
for all if I miss the old life. Maybe you need the same

thing—and you might understand yourself better, too, if I weren't around. I think you've started to get bored and uptight, Eve. I think you're missing what you might have had, and it could be that's what you need, too— to get away, get back. . . ."

Eve felt his weight shift from the side of the bed. She knew he'd gone, and she wanted to speak, to have the last word, to tell him. . . . But there were no words left in her. Only a cold kind of emptiness that made her wonder if that was the way *he* felt inside all of the time, and if so, poor Brant.

She didn't really want him to go now, but she couldn't stop him, either. She had no strength of will left.

"I'm taking the boat. Guess I'll sail around the coast to Colombo. I'll be in touch later. Take care, Eve. I'll look in on Jeff before I go."

The walls were falling down, everything was crumbling around her, and she couldn't seem to react. She heard the door close behind him, and she had still not found words, nor the energy to utter them. Absurd, the sudden surge of feeling that she wanted to follow behind him and remind him that he hadn't taken any clothes with him, nor even a checkbook. What did it matter? He'd managed before her. . . .

And at least she had Jeff, who had Brant's eyes, but with a difference. There was love and life and humor in her son's eyes—she would see that there always would be. The slow tears slipped out from under her closed eyelids as she began to cry again, softly this time and helplessly, unable to stop.

CHAPTER
THIRTY-SEVEN

LATER, lying on the patio beside the pool, letting the sun burn and consume her body, Eve tried to think about it all—the suddenness, the how and the *why*, and then gave up because her mind felt as bruised as her body, and thinking was as painful as too-sudden movement.

Brant had already left, of course. The baby's ayah had been curious (had she overheard Eve's screams, even through the thick, soundproof walls?), but Eve had not volunteered any information, and the woman, shrugging, had taken the baby to his room for his afternoon nap.

Eve wondered again if she would call him back if she could, but her subconscious mind gave her no answers this afternoon.

She thought again about Brant's almost unconscious arrogance—about the women who, no doubt, would flock to him now. She realized with a kind of shock that women—particularly the one whose name had started off a chain reaction, Syl—and her own jealousy had started it all. What she hadn't wanted to admit, even to herself, was that she was jealous. She had let herself become too arrogant, too sure of herself and of him. Maybe he'd been right and she had wanted, consciously or unconsciously, to be fucked, to be reassured in *that* way, at least, that he wanted her.

She moved restlessly on the chaise lounge and felt the aches in her body. Her wrists showed purple bruises already—what did the ayah *really* think? Oh, Christ, I must be a masochist, Eve thought, and fell asleep after all.

She slept until it began to get dark—the sudden dropping of a black curtain that was a tropical night without a lingering twilight. And then, of course, she couldn't fall asleep that night, even after she had stayed up as late as she could, reading.

The heat of the afternoon sun must have seeped into her body while she had foolishly lain out there, soaking it up defiantly. Now Eve felt her skin burn and sting in spite of the air conditioning. Even the soft sheets felt rough and scratchy, and the bed, she discovered suddenly, was too damned big—leaving her far too much space in which to toss and turn in her efforts to get comfortable. Insect noises and the high-pitched croaking of frogs outside seemed to beat against her ears, in spite of the insulated walls. She remembered how, during their early days here, she had felt deafened by all the noises of a tropic night.

Giving up on sleep, Eve turned the light back on and sat up, reaching for her robe. She might as well check on Jeff; surprisingly, he hadn't awakened and cried for his feeding yet. Usually he woke up at least twice during a night, and she'd hear, with half her mind, the ayah crooning to him gutturally as she patted his little bottom to soothe him back to sleep. Children were spoiled here, especially if they were boys, but Brant said it was okay—that kids needed all the love they could get, and it was most important when they were very young.

The hell with Brant! She wondered if he were already in Colombo, headed for the airport—or in some crowded little nightclub, dancing with Manel, the tall

Sri Lanka girl who'd given him so much attention at their housewarming party.

She hadn't paid too much attention then—she'd found it almost amusing—but now she wasn't sure, and the mixture of emotions churning around inside her amazed and infuriated her.

Tying the belt of her robe around her waist, Eve walked barefoot to the baby's room, noticing at once, with surprise and apprehension, that the light was on in there, shining under the door. She pushed it open and walked in, then stood silently on the threshold.

Brant lay on his back on the rug, the baby's pillow under his head, his son lying on his chest. The ayah had obviously been dismissed, and they were communicating in silence, watching each other with unblinking, identical eyes. Jeff looked fatly content, his head stubbornly raised so he could stare down at his father.

"What in hell are you doing back here?"

Eve's voice was taut.

"I found I missed you both. So I turned around and came back."

His eyes studied her, and she realized suddenly that she was still all oily from the cream she'd slathered on herself. Unconsciously, she put both hands up to her face, and his eyes began to crinkle.

"*Damn* you, Brant!" she whispered, but his admission had disarmed her, and her tone lacked conviction.

"I guess we all need to get all the pent-up questions and frustrations out of our systems, even if it means quarreling," she said to him later, when they lay together in bed.

"I don't know about needing to quarrel, but I suppose people have to learn how to communicate, and when you're used to holding things in, that can be difficult."

He was learning, she thought. He was so different

from the way he had been at the beginning, and all this time she hadn't realized it. Was *she* different, too?

Marriage was no standstill affair, thank God! You were almost forced to keep working at it; that way you kept learning, and she guessed that was the only way to keep any relationship *alive*, to be eternally curious about the other person, never taking him or her for granted. Maybe that was another form of loving, because you couldn't be curious unless you cared. And was that really so hard to say?

Eve tried the words out loud, curving her body into his.

"Brant, I love you."

Her voice held a stammer; the words sounded rusty and hesitant. The last time she'd said them had been to David—and then she had said them too often for them to really mean anything; she realized that now. Every time you said you loved someone, it should come as a fresh realization.

He said nothing for some moments, but she felt his arms tighten around her body as if he meant to hold her close forever.

"I guess that's what I was trying to tell you awhile back, Eve. But some words aren't easy for me to say."

"Don't say them, then. You don't have to. Show me."

And he did—renewing his lease on her, she thought crazily, all the time he was making such tender, beautiful love to her. Renewing it for the next hundred years, maybe. Which was the way she wanted it.

THE BIG BESTSELLERS
ARE AVON BOOKS

☐	The Thorn Birds Colleen McCullough	35741	$2.50
☐	The Insiders Rosemary Rogers	40576	$2.50
☐	Kingfisher Gerald Seymour	40592	$2.25
☐	The Trail of the Fox David Irving	40022	$2.50
☐	The Queen of the Night Marc Behm	39958	$1.95
☐	Sweet Nothings Laura Cunningham	38562	$1.95
☐	The Bermuda Triangle Charles Berlitz	38315	$2.25
☐	The Real Jesus Garner Ted Armstrong	40055	$2.25
☐	Lancelot Walker Percy	36582	$2.25
☐	Oliver's Story Erich Segal	42564	$2.25
☐	Snowblind Robert Sabbag	36947	$1.95
☐	Catch Me: Kill Me William H. Hallahan	37986	$1.95
☐	A Capitol Crime Lawrence Meyer	37150	$1.95
☐	Fletch's Fortune Gregory Mcdonald	37978	$1.95
☐	Voyage Sterling Hayden	37200	$2.50
☐	Humboldt's Gift Saul Bellow	38810	$2.25
☐	Mindbridge Joe Haldeman	33605	$1.95
☐	Polonaise Piers Paul Read	33894	$1.95
☐	The Surface of Earth Reynolds Price	29306	$1.95
☐	The Monkey Wrench Gang Edward Abbey	30114	$1.95
☐	Jonathan Livingston Seagull Richard Bach	34777	$1.75
☐	Working Studs Terkel	34660	$2.50
☐	Shardik Richard Adams	27359	$1.95
☐	Anya Susan Fromberg Schaeffer	25262	$1.95
☐	Watership Down Richard Adams	19810	$1.25

Available at better bookstores everywhere, or order direct from the publisher.

Mr/Mrs/Miss _____

Address _____

BB 1-79

AVON BOOKS, Mail Order Dept., 224 W. 57th St., New York, N.Y. 10019
Please send me the books checked above. I enclose $_____ (please
include 50¢ per copy for postage and handling). Please use check or money
order—sorry, no cash or C.O.D.'s. Allow 4-6 weeks for delivery.
City _____ State/Zip _____

AVON   THE BEST IN
BESTSELLING ENTERTAINMENT

☐ **Shanna** Kathleen E. Woodiwiss   38588 $2.25
☐ **The Enchanted Land**   Jude Devereux   40063 $2.25
☐ **Love Wild and Fair** Bertrice Small   40030 $2.50
☐ **Your Erroneous Zones**
         Dr Wayne W Dyer   33373 $2.25
☐ **Tara's Song** Barbara Ferry Johnson   39123 $2.25
☐ **The Homestead Grays** James Wylie   38604 $1.95
☐ **Hollywood's Irish Rose** Nora Bernard   41061 $1.95
☐ **Baal** Robert R. McCammon   36319 $2.25
☐ **Dream Babies** James Fritzhand   35758 $2.25
☐ **Fauna** Denise Robins   37580 $2.25
☐ **Monty· A Biography of Montgomery Clift**
         Robert LaGuardia   37143 $2.25
☐ **Majesty** Robert Lacey   36327 $2.25
☐ **Death Sails the Bay** John R. Feegel   38570 $1.95
☐ **Q & A** Edwin Torres   36590 $1.95
☐ **If the Reaper Ride** Elizabeth Norman   37135 $1.95
☐ **This Other Eden** Marilyn Harris   36301 $2.25
☐ **Emerald Fire** Julia Grice   38596 $2.25
☐ **Ambassador** Stephen Longstreet   31997 $1.95
☐ **Gypsy Lady** Shirlee Busbee   36145 $1.95
☐ **Good Evening Everybody**
         Lowell Thomas   35105 $2.25
☐ **All My Sins Remembered** Joe Haldeman   39321 $1.95
☐ **The Search for Joseph Tully**
         William H Hallahan   33712 $1.95
☐ **Moonstruck Madness** Laurie McBain   31385 $1.95
☐ **ALIVE· The Story of the Andes Survivors**
         Piers Paul Read   39164 $2.25
☐ **Sweet Savage Love** Rosemary Rogers   38869 $2.25
☐ **The Flame and the Flower**
         Kathleen E Woodiwiss   35485 $2.25
☐ **I'm OK—You're OK**
         Thomas A Harris M.D.   28282 $2.25

Available at better bookstores everywhere, or order direct from the publisher.